CROW

CROW

DONALD STEWART

CUTTING EDGE

ISBN-13: 978-1-957868-05-9

Previously published as *Strange Bondage*

Published by
Cutting Edge Books
PO Box 8212
Calabasas, CA 91372
www.cuttingedgebooks.com

CHAPTER ONE

John Dietche looked at his father's house, sinking in the vast lake of gray sand extending from the back road. He did not move to step into the desert: the pathetic view killed the sudden appetite for company that had brought him there. The porch had been chopped down for firewood, which left the front door so high off the ground it looked as if some invisible force were pushing the ruin out of the sand from below. The roof was beaten open. The old man was probably alive out there: straining his eye to focus on a tiny cream blur, Dietche made a chicken out of it.

He turned away, cured, and started making his way back to Myron Greenhalgh's farm.

Re-entering the birches at the top of the mountain above the back road, he remembered a little rite he had to perform. He sat down and lit a cigarette.

A week before at dawn, Dietche stood in the road mist on the fairer side of the mountain, looked about to make certain this was the isolated place he had known earlier in his life, then advanced on to the lawn and knocked at the back door. If Myron wouldn't take him in whose name for some reason stayed in his memory all those years, he didn't know that he wouldn't hang himself. As soon as Myron hinted that he was interested in hiring him, Dietche poured out the whole story—how he had jumped parole the minute he got back in the world, and how the police might be looking for him one day, but not soon, and not back there in the hills (the paved road running in front of the farm had not been the main road for many years). No one where he had come from knew he'd originated from these hills, he said, and parole jumpers aren't chased much anyhow. The truth didn't faze Myron. In fact, when Dietche mentioned the police, the little farmer seemed to light up a little.

The strangers faced each other, the skinny, vaguely hunted Dietche, his shoes soaked in dew, his hat pushed back on his red hair, and the small, black, alert, vaguely haunted Myron, dry in his white clapboard house, and they bargained—rather, Myron made terms—the screen door between them.

"I guess five dollars a week would be too much," Dietche drawled. His voice was light and resigned. "Two dollars?" he said. Dietche's voice was not servile; it merely indicated he'd serve. "Just let me have wine'n cigarette money, then, sport," he said.

Myron pointed at a tiny cabin beyond the barns. Myron's voice was high. He could command. "Give you that to live in, John, plus board. That's all. Why'd you come here?"

"I just happened to remember your name," Dietche replied. Whatever Myron had meant to Dietche, he didn't mean it anymore. "Don't worry, there's nothin' comin' for me, Myron. I told you."

"Don't you have no relatives or friends? What about your father?" Myron asked cautiously.

"Back up there in the sand still, ain't he, behind your mountain?" Dietche said. "There's a baby girl in Triple Cities. But she don't know me. No, it's just me, Myron."

Myron measured the famous local failure who stood like a dried flame on his wet lawn. Dietche had put quite a daring proposition to an upright man like Greenhalgh. The farmer's teeth appeared beautiful and flat and false as he spoke. "We'll give you a plate at the door every mealtime, John. And you can get your water up to the trough. Don't see why you want to eat with us."

The man in the prison-cloth suit and travel-stained shirt said, looking at the small, cell-shaped cabin, glistening in the distance,

"Maybe you'd give me a dollar now and then. Sometimes I might want a drop of wine with my dinner?"

Myron told him he'd give him all the drink he needed.

"We best give you another name in case somebody sees you around here," the farmer said, quietly, so the wife, who was standing around the corner of the pantry, wouldn't hear.

"If you think of one. I got a few in case you get stuck. But I don't think anyone'll want to find me," Dietche said and took his eyes off the cabin and turned back to the screen door. "Myron," he added doubtfully, peering down the dark pantry into the electric light of the kitchen where Myron had disappeared. "I was innocent."

And Myron replied without emphasis, invisible around the corner, "I don't care."

"I *was* innocent," Dietche said out loud on the mountain a week later. His boots lay far out on a skin of wet black leaves. The birch pole was rotten and sagged under his weight. The smoke from his cigarette rose straight out of the trees. He took off his felt hat and yawned, feeling lucky. He sat still and quiet, and after a time he felt he better get moving. Then the pole broke suddenly and he sat on the leaves. "Damn!" he said. He jumped up and gave the fence a long, looping kick and walked away, removing some papers from his coat pocket.

He dragged a match down several trees but the bark was soft and damp and he had to use the eyelet of his boot. He set fire to the papers and turned them this way and that to let the flames get them all and then he dropped them on the slick black leaf-and-mud hide on the dome of the mountain. He waited until they had burned to ash, and then he walked through the newly broken fence down into the high pasture. Myron's herd rose as he returned among them.

The mountain had originally been owned by a company of lumbermen. They didn't own it long because the trees were rotten. The soft female head of the mountain absorbed the melting snows, creating a perpetual swamp. On peaked mountains, which came *after* the glacier that left this mountain unmanned, there would be a tough blanket of dry earth and strong trees because the water would run off. Dietche's feet sucked the pasture as he walked through the corrupt vegetation where superabundant generations of reptiles flourished and were frozen off each winter when all Myron's land was white, and there was no contrast between this near-tropical slushy Eden of frogs, and the dry valley below where Myron lived.

The disappointed lumbermen sold the hunchback to Myron's father and vanished into the blue timber miles beyond. Dietche knew what it was that kept people going in this dud county. He passed a shack at the end of the pasture, brought by the lumbermen to serve as a cookhouse.

The county was settled in the previous century by optimists. When their sons took over the wheat fields they found that their fathers had had all the fun. Underneath the exhausted topsoil was an enormous bed of sand—the sons inherited a vast prehistoric lake bottom. It was worse in different places. Myron, a second-generation farmer, didn't have it bad enough to wreck him. He still grew things. But the house Dietche's father occupied, on the other side of Myron's parody mountain, lay in pure glass.

The sons became herdsmen and tried to forget the little historical joke that had been played on them, and when the first spring after the discovery came, newly bought cows were let into the old wheat fields and into sloped mountain clearings such as the one Dietche was walking through.

Cows didn't fill the cup either—another twist of the same blade—because of the sand, the grass in the pastures was weak, and so the milk was weak.

Nothing could have changed the nature of the earth in time to discourage the pessimism that came to flourish there. Myron could never exactly understand why Dietche had come back.

Dietche knew why Myron was there still. Dietche knew that even had Myron left he would have found no place to take himself to that would have improved Myron's particular needs. But that wasn't the way it ran for all of them. Still they couldn't know, never having been outside the county, that for every hell on earth there is a worse hell nearby. It wasn't that the land was worthless either. It was simply that the worthless land had changed the people.

But in each hell man creates his heavens, and in Myron's hell there was one for a time, until Myron found out about it. Not everyone settles for his fate. That heaven was the little shack Dietche left behind him following the inkassed herd out of the pasture.

After the first war, men who had submitted to the trenches and then to the burning ache of their dry, heartless yet satisfactory inheritance here in these hills suddenly refused to waste the dark night in sleep, as they wasted the day in work. They pried open Myron's shack. They put a bed and a retarded girl inside and for several seasons, through rain and snow, shadowy bloods drifted in from hills and towns around to drown themselves in her kisses and in explosion. But in each heaven in each hell there is somebody that will knock it, and one fall, midway through Coolidge's term of office (they had a picture of him, hanging upside down, in the shack) a file of outraged pilgrims crept up from the farm below led by the young Myron Greenhalgh, and caught the girl with John Dietche, who was just past twelve then. The raucous male voices singing in the darkness about the shack went silent, and Dietche escaped after them. And the girl was sent to the house of correction. Nobody forgot her. But the laughter and candlelight had gone, and the shack was boarded up and left vacant, spitting its nails into the wet earth beneath. No one knew what became of the lantern, the picture of Coolidge, the rugs, and her silken gown; Dietche, who'd come back the next night to salvage what remained of paradise, didn't remember any more what he'd done with the stuff. The memory had dissolved in prison time. And it was so long ago—and already another stage of his life was dissolving as that had.

He had grown up in this northern county, and in particular in this pasture. And then he tried to make a second life, free of drunkenness and pathetic, personal revolt, in a southern city, was framed on his wedding night by a couple of cheap thieves, and sent to prison for seven years. He'd had a daughter before the indictment, and the wife was dead.

The third stage of his life had begun a week ago. It would be the last stage and, finding it working out exactly as he hoped, he had, that morning, as a symbol of a new start, burned all his identification and parole papers.

So he did not look into the shack where years ago he'd begun to feel the lure of life, the lure of a life which was going to lick him at thirty-five, because it meant nothing to him any more. It no longer existed. Nothing meant anything to him, except not being molested, frightened, questioned, spied on, loved nor hated, and not being required for anything in life but his labor.

The cows would get down alone now. He had left the footpath in the woods, and was searching for a spring where pure water seeped up from the center of the mountain—he remembered the spring because he was thirsty. Finding the spot he took off his suit-coat and knelt, holding his coat against his chest as if it were a child, and sipped. Washing his haggard face and short growth of red beard in the crystal water, he rose and made his way down the mountain again. One of his eyes was blind so he walked with his head turned a little sideways, to see better.

He was a week old. And if that first week was what it was going to be like always, it was all right, he thought. Coming out of the woods, he checked to see that the cows were piling into the trough yard below the barns, and then went into the small white cabin.

It was April.

But there was too much work, and Myron would have to get more help since the farmer planted more than he needed or could afford to tend with just the two of them, and was intending to plant more still. Myron had written to New York for one of those tubercular tenement wops they advertised in the papers, to help out. Someone who wouldn't make anything of Dietche.

It was simple, hard work, beginning, as life had in prison, early in the morning. Dietche didn't have movies or his lovebird or his cellmate. But he'd brought a couple of bottles of wine with him to make up for the lack of company and conversation, to placate the novelties that beset him those first weeks alone in self-exile. Myron had promised to keep him stocked up. The good thing was that he didn't feel he was rotting. And even better was the absence of the smell of others rotting with him.

The tall, blood-headed man with the soft, disused voice had nothing to complain of except that every once in a while Myron reminded him of the guards, as any boss will to anyone from the stone colony. He put Myron's hardness of heart down to the farm, poorer than Myron would admit, and to the fact that Myron was doing too much in trying to make it go.

Week after week after week passed in order and in silence, in the kind of natural freedom men cherish who have seen too much of mankind. He got his plate at the back door three times a day and slept in the bare one-room cabin by the woods, and so he would go on doing, steadily working an unending procession of days the rest of his life, until he was deader.

CHAPTER TWO

Three months later the big square barn doors opened as usual and revealed the morning, and as usual Dietche released the stanchions and one by one the cows backed onto the runway, bumped into each other, and went slipping out the back door.

Along either side of the long walls the thirty empty stanchions hung like old, stringless harps. A long row of small windows shone a dull yellow down the side facing the road, their glass covered with years of spray and dry urine and dead insects. A cold breeze with dew in it carried off the incense from the gutters the cows had filled, until, with a creak, the back door, through which the woods and the white cabin and the last of the departing herd could be seen, slid in its track shut. Then Dietche took a shovel and cleaned the runway, scraping flat spats of excrement into the long, overflowing gutters which would be thoroughly dug out later and relined with dry dung and hay by him and Myron and Curtiss Lake and an iron-wheeled wagon drawn by one of the horses. Milking was done. The separated milk sat in two silver cans in the cooling vat. Cora would come up later to ladle out the private portion before her husband took the cans to the main road.

The hired man leaned the shovel on the bull pen and came outside and lit a cigarette.

"What's Myron doing?" the young man from New York asked. "I passed him on the way up and he didn't say a thing."

Dietche shook out his match. "He'll be writing up the coming romance in the breed book, I suspect. Or else it's her."

"What?"

The hired man brushed a pair of flies off his collar and said, "You'll see." A car passed the house on the seldom used road. Dietche turned his head away and when the car was past, he glanced slowly around at the diminishing license plates.

Curtiss walked inside to be by himself. By training, he resented it if someone didn't want to be friendly to him. By nature, however, he didn't want to make friends with anybody. He resented and coveted a man like Dietche. He couldn't have it both ways, of course, and couldn't strike a balance. Alone he was lonely; in the company of other people he usually wished he were alone. He smoked inside by the milkroom and compared himself to Dietche. The hired man was less educated and uglier and he was always picking up nails or stray bits of strap and putting them in his pockets, as if he were going to make something out of them. That's all Curtiss knew about him. Not that he wasn't perceptive. He wasn't curious. His curiosity, so to speak, was not plugged in. Dietche wasn't all that communicative either.

"Hey!" Dietche called inside. "Go on down and tell the boss we're waiting on him. I think he's forgot us."

"He hasn't forgotten."

"No, I think he has," Dietche said, smiling. "Now go on down, son, and tell him we're waiting on him." He stared in at Curtiss.

"Nuts to you," Curtiss murmured, frowning where he stood on the runway.

Myron was boring and his wife stayed indoors all the time and Dietche wasn't allowed in the house. It was three months since he'd seen a new face; although he knew he shouldn't make any kind of contact with the kid, Dietche's curiosity was alive. He watched him hovering in the darkness by the milkroom. He sure wasn't a tenement child. Curtiss was educated, and wore an expensive pair of jodhpur boots to work, but he had a manner which by now had quietened their fears that he would become nosy and put a few things together in his expensively trained and, therefore, to Myron and Dietche, intelligent and perceptive head. No, Dietche reflected, the boy was all to himself.

A sullen mouth and a quiet voice and a head of careless mouse-brown hair—Curtiss's whole being, from his slow walk to his low, guarded tone of voice, was a reflection of resentment, resentment of the love he'd had from his fast-driving parents, a love which, to his undying disappointment, he couldn't ever return because at the moment when he was learning to respond and return their affections to his own satisfaction, they suddenly smashed the car—into someone else's parents—leaving the boy in the care of a loving but familiarly and utterly impractical uncle and aunt whom he could not permit himself to love because Grace and J. J. Tavener were poor and not *his*.

Curtiss was quiet and disinterested, which Dietche and Myron, in league against the law, appreciated and which was all they knew and needed to know about him. However, before entertaining even his natural curiosity about Curtiss, Dietche had seen a chip of the young man's shoulder that, retired from the world as he was, Dietche knew he should not knock off. Instead of being offended when the young man said, "Nuts to you," Dietche had to say, "I do think Myron's forgot us," and laid the cigarette on his lip. He felt he was in for trouble.

Curtiss had slept only four hours the night before and as a result didn't want to sit down because he was afraid he'd fall asleep. He went down to the house to find Myron. Dietche grinned at him in the hard glare of the morning.

When Curtiss had gone indoors, the hired man glanced up into the sky, by habit, as if there was someone, not very far away up there, he could see.

Their feet moved over his head.

"I can't find it," she said.

"You best, that's all," Myron said.

The young man walked nervously around the kitchen, hating arguments. Everything was white except the brown-and-gold cuckoo clock and an old wall telephone and the floor. White stove, icebox, table, and garbage pail. She scrubbed the place mercilessly. Through a door by the big white sink was the living room where he had not been, and which was not in use and which smelled of sour, coffin air. A pair of upholstered armchairs with shiny wood arms, a huge radio cabinet, a dusty sofa...the wall paper in the room was rosy and through the half-lidded windows he could see the stomachs of the trees on the lawn by the road. The living room was about what Curtiss looked like inside.

Myron's small boots clattered on the stairs. "You waiting for me?"

"Yessir," Curtiss replied.

Myron put the breed book on top of the icebox and laid a pencil carefully beside it so it wouldn't roll off. They went outside together.

"If you see a scrap of brown wrapping paper with a telephone number written on it, you give it up, will you?" Myron asked. "Fella called this morning and left his number with my wife and she's lost it somehow. It ain't important, but I don't like to lose things."

Curtiss said he'd do that.

"You getting along?"

"I suppose so," answered Curtiss.

"That's good. You do a good job and we'll all get along."

"I am."

The farmer put his hand to the side of his mouth "Bring her down, John!" Dietche ducked away off the barn wall. Myron put his little black eyes up at Curtiss. "He speaks French," he said in his high voice.

"I speak a little French myself," Curtiss replied. So he speaks French, he thought. Well so what?

They went into the stalls and stopped by the bull pen. So nothing, Curtiss decided.

Suddenly, at Curtiss's elbow, shaking the young man, came a hoarse, wet bellow. Again and again, the sad male horn issued from the pen behind which the enormous white pasha was slowly revolving. The gate went away from his view and he stepped off the hay blowing through his scalloped nose, and slipped heavily on urine-wet hooves down towards the square of light at the end of the barn. Myron and Curtiss followed him.

He stopped half outside the barn in back, blinking rapidly in the bright light. He looked up at Dietche who was sitting on a rock wall above him and then ahead at the small black cow. The ground shook: he'd left the doorway and was trotting at her. She had her butt to the stone wall—Dietche raised his hand and kicked at her—she shied away, and there was space all around her and the bull was able to begin doing his stuff.

Dietche glanced at Curtiss. The young man was intrigued. He looked at Myron. Myron's faded blue cap was pulled over his forehead, concealing his expression.

The bull buried his long, raw, dripping cue in the heifer's back, and Dietche put out his cigarette and walked up over the hill, into which the three levels of the barn were built, to open the trail to the woods. The little black cow followed him nimbly.

"Huh," said Curtiss.

Myron looked into the sky which was pale blue and cloudless. "We'll put the bull back, Curtiss, and clean the gutters," he said.

When Dietche and Myron went up together with the red horse to get the manure wagon which was parked in the smaller of the two barns, in as casual a voice as he could manage, the hired man asked if Myron had received a telephone call that morning. He'd heard the thing ringing.

Live emeralds coated the horse's rump. The thick hair-tail swung up and whipped them away, and Myron replied "No."

"If you do get a call and it's for me, come tell me, Myron," Dietche said.

Myron opened the doors of the small barn and turned the horse and pulled it back into the shafts of the wagon.

" 'Cause you see I *heard* the phone ring this morning," Dietche added.

"I can handle it," Myron said.

"Oh no you can't."

"I thought you said no one'd come for you."

"Well, no one has come for me. And no one will, if you leave it to me."

"The call wasn't for you, John."

"So there was a call. I knew I heard ringing."

"Yes, there was."

"I can be stubborn too, Myron."

The horse stamped the ground, ringing its harness.

"Well," Myron said. "Anyhow, my wife took it."

"Why don't you tell me who called? Did they give you a number?" Dietche asked.

"You might decide to run and I can't get another hand this summer," Myron said calmly.

Dietche shook his head. "I ain't going to run. I'm through running. But if somebody *is* going to come here, I've got to know who it is and why he wants me. I can handle it if I know what's it all about."

Myron shook his head. "No, you'd run," he said.

That afternoon, Dietche found the telephone number on his plate when she gave him his lunch at the back door. He didn't know why she did it. Perhaps she wanted to get rid of him. Perhaps it was an accident. The wrapping was buried in the succotash and the number was illegible.

He wondered if he could get to the phone if it rang again. He was so fixed in his isolation, he did not realize that if his voice ever went into Myron's telephone it might not be very long before people'd drive out to see who the stranger was.

A few days later, on the first of July, a Wednesday, a letter came for the young man, postmarked Ohio. Cora examined the penmanship and the return address. It was from Curtiss's uncle. There had been one before this, postmarked Pennsylvania or New Jersey or something. She figured his uncle was looking for work. She was interested in Curtiss since she perhaps might never have a child. "Letter for him, Myron," she said, turning the envelope in her fingers. "His people are in Ohio."

"What?" Myron wiped his lips on his bare arm.

"Letter for the boy."

"Well leave it be. You'll lose it like you lost that telephone number." He reached out his hand. "Bread." She put the letter on the plate before the empty chair and passed Myron a loaf of bread. She was taller and heavier than he was, but her face was almost smaller—possibly it seemed smaller because it was framed in such a mass of red hair. Her skin was smooth as a child's, and when her face registered in any way, white thin spokes curved over the abutments of her cheekbones in tiny individual slashes. It was a face that withheld nothing. Nothing. And the rust eyes seemed as you looked at them to be eternally fading. "I wish you wouldn't go on about that number, Myron."

"What did you say?"

"Why don't you *fire* him if he's causing so much trouble?" she asked.

"But he isn't, Mother," Myron said.

"The telephone got you all upset."

Myron leaned back. He put both his brown hands on the table. "My God, you," he said. "Dear dear dear. Listen."

"Myron, I believe everything you say."

"Well then, shut up." After a moment he laughed. "I mean it." He grew quieter. He rinsed his mouth in the sink. "Listen," he said, "if I tell you something, it's the truth. Now don't *never* let on to him about the phone." He left the house.

She felt badly about giving Dietche the wrapping paper now. She didn't know why she'd done it. She wished Dietche was gone. She had a definite feeling she shouldn't have given him the number, although Myron hadn't told her not to earlier. It was a mistake. If Myron found out, she would be punished. Just as Myron would be punished if he made a mistake, she thought. She didn't quite know who would punish Myron.

"Well," she sighed, and forgot his harsh words by a special process she had and cleaned off the breakfast table.

If Cora had any ambition, it was sunk deep in her. Evidence of complexity infrequently appeared. She liked flame. She loved the winter. There was the kitchen's extraordinary brightness. She would have been famous for that had they any friends.

Myron was gone when Curtiss arrived downstairs for breakfast. Again he had not slept. There was nothing to do after work except smoke or abuse himself. He would try and sleep like everybody else at nine-thirty, but his city body was set to sleep at midnight. As usual he tossed and sweated and sat on the sill and then went for a long walk. At two he collapsed finally. And as always, at six, she knocked on his door whereupon his leaden legs swung over the high quilted precipice, dropped into his jodhpur boots, carried him down the hall to a basin of cold water, jerked him downstairs while he tied up his blue jeans with a pajama cord. He retrieved sleep on Sunday afternoon in the hay; at the end of his first week he had rings like leeches under his eyes.

The legs dumped him in his chair; he opened the letter from his fifty-year-old uncle, and automatically began growing cold.

Dear Curty,

Just a note to let you know where I am. Don't have a secretary yet—ha ha—so excuse the bad handwriting. I'm sorry we all got so tight the night you came home. It meant such a lot to us. We were wondering what got your back up so to leave us without even saying goodbye. Gee, not even a so long to your poor old uncle. Ha! Never mind.

Hot. The fella that wants me to work for him there in—what state is it—Ohio?—is on a hunting trip. "In June?" I asked the girl.

Don't think I'll ever see your Aunt Grace again, Curty. She's moved in with her sister. It sounds alright. They only fight when I'm there. By the way she dropped that suit against me about my hocking her phonograph.

I'm fine. How are you? Happy Fourth of July. Write me will you for God's sake. Whenever you get the time?

LOVE,

J.J.

P.S. Maybe you ought to know what's going on. We are in a hell of a fix. I owe so damn much money. Some bozo from the liquor store around the corner—Calahan's— told my boss I hadn't paid my bill. My boss, my ex-boss, asked how much we owed. Calahan said two thousand dollars—well, he couldn't of been far off—sister Polly used to come over a lot. So I was canned. Now I'm here and I haven't a mother loving nickle and the bill collectors are after me. Whoopee. Hot. It's hot out here. Excuse me, I'm going to get another drink of *water?* Hell no.

OK I'm back. My hand's tired, so I'll just send this off. Can't write no more. I wish you were here. You got a great future kid. I don't exactly know what you're going to do, but it's going to be a great future. Think of all the great fun ahead, all those marvellous years before you.

I'll write you again when things get a little organized at this end, and I can see the inkstand.

LOVE.

Curtiss put the letter in his back pocket. His coffee had cooled while he was reading.

Cora asked if he had had bad hews. He was thinking about asking Myron for some money. "I beg your pardon?" he said. "Bad news," she asked. "No," he said, "I don't think so." He got up and threw his napkin into the white receptacle under the sink.

"It's nice to get letters," she said, turning, but he was gone.

Hotter that morning. Halfway to the barn he was sweating. The sky was a clear blue, across which flew, like pepper in his tired eyes, a flock of crows. They circled and broke high over the barn, rising to avoid a possible spray of buckshot, and disappeared into the mountain where the herd was spread in a long string on the trail to the woods. Curtiss knew he was late again if the cows had got that far up.

While he was taking a drink at the trough Myron rolled up to him. "You're late."

"I am?" Curtiss said.

"Me and John can't do all the work."

"No, sir, you can't. Say I was going to ask you—do you think you can let me have some of my salary in advance?"

"Ain't you got any money?"

"I used my last twenty dollars on the bus fare. I want to buy some work clothes."

"Ain't you got any?"

"No, I haven't. I do have a few things but they're too good for this kind of work."

Myron asked how much the boy wanted, never speaking above the volume necessary to hear himself.

"Five dollars."

"Won't be enough."

Curtiss stepped closer to the hot, shaking tractor. "Excuse me?"

"I say you'll want more. I wish you'd listen. They got many more like you in New York City? Anyhow, I can't let you have any money now."

"But let me remind you that I get my first pay in one more week. On the tenth of every month."

"Maybe I'll have some money then. Now I ain't got any. You go on up and help Mr. Dietche dump oats. And don't get up so late." Myron took hold of the accelerator and pressed the clutch. "You get to work on time," he said, and the machine lurched down the gravel road carrying away the little blue emperor rocking between its great rubber ears.

"You waiting for me?" Curtiss asked Dietche outside the large barn.

"Sort of—"

"Well, let's go!" the young man cried. "Jesus, everybody waiting for me today. I must be a very important person. Don't get them damn oats done whole world'll blow up! Come on—"

"Take it easy!"

"Well Jesus, John," Curtiss sighed. "I mean it." Dietche was leaning on a broad pile of sacks lying outside the tall doors, trucked in the evening before by the feed man while Curtiss was driving the herd down from the mountain (Dietche's old job) and Dietche was hiding on the floor of his cabin. Dietche removed his hat. Matted from the heat of the hat, his hair looked poured over his skull like dried blood from some hidden spring in his head. He rubbed his neck and forehead and returned the hat and all you could see then were the long jaws and the chin which all his life had been a perfect target. "O.K.," he said ruefully and grabbed two corners of a sack and jerked it onto his hip with a grunt. "C'mon," he said, going lopsided into the barn.

Inside, in the shade of the great lofts, Dietche took two strings at the top of the sack and pulled them and the pale yellow feed appeared. "It's them two red strings. Don't pull too much," he said breathlessly, tipped the bag, waited, and then draped the empty sack on the loft wall. Curtiss pulled his strings, raised his sack, and directed the snout to the tiny hole in the runway. The oats vanished and the bag was limp in his hands. Pleased, he shook the sack and laid it on Dietche's on the wall. They hoisted and carried and emptied for another quarter of an hour. "Why is Myron so close with his money?" Curtiss asked.

He repeated his question a second and a third time and at last Dietche replied, the last of the pile going loose. "You're a pretty rich kid, Curtiss, ain't you?" he asked, panting.

"No," the young man answered, which was the unfortunate truth.

He must have been around money in the old days, Dietche figured. It was written all over him. "Where'd you get the fancy boots?" he asked, picking up the loose red strings from the dusty boards.

"They belonged to a relative of mine who died." Curtiss had never met anyone who could leave the atmosphere so suddenly, so effortlessly, and still be where he was. He tried to bring Dietche's attention back. "Doesn't Myron have any money?" he said. "I mean why did I come to work here if I'm not going to get paid?"

"Why come here to work anyhow?" Dietche asked.

"I wouldn't work in New York. I know too many people there."

"You ashamed of working?"

"I'm ashamed of having a nothing job."

"Thirty dollars a month is a good job, Curtiss. Are you nuts?"

"It's the kind of job, I guess. There are certain jobs which don't matter."

Dietche took a broom and swept the stray oats carefully into the tiny hole. "We'll go on down now," he said, and pivoted a slat back over the hole. He felt the more attention he paid him, or contrarily the more he ignored Curtiss, the more Curtiss would close in on him. (Half of this was correct diagnosis, half vanity.) Something would have to be done about it, he thought. He would need to strike a balance somehow.

The earth drew closer to the sun and the sky became the color of ether. Far away in one of his fields across the road Myron steered his tractor ahead of a wheeled box. A dry white chemical dust dropped from a slit in the box and historical dust spun up from the wheels and both white and brown dust blew away over the river behind Myron. "Windy out there," remarked Dietche without pity, drinking from the faucet at the trough on the side of the hill that carried the barns.

"Could do with some rain," Curtiss said, watching Mrs. Greenhalgh run down from the milkroom carrying the dripping ladle in the direction of the house.

"Telephone's ringing," Dietche said quietly.

When Cora came back out again, Dietche was there. Her lip flew into her mouth and she stopped dead still.

"Where's the fire?" he said.

"Telephone call," she said.

"For Myron?" he asked, his good eye fixing her, the blind sightless eye watching the pitiless way the paintless eyes of statues do, and his lazy voice rasped, "Or is it for *me*."

Her dark red hair was brushed now, after breakfast. The red hair had life in it. "The call's for Myron, I said, didn't I?" she said.

"Mrs. Greenhalgh, it's for me, ain't it?" Dietche said patiently. "It's written all over your face."

"Curtiss," she said, "go tell Myron he's wanted on the phone. Tell him to hurry, hear?"

Curtiss walked a few steps and looked around. Dietche had gone into the house for the first time since he'd been there.

"It's for someone called Myron Greenhalgh," she called in at him. "Myron'll know what to do to you for this, John!" He'd been there three months, but Myron never talked about him except in his sleep. She was afraid he'd leave dirty tracks. She did not know what to do until she started to run across the road past Curtiss, who had stopped, absorbed in the mesmeric motion of the distant tractor which was turning down the river bank into the next stretch of field.

The screen door slammed. Dietche joined him. By then the tractor had halted and was waiting, riderless, in the distance. "What happened?" Dietche asked.

"I don't know. They've disappeared," Curtiss said crossly.

The hired man shaded his eyes. Myron got back on the tractor. The noise of the engine grew louder and the machine rolled on. A moment later a puff of dust appeared where the tractor had been and Cora stood up in it.

"What was that all about?" Curtiss asked.

"Don't you never lose your temper?" Dietche said.

"I don't want him to go hitting me, by God."

Dietche had no reason to dislike the young man, he realized. But it was imperative for his own safety that he resist the urge to communicate. It was like being on a secret mission. (He hadn't Curtiss's training.) "Do your job, kid. Myron's O.K.," he said and went across the road.

"Oh, he's *O.K.*," Curtiss replied. It wasn't a bad life, the young man reflected. He looked at the woman walking across the field, waiting to see her expression. He had an assortment of women's expressions in his memory—looks of casual amusement, of boredom, of placid contentment, of self-amusement (he could not remember looks of hate or fear), expressions he found on the cows he tended—but she altered her path so she wouldn't have to meet the two men by the road, not wishing to see anyone until she had got some soap and water on her knees and hands and mouth.

'Damn,' thought Curtiss. The bit of unseen activity behind the tractor had disturbed his emotional privacy. The other part of the story—the telephone call—didn't matter. With effort he pulled his spirits up: he was superior to all this. He wasn't involved in these people's affairs. He did not owe them anything except his labor, nor they him anything save their money and lodging. He could remain a spectator if he was careful and he could leave whenever he chose.

Under the big elm tree across the road it was cool where he and Dietche had gone to wait for Myron, now driving in towards them, and each of the flies that landed on their skin was cold.

"Not so hot in here," the young man said.

"That's right," Dietche said, the pleading foreign voice of the person at the other end of the telephone wire echoing in his emptied mind.

CHAPTER THREE

They stood working on the gravel driveway, between the garage which housed Myron's car, and the house.

"Who was he?" Myron asked again, fit to be tied.

"You got nothin' to worry about," Dietche replied.

"Damn you," Myron cried, "You got to tell me! Else I'm going to call the troopers and tell them to take you back."

"Haw, haw," Dietche said, mulish. He wanted to go to town, Myron wouldn't let him. So to hell with him.

"I'll have you back in prison so fast you wun't know what hit you," Myron said.

What, Dietche wondered, keeps him going at me? "I'll tell you who called when I'm damn good and ready," he said and pushed his hat back to dry his forehead. He'd had lots of wine the night before and was full of water.

The sunlight died when it hit Myron's teeth. "John, I'm going to *make* you tell me," he said.

Before Dietche could reply Curtiss walked into earshot, yawning.

Dietche measured the tarred seed corn which he had been stirring into the four red pails Curtiss dropped. The black, acrid-smelling kernels gleamed and rattled like blue pearls spilling into the pails. Myron told them to take the seed to a field across the bridge and went up to the barn to get the hoe.

As Curtiss and Dietche were crossing the highway with the pails, honks came around the curve that led into the hills.

Cursing, Dietche put his pails down and walked quickly away and lay in the clover just as the cars appeared.

In the center of the parade rolled a long black limousine with tobacco juice windows. Curtiss caught a wedding dress inside. A pale, scared face looked out at him as it went by and then the whole contingent went jerking away through the valley and dissolved into the succeeding valley.

"Wedding?" Curtiss asked, turning. "What are you doing over there?"

"Looking for my good-luck charm," Dietche mumbled. "Yes that was a wedding. You ever hear honking at a funeral?" Thank God she was getting married, otherwise he wouldn't have had a warning. It was a close scrape. Where was that car coming from?

Myron caught up as they crossed the bridge, and the three men came to an area the size of a football field embroidered with small holes in such wavering lines it looked like Myron had been thinking of something else when he dug them. Most farmers hoed straight as rulers. Beyond the field, in. the near distance, something Myron never saw anymore, the arctic-colored hills that walled in the valley.

Myron pointed to the first row of holes. "I want you to fill and bury them with the corn, John. By the time you've done all the rows, I'll have more dug. You can follow behind him and watch, Curtiss."

"You pay him to watch?" Dietche asked. "He can be planting the row next to me."

But Myron had walked off to break another row in the dry surface of the earth and wouldn't be sounded.

"I'll do the next row," Curtiss said.

"No," Dietche said.

Next to them was a field of foot-high corn. The leaves were yellow-tipped. Each of the thousand cockades was dying as it grew. The end of the process, Curtiss reflected dully. He didn't see the point of any of this. It was a ridiculous existence, he thought, following Dietche uselessly down the row.

Dietche came to the end of the first row, dropping the yellow, tar-coated, teeth-shaped gems in the earth—the beginning of the process—thinking about Saturday, which was tomorrow, the Fourth of July. A coincidence had occurred between him and the outside world: a dewy yellow car driving out of a telephone pole that morning on his way to get his breakfast plate at Myron's backdoor heralded deviltry, dare-deviltry, at the fairgrounds, and he found he knew one of the drivers listed on the poster, a man calling himself Jesse James with whom he had shared a cell.

At the end of the row, Dietche stood up straight to pull the knotted muscles loose from his back.

And Dietche's daughter was going to be there, too. Those were the people who had her.

He'd told Myron he was going to see her—he was going that night. But Myron had said no. Myron believed Dietche would come back and he almost believed him when he said that his little cell-like cabin was more important in the long run than a daughter. Myron said no for another reason. For the telephone call.

This desire to visit people seemed to contradict Dietche's point of view. When he had passed the poster, which seemed to have appeared as suddenly as Myron's new manner, it attracted the hired man a little in the way water bubbling up between the dry feet attracts a man rowing a boat. So, acting on a hunch, he told Myron he'd like to go. Not because he felt responsibility to the girl or even to his ex-cellmate, Jesse James, but mostly because of this nuance he felt in Myron. Trained in the portentousness of the innocuous, Dietche simply heard a new tone in Myron's voice, reminiscent of some of the hundreds of prison tones he'd learned could mean trouble. He'd take the weekend off, get away from Myron a bit, see the people he'd known, and replenish his faith in their uselessness. It was probably his own superstitious nature anyhow, he figured, that made Myron seem more than he was. But Myron said that if Dietche went to the fairgrounds (he'd planned to go in the night, traveling in the comfort of his much-loved darkness) Myron'd sick the troopers on to him. Dietche did not know what the hell to do.

Fortunately, however, there was the matter of the unsolved telephone call which snowed Myron. As long as Dietche kept silent about it, he might just have his way, might make a deal.

The fields were without shade. Curtiss wrapped a handkerchief around his forehead. "Jesus," he said, protesting.

"What's the matter, old boy?" Dietche asked, halfway up the second row.

"Hot. Lemme do something."

Dietche said, "Carry the bucket."

Myron saw Curtiss take the pail, and held one hand at his mouth so his light voice would carry to them. "John!" he called.

"Whut?" Dietche called back.

"Take back the pail."

"Pail," Dietche said to Curtiss.

"And—!" Myron appeared to be smiling at them, but it was just that the sun was in his eyes.

"What?" Dietche asked.

"I told you to fill them holes too."

"You got the hoe, old boy. No point in doing it by hand."

Myron said, "I'm using the hoe, John."

Dietche turned his back on Myron. "I can wait," he said.

"I can't," Myron said.

Dietche turned nervously. The little jerk's got good ears, he thought.

"You go back to the beginning of the first row and cover everyone of them holes by hand."

Curtiss suggested they get another hoe.

"Other's broke," Dietche said and raised his voice. "There's an awful lot of work here, Myron. I ain't no monkey!"

"Get to it, Johnny."

"Use your head, Myron!"

"I'm usin' it."

"It'll take me all night!"

"You ain't going anywhere's tonight."

"What's the matter with you?" Dietche cried.

"Crawl, John."

Dietche was so relaxed from disbelief in what was happening he seemed to hang on the ground from a hook. "I get it," he said at last.

"Yass, O.K.," Myron replied dully, dropping his small hand from his mouth and lifting the hoe again and sinking it in the sand.

Dietche ran to the head of the row. He dropped on his knees and swept the dust onto the black lives in the first hole and stamped the spot with the heel of his palm so hard the dust flew. He did another in the same furious way and went on to the next.

Curtiss walked across the bridge to get out of this.

Myron called to him where he was going.

Curtiss shrugged his shoulders.

"You can't just wander around, son," he said. "You sick?"

"Why do you ask me if I'm sick?"

"Don't mind him—he's a little touched by the heat," Myron said, which was undoubtedly the truth, then went down to Dietche.

"Who was that called yesterday, did you say, John?" Myron asked again.

"None of your damn business."

"Was it the police?"

"You tell me if the police are going to call up and ask if I'm here."

"I don't know," Myron said, "I just wish you'd let me know who called you. I'm responsible for you."

"If the police want me they won't call. And if it wasn't the police what do you care?"

"I don't want to lose you."

"Oh boy," Dietche whistled. "Look Myron, I'll make a deal with you—I'll tell you who called if you let me go to town tonight."

"No."

"Well then, go to hell."

"I told the boy you were a little crazy. That'll help explain your strange behavior."

Dietche looked up at Myron. The sun was right behind the boss's head. "I figured if he thought you were a little touched it'd help," Myron was murmuring.

"Don't need to tell him that, you damn fool. We'll get along without playin' games."

Myron flushed, his tan cheeks going rosy. With a kind of tortured movement of his arms, as if they were paralyzed, he lifted the hoe and cut open one of the holes Dietche had filled. He stepped back and opened another. Slowly he cut open four more.

"I ain't gonna take much more of this," the hired man said.

"Nor I."

Dietche heard Curtiss laughing at the bridge. He got up off his knees. Myron went quickly down the row. He handed Curtiss the hoe.

"Fill the rest of them holes he's seeded, please, son," he said and crossed the bridge.

They neared the highway, Dietche walking just behind him. The hired man struck a root under the elm because of his blind eye and stumbled against the tree. Myron snapped around and held still, his house behind him across the road.

They could barely hear Curtiss laughing now because of the wind and the distance.

The hired man advanced, a circle of dust around his mouth, his hat upside down in the dirt behind him, up to Myron and asked him where he was going. Myron told him he was going to call the state police. Dietche said, "You ain't. I'll tell you what you want to know."

Myron did not speak for a minute. Then in an agonized voice, his face confusing pleasure with pain, he said: "Why didn't you see fit to tell me before?"

"Didn't suit me."

"Why didn't you come right out and save all this from happening? I was going to send you back to prison!"

"Don't cry."

"I don't like getting tough with you."

"No, you don't, do you. One of these days you'll bust, keeper." Dietche snatched up his hat and removed a handkerchief from his hip pocket and wiped the leather liner clean of dust. Then he opened his shirt pocket and gave Myron a piece of brown wrapping paper. He said he'd found it. "It was a Jewish fellow," he explained. "An old friend from the old days. He ain't comin' out here and he ain't sending anybody out. And he ain't no cop. You got nuthin' to worry about. Now lay off me. I think it's stupid of you to get so upset over a telephone call." He added that the Jew probably got Myron's name from Dietche a long time ago. He'd never get to town now, he knew. He didn't care. He hated himself for being such a fool.

"Why didn't you come to me sooner?" Myron asked.

"Don't know no better," he said, walking away towards the barn waving his long skinny arms.

Curtiss held the hoe, shook his head like he'd seen Henry Fonda shake his head in a farm movie, and spat. It was hard work declining these insistent invitations to go; yet he managed to depreciate Dietche's anger (he took Myron's side), as he had Myron's a few days before when he saw Cora fall not far from where he was standing. He was somewhat curious now about all this.

In an hour he and Myron finished twenty new rows, he planting, Myron filling. Myron wanted to talk. When grown, about a twentieth of the crop would be put up in jars, seven-eighths sold and the rest fed to the pigs he bought each fall, Myron informed him.

"Really?" Curtiss said sincerely.

And then Myron surprised the young man by telling him he could charge as many shirts as he liked and get some boots too, and pay him whenever he liked. Curtiss thanked Myron twice—unbalanced by this uncommon generosity—and said he'd go to town the very next day. They crossed the road together.

Myron had planned to lie down for a while, but he found himself accompanying Curtiss to the barn.

Dietche put his fork into the loft hay, lifted, put the fork in again, lifted, and stuck it still deeper until a bundle that would come out twice his size was hooked firmly on the tines; then he braced himself, slipped one hand up on the iron neck and hoisted the wad without effort out and up into the dark air above his head and floated it forward, taking the streaming mass to the box mouth of the chute, where he let it fall. The iron jacket hit the wall of the box, the hay slid off the downward-pointing tines and disappeared; dust fountained out of the chute, the flakes turning in the bars of sunlight pouring through the open hatches in the roof. Dietche moved through these pillars of light on his way back to the part of the loft he was working on. He didn't see them come in together.

"John," Myron said.

"Hello."

"You be careful when you go into town tonight."

"You mean you're letting me go? I was going anyhow—" Dietche said all at once.

"Yes, you can go," Myron said.

Not less than an hour ago, Myron would have sent Dietche to prison. Dietche wondered if Myron maybe didn't have Jap blood in him. He stared down at the boss, wondering what made him change his mind. "I'll be careful," he said. He realized he'd resisted Myron too hard in the field. Now that Myron was letting him go to town, a terrific sense of gratitude swept over him and he had almost fallen on his face, a second time, there in the hay. This was the way they got you. "I'll be careful," he said coolly. He wouldn't resist Myron so hard any more. He watched the small, hopeless brown face below him and felt gratitude change into its opposite feeling. He turned away. Slaves are made by making men pity each other.

Dietche's self-possession, supported with wine, was almost his whole character. He believed he was entirely self-sufficient, like one of those machines that repair themselves. He had just repaired himself.

This main aspect showed in every facet of his being—his cleanliness, his watchfulness, his singleness of purpose.

"I'm supposed to help you," Curtiss said from the wagon run. Myron had gone.

Dietche gave him a hand up.

The young man spilled his first fork all over the runway.

"Don't put your fork in deep until you've loosed the surface," Dietche told him.

The second time Curtiss dragged out a sufficient load, but it was not set tight enough on the points. The hired man, who wouldn't mind talking a little himself, noticed Curtiss's silence. "Myron told you to keep shet of me?" Dietche asked, stopping for breath, wheezing.

"No."

"He told you I was crazy didn't he?"

"He said you spoke French too."

"He did?"

"He said you spoke it," Curtiss said, returning to work.

"I do."

"Where'd you learn French?"

"I picked it up." Dietche jumped onto the runway and lit a cigarette and shot the match out the doorway.

"Shit: you don't know any French. You?"

"*Merde* to you too," Dietche said.

"That's some French you know."

Dietche blew out a thin stream of smoke. "Curtiss, you certainly are a pleasant fellow. I bet you'd make a dandy hostess, the polite charming way you keep a conversation going."

"*Where'd* you learn French?"

"In a classroom, like everybody else." A classroom with three-foot thick walls.

Dietche's hayseed, splotched face, spiked with short red-gold quills, looked about as scholarly as a harmonica. He laid the cigarette on his lip and began cleaning his nails with a bit of wood.

Before that afternoon, Curtiss feared him. There was no more fear now, since Dietche's surrender by the elm tree. He'd seen him cringe. He was pathetic now. Ripe for sympathy. "How come," Curtiss began, "you and Myron out there under the elm tree—"

"Never mind."

"I thought you'd want to talk about it."

"What's there to talk about?" Dietche asked, bewildered.

"You didn't hear nothin'."

"Well," said the young man. "I don't know. Let's forget it, then."

Dietche pulled his hat tighter on his head and put out his cigarette and replaced the butt in his pack.

"I wouldn't of told," the daring young man said. "No matter what Myron did to me, I wouldn't have taken it."

"But you don't know nothin' about it," Dietche protested. "How in hell could you know what's going on between me'n Myron—which there ain't—if one of us didn't tell you?"

"I got eyes."

Dietche climbed up the wall. "What good'r eyes if no one's told you what you're lookin' at?"

"Oh, I don't care *what* it's all about. It can't be anything important. I mean really important. But just *why* did you do it, Johnny?"

"Say, you don't want to call me Johnny neither."

"I wouldn't of told. I'd of quit'n gone home."

Dietche was baffled.

"I'd of quit," Curtiss mumbled, looking with phony detachment at the sun-filled hatches.

"You know what I think?" Dietche said.

"What do you think?"

"I think it's time you shut up."

Curtiss ignored the warning.

Whether the young man was really sympathetic or whether he was preying on the hired man, it was all the same to Dietche.

There had been a religious motto over the entrance to the dining hall in prison. The prisoners had got up to it somehow and scratched out the words, which were "Come Ye Unto Me," and scrawled in pencil underneath "Go Fuck Yourself." The warden erased that and put a plastic cover on the sign. The motto appeared on the plastic. Time and again it was erased by the authorities—God knows how the men got up that high—and time and again it was rewritten, until by the time Dietche was there, the derisive response was a permanent groove. The plastic was replaced. And so the next day was the men's response.

Eventually a more sophisticated priest succeeded the bored old robot who had given up the fight and who never looked up any more on his way into the dining hall, and the whole sign, plastic cover and all, was taken down for good. There were a number of conversions. But throughout his prison career, Dietche knew he was innocent, which many of them did not. He stayed on his feet. So naturally, upon seeing the sadistic smile like a motto on Curtiss's face, he got sore. And when Curtiss made the further mistake of saying softly, with the Jesus look, "I'm sorry for you, John," Dietche's lips became the thinnest, most satirical phase of the moon. The young man became frightened, and life, whose invitations he had so often declined, came to collect him for a party.

"Just what do you want?" Dietche asked him, floating a foot away from Curtiss, one eye full of a crazy self-amusement, the other one bland and cold as marble. Both men rose up and down slightly on the pliant hay.

"Don't want anything," Curtiss replied with an aching smile on his dreary face.

"Why've you bin askin' me all them questions?"

"I wanted to make friends."

Dietche grinned. Curtiss's elbows and knees hummed.

There was a long silence.

"What's the matter?" Curtiss asked.

"I'm waiting for you to start something."

"Start? Start what?"

Dietche stepped on Curtiss's foot. The young man tried to pull away and let himself fall over backwards, complaining loudly.

"Didn't do nothin'," Dietche said.

"The hell you didn't."

"Calling me a liar?"

"No, I'm not calling you a liar," Curtiss replied. "I'm not afraid of you, you know," he added. He was not, he hoped, a coward. He'd never fought a man before. "I'm not afraid of you!" he made himself shout again and was amazed to feel energy spurt into him because he yelled. He got to his feet.

The hired man braced himself on his back foot, holding one arm across his chest, waiting quietly, self-controlled, leaning on the air.

Curtiss, wanting only to make the gesture of fighting, charged lightly.

Dietche pushed him away.

Curtiss went at him again. Dietche hit him in the chest. That stirred up a glorious, windy fury in the young man. He began lashing about, the blood racing in him. "Come on, you coward!" he yelled, and managed by accident to catch Dietche in the eye.

Dietche's emotions were far from cold—that's why he was up there on that farm. "I'm coming," he promised. He took a step forward, feeling cruel, his bony right hand gleaming like a knife at his side. Desire flamed in him, burning his self control. 'Lord,' he thought. He felt like murder. He bent over to get the pitchfork at his feet, and then, with great effort, stopped dead, his hand stretched down, head tilted up, bobbing as if on a string, hat slid over his eyes, fury twitching on his cheeks. "You," he muttered, and stood up and took a deep breath which cooled his lungs, "You come to me," he said.

Curtiss came and cocked his fist and launched it. He missed. 'I can't hit him,' the young man thought. He aimed and fired again. He fired again.

Dietche stood quietly, holding him off, tangling him up so he couldn't get in.

As suddenly as it had come, the spirit began leaving Curtiss. He fought against the outgoing tide, swinging his light fists but missing. And Dietche, motionless, watching, waiting, was quietly taking more and more control, and at last found room to be amused by this desperate, thin-mouthed boy use-lessly defending some vague sense of self-honor. Curtiss had lost. Dietche was stealing his fire simply standing perfectly still doing nothing, waiting to make sure the kid wouldn't ever bother him again, wouldn't try to "know" him in any way, either in pity, love, false friendship, or in hate. Curtiss swung on and on. If Christ's compassion rots men's souls, conscience rots their hearts. It was not to rid himself of guilt and remorse that he lived alone—it was to avoid them. The one idea he'd cultivated in prison—being innocent and yet having to behave, because he was human, like the guilty—was not to feel obliged. Love and hate and their intermediate states bring trust and trust brings thieves. So he went at Curtiss a little angrily, being human, but also like a tired surgeon at the end of the day, want-ing to cure him of an illness with which the young man was undoubtedly trying to infect him. "Come on!" the young man cried pitifully.

Not because they were bad things, but because they had almost destroyed Dietche's life.

"You come here," Dietche said politely.

"You come here to me this instant!" Curtiss cried.

Dietche turned his back and walked off with an insulting remark.

"What did you say?" the young man protested, stumbling after him, his hands raised, eyes shut.

With quick movement, Dietche knelt. The charging Curtiss tripped over him. Dietche leaped and pinned him.

Curtiss tried to pull him off his chest. The hired man was light and almost went off, but he cottoned onto the boy's shirt.

Curtiss asked what was going on.

'Just one,' Dietche said to himself.

"You gettin' off?"

"No."

"Get off!" Curtiss cried angrily, his teeth crossing the air.

With utmost care, Dietche raised his right arm and brought the fist at the end of it down fast, cold, and controlled into Curtiss's face.

"Jeedis," Curtiss said; bright red blood came out of his mouth and ribboned down his chin, and Dietche asked, watching him bleed, "Now will you leave me?" and got off and walked away. "Just leave me be?" he asked again and began closing the hatches with a long pole which made it dark then in the lofts. The day stopped timidly at the great open doors. "Just leave me be, huh kid?" Dietche asked somewhere.

"Oh, I'll leave you be," Curtiss said, spitting blood onto the hay.

"Well, that's what I'm hoping," Dietche replied.

Curtiss jumped carefully onto the runway and walked down to the trough, arms and legs shaking with shock, and sunk his face in the cold water. He lifted his dripping head; he'd heard the screen door slam below. Myron came out of the house and called up that it was long past the time Curtiss should have gone for the cows. Curtiss ducked his head once more. The cut shrank and gradually the bleeding stopped. He ran his tongue across the cut.

Dietche went slowly to his cabin by the woods. He had dealt with his feelings peacefully, without much violence, although he had to hit the young man violently. The great calm had broken when he wanted to push the fork through him; had broken like a first fish breaking a lake at dawn, and that was probably more Myron's fault than Curtiss's; but after that moment, the water became flat and reflective again.

When he got inside the bare room, he was surprised to find a cot Myron had been promising him. Myron was a puzzle. Dietche figured the boss just didn't know how to be a nice guy. He pushed the cot under the window. A long night's walk lay ahead of him, which he knew he could handle with a little rest. He lay down stiffly and neatly, like a mechanical man, folded his arms across his face, and fell into a peaceful sleep.

Against the white beaverboard walls, the long files of empty glass bottles lit by the sun, one bottle falling into shadow each time the sun fell.

CHAPTER FOUR

She heard the feed man turn into the driveway the next morning, the Fourth of July, and went to the back door and watched him drive up towards the barn, thinking how she had seen him come every two months for years and had not exchanged more than ten words with him. Sometime, she decided when he left each time, she would get to know him; and that morning, for some reason, when the curvaceous orange door swung out and smashed the sunlight, she walked outside.

Jim Lace stood by his truck and watched her coming up. Nice red hair. Hadn't given her much thought. Lace liked flair. One dawn years ago he'd found himself on Forty-second Street, his legs knocking one hundred and thirty dollars cash around in his pockets, looking for flair. He found it soon enough and one month later dropped penniless from an empty boxcar, tiptoed through town, and reentered his brother's house where he rented a small room. He never went away again. He still sought flair, though. There was a property on Kean Lake belonged to a Californian. Jim'd trucked in cement to build the swimming pool, and one day he had been invited in for a drink. He remembered a thick blue carpet with white deer running across it, and an abstract painting which the owner, Grantz, helped him understand, and the heavy tumbler of green glass with bubbles not only in the whisky and soda but in the glass itself. "If you don't mind my asking, why are you building a swimming pool when you've got all that lake front?" Jim asked.

"Good question," the man said and crossed his bare legs and picked his heel. "I suppose you folks think us strange."

Lace replied, "What you do here is your own business. We're all the same without our clothes on."

"That's a fine way of putting it, Jim," Grantz said, and looked through the modern window to the far side of the lake. "Men all right?"

"You paid them."

It was 1937. "I mean are they happy?" he asked wearily.

"Sure," Jim answered.

Grantz got to his feet. He swung an imaginary tennis racket for a moment, then suddenly confessed: "My wife does not like walking in mud, Jim. When she goes swimming in the lake, beautiful as it is, she is afraid of stepping on broken glass. She was cut badly when she was a little girl. So I'm building her the pool." Lace jumped to take the extended hand. Now that was flair. Nobody ever saw Grantz again, after the pool was built. The wife lived alone with the children up there. Jimmy looked in on her two or three times a year.

He stood black and fat against the orange truck, peering about for a glimpse of John Dietche while his short fingers felt his shirt for tobacco. Cora came up and stopped ten feet from him, and shaded her eyes. "Myron'll be along directly," she said.

"Fine. How you?" he asked.

"Fine," she said.

"That's good," he said.

She asked about his older brother, Howard, who owned the truck. "Howard's not well," he said.

"Maybe he smokes too much," she suggested, not knowing if he smoked at all.

"That, or he's dying this time, which'd be just cute."

"You tell us if he dies, won't you, Jim," she said and walked close to him.

"Why sure—" Jim said, surprised, looking up at her.

"We all got to die," she said.

"I don't see why," he said. He knew the rural phrase book by body, heart, and soul and spoke to her as easily as the wind blew while he looked her over. Tall, lusterless, a peculiarly unused female. She was like a brand-new piece of store merchandise nobody'd ever bought. He'd buy her. He'd had lots of merchandise. And she really wasn't all that bad looking. Hair was lively—red gold, burning, smelling of the strange human perfume. Gradually, he began to warm to her. Anyhow it was up to her. If she wanted it up her, O.K. He'd had so many. Used to be that the slightest sign in a woman's face would drive him miles out of his way. Used to be everytime he saw a poor farm or a poor herd he'd get hot and circle and move in. Myron's place looked too good for that—but Jim knew what Myron owed. He figured he'd have Cora Greenhalgh as easily as he'd catch cold. But it was getting to the point where he didn't really want it anymore. "Warmer today," he said and tore open a fresh package of cigarettes. "Cora—" he said, calling her Cora for the very first time. He paused and she looked at him, surprise moving into her dignified face. "I can *call* you Cora, can't I? Tired of calling you Mrs. Greenhalgh."

She scratched her elbow where the soap burned. "I guess so. No harm in people who've known each other ten years callin' each other—" she took a breath—"by their Christian names. 'Sides I call you Jim."

"You don't get about much to let folks know you."

"We got too much to do to get about."

He thought he'd about die if she said another faded thing like that in that typical faded voice. "Everybody's got a right to keep to himself, 'specially when they got lots of work," he said. "You put in a very big crop here, considerin' you do it all alone."

"We got help," she said.

"You can't trust help these days."

"He's new at it, but Myron figures he'll come along," she said.

"Where's he been—in jail?" Lace laughed, his gaze locked on her face.

"No," she said.

"I see," he said.

They grew silent.

Myron was across the main road under the elm tree, making minor repairs to the tractor which was forever breaking down. As he tore away a board holding the air filter erect, pitying himself slightly because Dietche was gone to town and sore at the anarchic symbolism of Jim's pickup truck, orange and radical as a whore by the barn, he thought: 'Jim Lace's got a soft job of it jawin' to wimmen all day.' He opened his pen knife.

"Myron could use a new tractor," Lace said. "Howard's seen the new line to Franklin—them little baby gray Fordson tractors. Take one to bed with you, Cora." He felt gay. He did a little dance step.

She laughed. She saw Myron watching them. "Jim Lace," she said severely. But she'd laughed; and she did it again, right out of the blue, and put her hand over her mouth.

"Don't let me keep you from anything," Lace said.

"My, my," she said and picked a loose filament of red-gold and wound it in place behind her ear. "Whew, it's hot." All morning the sun lay behind a vast haze, like an assassin.

"What's your hired man's name?" Jim asked.

"Don Jie—" she said absently and stopped and gripped the earth with her toes through her slippers. She had nearly got it right.

"John Dietche?" he asked.

"Curtiss," she said, "Lake."

"You said Don somebody."

"That's a boy Myron hired a few years ago." She looked at him. "Boys come and go. I forget them all. You know what I mean?"

"Ah," Lace said, suddenly warmed. He always preferred a more intimate level of conversation; and his mouth ached from smiling. "If you had a boy of your own—"

She turned away abruptly, closing her mouth as if she had a bird in it.

"Cora," he said in a cajoling voice. "You can talk to me," mistakenly thinking it was a son she wanted. It was just *talk* she wanted. Just a new voice, a new face, a new—Lord, a different-colored sky is all she wanted, she thought. "What in the world would I have to talk about?"

"Everybody's got troubles."

"I don't know's I can make out what you are driving at," she said.

"If you had a boy, you'd have something to look forward to in your old age."

"I declare."

"You'd like a son."

"Well, who wouldn't?" she asked, not to be impolite.

"Uh huh," Lace said, thrilled by his charity. "I knew it."

"Did you?" she said. "You certainly are an interesting person."

"Me?" he crooned and looked her hard in the face; he wasn't sure if she was kidding him or not. She couldn't be—big red horse with misty eyes—washed-out woman with a head of hot hair—not dumb, but not all there either—no, no, she wasn't kidding him. "Me? I'm nothing," he said. "Got no wife. Don't own nothin'. Why I'm so light and useless," he said, stretching his arms, showing her a whole busload of teeth that she could tell didn't come out at night, "some mornings I stay in bed for hours and hours slowly turning on the warm woolley spit. Well, that's fine for a lazy fellow like me. But what about them that have to work? Why're they so dry and hard?" Words flew off his lips. "There's a terrible emptiness in these valleys, Cora. Emptier than churches. What causes it? Am I keeping you from anything?" he asked in mid-flight.

Holding one hand at the side of her mouth, the little finger between her teeth, the red woman looked down at Lace as if she were deciding whether to purchase him or not. "Go right on," she said.

He stepped closer to get under her bleak stare. "This is the way I see it, Cora. We are born with a little drawer in our hearts and in that drawer is a packet wrapped in silver paper and around that silver paper is a soft, pink ribbon. And inside that packet, wrapped neat and tidy in that pink ribbon and that silver paper, is a live square of pure love."

"Sounds like a piece of cheese," she laughed.

"Our life on earth," he said, "is only a means of using that cut of pure love right." Moved, he put up a hand for another cigarette.

"You got the gift of gab," she said. "Go on."

"There ain't much more. Now you love Myron there. And Myron…loves…you." He couldn't go on. Spotted corn, tired old gear, two cans of milk standing in the cooler where on farms with love there would be six cans now and twice six in winter. No children. (Where in hell was John?) Lace had a particular view of life: into the gap that exists between reality and hope that people fill with religion or science or alcohol and which Myron filled with Dietche, Jim Lace put his own aromatic, cinematized, big red amorous heart. Without love between men and women there could be no happiness for mankind. Myron and Cora unloving, therefore the dry fields and decimated regiments of cows and cans. He could explain it badly enough. The theory was nonsense. A self-confidence born of leisure was the motive force. Not many had either, at least none of those wives he fostered. The only thing Lace did well, the one thing that brightened his life and made him feel king of the beasts, was making love to their women; he had the leisure. And now, once again, although it was merely an echo of old thunder, Jim was warming to this not-beautiful woman. So many times past a poor field had told of a woman without love who'd welcome a man in an orange pickup, and it would happen again, even though he was rounding fifty. Often, however, although not in the case of Cora Greenhalgh, it was not what he thought at all: often a woman would welcome him who had nothing except love. Jim had a theory that love was abundance, that was all. And he had a truck which his indulgent brother let him do what he pleased with.

The approach of Myron retired Lace. He figured he had touched her. It looked all set.

"Could have been loading them empty sacks for me, Jim, couldn't you?" Myron asked.

"Sorry," Lace said. He never did any work he didn't have to. "You have such an interesting wife I lost track of the time."

Myron climbed into the pick-up and Jim drove him to the top of the hill. On the way up, they passed an old, disused chicken house. The door hung open like the mouth of an idiot. It hadn't been used for years. No love, Jim thought.

Myron suggested that there was no need to hurry to pay a bill two years outstanding.

"No, hell, Howard don't care," Jim said, and pulled the emergency brake to and followed him outside. "If he dies, though, the banks'll get on to all of you, you know," he said.

"If Howard dies it'll kill you as well, Jim, won't it?" Myron said and went in to the barn to get the empty sacks Dietche and the boy had hung on the runway.

Lace came off the running board with a black bill-book in his hand. He heard footsteps behind him. "John?" he inhaled and swung about. "No," he said relieved.

"Curtiss Lake," the young man answered, out of tune.

"You ain't from around here, Mr. Lake?"

"No, I'm from New York. Are you going into town this morning, Mr. Lace?"

"Yes, I'm going to take those sacks back. How did you know my name?"

"You've got it painted on your door. Can you give me a ride?"

"Sure—"

Curtiss yawned. "That'll be very good of you," he said, and was about to walk away, dragging his cloud behind him, when Myron came out with the sacks.

"You can go to town with Jim," Myron told him.

"We fixed it," Curtiss said.

"You know where to go?" Myron asked.

"What?"

"You know what store I got my charge at?"

"Your charge, Myron?" Curtiss asked with a glance at Lace. Nobody got it.

"My charge account," Myron said.

"No, sir, I don't," Curtiss replied.

"Let him off at Carmichael's," Myron told Lace.

"Curtiss going shopping today?" Lace asked.

"Yes, he is."

"Well, today's the Fourth of July. No stores'r open today."

Myron's mouth opened. The holiday had come round all by itself. "That's right," he said. Something had happened without him; he felt the same strange, helpless release he got from lightning.

"I wouldn't lose any sleep over it, Myron," Jim said and turned to the young man with a friendly smile. "You come to town anyhow. We'll find somebody open. Everybody's looking for an excuse to do a little extra business these wonderful prosperous days."

"O.K.," Curtiss said and turned on his heel and walked quietly away.

"Touchy, ain't he," Lace said, watching Curtiss go off.

"He's touchy today," Myron replied after a moment, and laid the sacks on the back of the truck.

"Nice boy?" Jim asked.

"Yep."

"Hard worker?"

"Nope."

"Quiet, ain't he?" Jim asked.

"What do you want, Jim?"

"Orilla Ano said she'd seen somebody here on Wednesday she never seen before," Jim replied evenly.

"Who's Orilla Ano?"

"She got married last Wednesday and passed by your place. She says she saw John Dietche here."

"Who?"

"The pride of Garfield County. You remember. Lit out about fifteen years ago. Father lives over in back of your pasture where you and your Pa and the others drove him after the first war—old Dietche, the Kaiser's secret agent, they said."

"That was a long time ago—"

"There is talk in town his son's come back."

"They seen him?" Myron asked.

"No."

"He was in jail, wasn't he?" Myron asked.

"Yes, he was. In the penitentiary."

"Maybe he's going to settle up for what you and Pa Greenhalgh did to him and his Pa."

Myron grinned. Dietche didn't care about that. Myron knew him well enough to know that very likely it was precisely that blinded eye which made Dietche choose Myron to live with. A man like Dietche wouldn't trust his life to a friend. "Would I tell you, even if he was here, Jim? The police might want him."

"I hadn't thought of that."

"This is funnier'n hell. Who's that says she saw him?"

"Orilla Ano. Her folks live up by the chasm. She got married Wednesday to Gene Devereux."

"Who?" Myron asked. He jabbed his finger down the stacks on the truck, checking the bags with the credit slip Jim'd given him. Had he been on trial for murder, the torture Myron endured at Lace's cross-examination couldn't have been more exciting.

"She *said*—"

"Who said—?" Myron murmured.

"Orilla said—leastways she confided in her Ma, and her Ma's got even a bigger mouth, said Orilla seen Dietche from her car when they all come by your place on the weddin' day."

"Yesterday?"

"Wednesday."

"Sounds silly to me."

"Doesn't it?" Jim said.

Myron turned, surprised. "You find it silly, Jim?"

"God I think it's stupid. See, she was stuck on Dietche as a young girl, wasn't she?"

"Was she?"

"Yeah." Jim paused. "I got a theory—"

"One of those theories of yours, Jim?"

"Yeah. I figure people can see anything they want to see."

"Do you?"

"I figure Orilla saw Curtiss Wednesday—her wedding day— and wanted so much to be married to John Dietche—Curtiss is about John's size."

"That all sounds pretty sensible to me, Jim."

"That's what happened," Jim said confidently. "She still wanted John so bad in her subconscious mind, specially on her way to the wedding and all that excitement and everything. I don't guess deep down she loves poor Gene after all."

Myron said, "Must be lots of women in that fix. He was quite a sport, wasn't he?"

"Oh I don't know," Lace said after a moment, a little haughtily. "He did all right."

Myron folded the slip and put it in his pocket. "Where do you think he is?"

"Probably in some big city'r other. If words was flesh and blood he'd be all over here cause everybody's talkin' about it." Jim rolled down his sleeves and buttoned his cuffs. "Mind if I use the phone?" he asked. Myron said he didn't mind. He watched the truck spin round the small barn, pass below him and pull up between the garage and the house. 'It is getting worse than I expected,' Myron thought. 'What will I do?' His first thought was typical: 'I might get some folks over tomorrow and show them around. If everybody's heard, like Jim says, they'll come looking for Dietche, and he won't be here. I do hope he keeps hid at the fairgrounds and to Avalon. I oughten to of let him go, but what could I do?' The warning threw Myron. Taking the fugitive in at the risk of his personal safety had proved delightful. Owning him, owning a soul, had proved an extension of the initial pleasure. But keeping the world off him .... Myron was in this up to the hilt.

And being Myron, he decided to play it for all it was worth. The capacity for total abandonment to one's fate is rare in people, and even though one tries to guide the rush with a fragile leash of reason, nothing can diminish the roaring, terrifying blackness of the experience. If abandonment is what it was. Myron seemed to have a lot of courage; more perhaps than he knew. Certainly more than Dietche who would never have faced such a problem except with his rear end. It appeared to be abandonment; but actually Myron was convinced, irrationally, that he and Dietche would never be caught. And people who are unalterably convinced of their own sanctity are hiding something, and one cannot abandon oneself when one is hiding something, whether a man or a secret. Roaring blackness might be Myron's, but he would walk into it with the faint smile of the self-assured. There was no question of courage. It was pure arrogance. So long as he knew where the attack was coming from, he felt he could not be unseated.

He decided to kill the rumor by inviting—his first thought— a few chosen and undoubtedly suspicious gossips to a lawn party the next day. From there on, he went about like one of those old kings who knew they would win because God was on their side; and as often as not lost.

The feeling was like a long parachute jump, and he felt anxieties assail him like Jap pursuit planes. What if Dietche turned up? Well, he would say he hadn't known John was on the run. But no one held Myron in their doubtful affections as so many people held Dietche. Therefore what if Dietche accused Myron of hiding him, and what if they believed him?

He wanted to tell somebody how brave he felt. It annoyed him a little that he couldn't tell anyone. He headed across the flat towards the small barn.

The young man stood in a corner of light, reading a letter. "You ever going to town?" Myron asked him.

Curtiss walked through a hundred tiny rays of light to the door.

"You get up on the wrong side of the bed this morning?" Myron asked.

"I don't feel so well, O.K.?" the young man replied.

"What's the matter?" Myron asked.

"I just can't sleep." The fight kept going through his mind.

"I got some pills, Curtiss, if you're having trouble sleeping."

"Do you?"

"I'll give you a pill tonight."

"W—will you?"

Myron nodded and then spoke quietly to him, in a confidential tone: "Lissen: you lissenin'?"

"Yes, sir," Curtiss said suspiciously, licking the healed cut inside his cheek.

"Don't say anything to Lace about John ... don't even mention he's here ... don't in town neither. You buy yer stuff and get out. Don't say *nothing*."

"No, sir," Curtiss said.

"Remember!"

"Oh yes."

"You goin' to remember?"

"Yes, *sir*." He'd yessir him till the cows came home, until he got that pill. He went down to Lace's truck and got inside it.

Before he walked down to brush the horses, Myron remained alone on the flat, grassless earth between his barns. Life had never been quite like this before. His small dark face automatically counted his cows emerging into the high pasture on the mountain above him. Bluebottle flies turned their beautiful glistening blades around his head. The great temple doors of the big barn clapped softly behind him.

Meanwhile Jim Lace was down in the kitchen holding visions of delight before Cora's indisinterrable eyes. "Lois Van Meter has eight kids—killed her old man," he said, raising the glass of water to his lips. She didn't remember how or when he'd got in. She sat with one arm out flat on the table as if strapped down; in among her fingers smoked a king-sized cigarette.

He sat the glass on the enamel table. "You know the Uffords?"

"We don't get around much," she said.

"Everybody's heard of Doady Music."

"I heard," she said.

"She's a bad woman and a sore on the face of the community. Never mind: she's *happy*." He pulled another cigarette from his pocket. "Her and Sam got four boys in military school." He opened his gold lighter. "They got a good income from the hotel and a perfect insurance. I might add"—and he smiled through a cloud of blue smoke and kicked his leg up and down—"it is warm in their place all winter long."

"What is so surprising about that?"

"They got a whole hotel to heat. Used to be a whorehouse, you know—did you know that?"

The ash dropped onto the table and broke. She looked him in the eye. "What is your business with me?"

"I'm talkin' about love, Cora," he said. "Without love," he said, "the world would dry up and fall to powder." One of his best lines, composed in the hot stare of a girl in Peru. He was in love with love.

"We're wasting our time," she said.

"Maybe we are," he said and scratched the thick shiny black hair on his neck. He stared beyond her out the window, suddenly tired.

They did not speak for several minutes. She did not notice the hot coal drawing the web between her fingers. He'd made her light it, although she didn't smoke, to keep her still.

"When the earth was still very hot and no life yet abroad, there wasn't any love either. But when the first things came out of the sea, love came too. Then came the monkeys. You heard of Romeo and Juliet." It was about the shortest history of the world to date.

"Yes—we read about it in school," she said.

"Take them. Take the Trojan War."

"Sure."

"Ajax and Lysander whackin' each other because of their love for Helen." His lecture was a very crooked path leading to the bedroom, so it wasn't entirely the rural woman's lack of attention—divided as it was between wondering when Myron would catch her and the sexy drip in Jim's voice—that caused the extraordinary shifts in the narrative. After he'd told her how Don Juan'd taken Elvira's clothes off piece by piece and seen she still wasn't listening, he began a story about himself. "When I was a small boy, Cora, I made friends with a pussycat I found one day on the road." She looked up for the first time. "My father was agin the cat and so was Ma, but I cried up a storm and they let off. I was five." He stopped, feeling suddenly tired and unenthusiastic again. Why was she interested in *this*, he wondered.

"Go on," she said.

"We was livin' up to Saint Marie," he continued. "Well, I loved that cat and took it around with me wherever I went. One day I was playin' in the loft and Pa come and rolled the sliding doors to admit a wagonload of hay and my cat got her head caught in the jamb. There was a considerable squeal. I come scampering down and there it was, blind as a bat, walking along, tripping itself up, its little legs all out of kilter. 'What are we going to do?' I shouted to make myself heard above the laughing. The men looked down at me of'n the rick, and Pa said, 'It's yourn. Kill it. Lessen you like it that way.' 'How, Pa?' I asked, and he told me to sink it in the rainbarrel. So I took it in a blanket so's it wouldn't scratch me and put it in the barrel, which was full in them days. It swam, of course. Then I hit it with a piece of wood. And when Pa come in the next load he called me an awful fool and a coward. And took a hammer. That did it. I wasn't much use to anybody for a couple of days. Then I come round and apologized."

"Why'd you apologize?" she asked. "You didn't do anything wrong."

"No, but my folks seemed to like it if I just apologized for things."

"I sure feel bad about the kitty," she said.

"What about me?" he asked, but before she could reply the coal struck her fingers. "Ow!" she cried, yanking her hand away. The cigarette fell to the table.

"Didn't you feel it coming?" he asked, beginning to laugh, amazed to see how little the butt was, how close the coal had burned without her feeling it.

"Shush!" she said, terrified Myron was near. "Stop that laughing, Jim! You want everybody to hear?"

"I clean forgot that cigarette."

"You and your chatter. Ought to be ashamed pestering an old woman like myself."

He walked behind her to the low window. "You ain't so old."

"No?" she asked, sucking her hand.

Outside he saw his truck waiting for him, burning up the sunlight. He turned. "Let me see that."

"It's nothing," she replied and held out her hand to him.

He took the hand. "Cora," he said. He squeezed and looked deep into her flameless eyes. "Cora," he said again.

"You haven't looked at the burn yet," she said.

He looked and returned his intense stare to her face. "Stop," she said.

"Stop what?"

"What you are doing."

"What am I doing?"

"Looking at me that way."

"I am not looking at you in any way at all."

"Let go of my hand."

"I can't," he replied. She was making it so dignified, he thought, wishing as usual he were taller and had not shaved off his mustache the year before.

"Let go," she said in agony—not since the first weeks of life had she been so lost—so free—so abandoned to the bald spaces of the present. She felt just about perfect. And miserable, and scared to death of what there might be for her to do beyond just sitting motionless in the chair, her back to the window. She withdrew her hand.

The short man with the sweet pants and the ginger-haired woman were silent, he standing, now unconnected beside her, she sitting in a pool of her own stillness, while their emotions clattered about in old rusty armor, and far down below them waves swooped up against the fantasy tower and gulls shrieked in block-and-tackle voices—which were only the sounds of the singletree banging down the drive outside between Myron and the horse. The little farmer held the reins as if they were the train of a bride and passed the window without seeing them together there in his kitchen. He was figuring out who to telephone for the party, and worried about his tractor which had broke down. He'd forgot Lace.

The black knight watched him go out of sight and reached an arm to his lady. "Cora," he said and touched her shoulder.

"Stop," she said. 'Just stop right there forever—you needn't go on,' she thought, entranced by the sudden absence of pain and fear in her while the miracle hand rested on her.

"We ain't got much time," he said.

"Time?" she asked.

She didn't know even the littlest tricks, he thought. But if she didn't want him there she should have thrown him out. She certainly was a puzzler. Perhaps she was teasing him. "We are attracted to each other," he asked the back of her aromatic head. "Well?" he said when the silent creature did not reply.

"I-I—," she muttered.

She suggested he talk some more.

"Talk," he grunted and took his hand away, announcing in a voice full of boils, "Promise me when I come back I can make love to you. You give me your word? O.K.?"

She felt dirtied. She stood up indignantly. "I don't promise nothin'. I don't know what you mean." The endless days of the future ran greedily up to queue. "I don't have to promise anything. Go on now, Jim," she said. "Before I tell Myron what you said."

"Cora!" he cried, disappointed.

"You aren't the first that's talked to me that way," she said, intending to walk stately out the screen door.

"No sir," he said, coming up behind her. "You let me touch you," he was saying.

"But that's all, Jim," she said.

"That's a sign you want more," he said.

"I ain't attracted to you, Jim," she said.

"Why'd you get so hot then?"

"Oh I didn't get h-h——," she protested and started to go out. He grabbed her. It was the old familiar sort of touch now. She kept walking, hoping to pull the hands off her. And then, without warning, he let go. She fell forward, onto her knees, on the floor.

The china tittered on the sideboard.

"You all right?" he said, watching her gather herself on the linoleum.

"You go on," she said, breathing heavily and not looking at him.

"I guess I'll go. Get to town," he said and stepped past her and out the screen door.

Outside he tried to shake an oncoming depression by whistling. He felt tired and failed and full of unreleased seed and the desire for revenge which were pretty much the same thing at that moment. Well, sometimes you don't get away clean, he thought, and leaped youthfully into the truck and slipped and almost fell on his face.

It would not have been necessary for him to worry about her, had it been likely he would worry about her. It was all taken care of. She was standing at the window. She heard him whistle, thinking what a nice man he was and how he came this way every odd month or so for years and that she'd got to know him a little now. She put the cold cigarette butt in the garbage can and wiped the face of the table clean and smiled. She had forgotten what had happened. The bad moment had disappeared, swallowed up in shadow. Thus she had put out of her thoughts Myron's blow in the fields and remembered now only how lovely the sky had looked on her back in the dust. The story Jim had told about the pussy—ah yes, she remembered the story, and transposed it into the fabric of memory for a rainy day. She took the ironing board out of the pantry. In a moment—in an hour—if someone were to ask her when she'd last seen Jim Lace, she might very well stop and think and say, "Why, wasn't he just here?"

The plug went into the wall, and soon the iron was hot and sliding back and forth over her husband's shirts. Once, only once, she stopped ironing and put her hand absently to her shoulder, but she felt nothing because both shoulder and hand were hers.

CHAPTER FIVE

At the fairground, six loudspeakers spoke. Men with sunflowers sewed on their backs heard it on the track and three thousand people listened from their seats in the grandstand. On the track stood a car with a chicken wire windshield, about to start off with a man in a white helmet lying full length on the hood. Because of the helmet, he was the only one who didn't hear the loudspeakers say: "If there is a doctor in the grandstand will he come to the main ticket office immediately!"

The announcer repeated the message and then said to a friend next to him in the booth that the doctor was for Howard Lace, who was dying. But he forgot to shut off the sound, so everybody heard. The grandstand grew silent.

Answering the loudspeaker's request, three doctors picked their way down through the crowd. They noticed each other and felt a little silly to be all going and actually started to turn back before they realized that that would look even worse. They met at the bottom and walked away to their cars.

Would the doctors be in time this time? People wondered. By means of his self-made feed-and-lumber concern Howard Lace had become the most precious man in town. His death would shake the rural economy. The farmers were worried about a bigger man than Howard who lived in Avalon with a vast milling empire stretching across the country. Now Howard was dying, the big man might move up there and occupy Howard's bank and warehouses: he could call in all the unpaid mortgages because he didn't know anybody in the town or the valleys and needn't fear what people thought.

The townspeople knew Howard intimately and they were worried over the loss of a friend and an example. Everyone knew he was the only real businessman they had, and that he was a man who understood their problems, who understood how impossible it was to improve things, who allowed people to run into debt, sold them fair goods, not first class, playing the game as life had played them all. What would his death bring? A big man with a terrible reputation for improving things. They were sensible people. They dreaded the cheerful.

And something else, a kind of indigestible hors d'oeuvre to this latter piece of bad news, a rotten young man named Frank Daville turned his car onto his neck the night before in an attempt to get home by not using the road.

And that came, coupled with the news of Howard Lace's imminent death, in time to join the rumor of John Dietche's presence in the area, the name that was a symbol of all that was unholy.

"Needn't listen for more," a man in a black suit said nervously to his brother, whose eyes were latched into the loudspeakers. "We'll call tonight."

"Shore," the brother replied. "What's going to happen now Howard's done?"

"Howard ain't done yet," another said from the seat below.

"Oh? I thought that's what the doctor said last time—next time he's done for."

They laughed harshly when a kid suggested that Howard's brother Jim might take over the business.

The old goats to whom death was a dear friend hated to listen to the gravediggers converse so coldly and halted the work where they could. "Wall," they said, drawing the word out loudly to cover younger voices and then, when the young were silent, croaked on quietly, "I hope he don't kick."

"Yaas, me too. Don't do no good guessin'."

"Wonder if it is his heart again," murmured an ancient who had heart trouble.

"Waal, Franny don't seem to think so." Franny was Howard Lace's secretary. "Let's all wait and see and enjoy the cars. What do you say? How about shuttin' up on Howard?"

So the talking died and without much interest they thumbed open their programs. The next event was a death-defying crash of a man's head through a wooden wall. The car started rolling forward below them.

The truck mused around a curve. Straight ahead down the black asphalt aisle, trees waited. The truck went through them and they fell away as if blown off their feet.

The wreckage of a roadster passed, wheels-up on the side of a rocky embankment. Frank Daville's car, Jim said and explained what had happened. A skinny deer rippled his ribs across the road in front of them and dissolved. Curtiss sat up. "Do you have a gun?"

"Hell no. It ain't season anyways."

"It was so fast! God!"

"Oh, they're fast all right," Lace said with a smile.

"Marvelous," Curtiss said and relaxed against the seat.

"He's on his way to the lake."

"Marvelous."

"Awful thin, didn't you see?"

"Marvelous," Curtiss said patiently.

"We're all thin around here," Jim said, happy that the boy was talking at last. "Spiritually, I mean, we are practically invisible." Jim swung the truck around another sharp curve, shifted down into second, and then back into third. "If you ask me," and Curtiss had not, "it's a boneyard, this particular part of the world. And it ain't so terribly different on the outside neither. Son, it's black as the inside of a wrist watch in Garfield county.

I seen it all. Watched this comin' since I was a kid. They've lost somethin'."

"You're luckier than most, I guess."

Lace lit a cigarette. "When a farmer gets to the state of affairs where he dries," he said, snapping up his lighter, "the first thing happens he starts to mistrust me. Stops speaking to me. I try to help them. But they just don't care."

"Well."

"And I'll tell you why," Jim said.

"They can leave, I suppose. I'd leave," the young man said and yawned.

"They can't leave. They're all in hock to my brother Howard. No, it'd be all right for one thing: if they hadn't lost the capacity to love each other, they'd be prosperity around here."

"You say there isn't any *love*," Curtiss said, putting his finger in the syrup, "and you say it's—no, you say that the farms are poor because the farmers don't love each other? Is that what you said?"

"Yep." They swept silently through a gallery of tall pines crossing out the sky, and then the chamber emptied into the sun again. "How many times have you been in love?" Jim asked simply.

Curtiss swore under his breath.

"What did you say, son?" Jim asked.

"I don't think I said anything."

"I asked you how many times you have been in love."

"Don't recall."

"You never had a girl?"

"Sure."

"You love her?"

"I don't know what you're talking about. You can't just go around throwing phrases about, Jim. You mustn't be so vague."

"You don't know what I mean by love?"

"No."

"I can see you're one of those sophisticated city fellows."

"No," Curtiss said. "Why would you say a silly thing like that? Just because you come from up here, Jim, shouldn't make you jealous of people who don't share your point of view."

"I won't argue."

"I don't think this is an argument," Curtiss said inaudibly.

"Can't you believe in the one power that binds us all together on earth—that holds us spinning right and true—that gives us hope for the future? You deny that, son, and you deny everything."

"Well then, I do. I can't make it up."

"You're foolish not to *believe* in something."

"On the contrary."

"Where do you get that nonsense?" Jim laughed.

"But I haven't said anything at all!" the young man protested. "What do you mean, nonsense?"

"I don't get you," Jim said.

"Well, I do. Just keep on the road!" Curtiss said, sucking in his breath with fear. Jim swerved in and out of a ditch and slowly began to unfurl another banner.

"Son," he said, "when you get below the surface of life—when you get a look at the whole picture here—"

Curtiss's attention wandered. He drifted away while Lace continued, in a low, singsong, poet voice, to rebuild his house of face cards, until bit by bit the gravity of logic and reason was once again defied and something seemingly substantial reappeared in the shallow basin of his music-hall mind. "You," he whispered softly with a smile, "see you got to believe. With love in you, you can understand the speech of birds. I can. Hours I've sat on the roof of my brother's house and counted the swallows in the spring and the geese in the fall and understood what they had to say. Because I love them!"

"But what is it you love *precisely,* Jim?" the young marksman asked. "What is *love?*"

"Everything. All of life. All life is what I love." Jim said.

"You win," Curtiss said. "You got to win."

"I can see you're one of the loveless kind."

"I am, Jim, I am. But it's nothing for you to worry about."

"Ha ha," Lace said, embarrassed by Curtiss's flat rejection of everything he said. He mashed his cigarette in an ash tray suffering from old butts. He wouldn't say another word. Tap, tap.

"What was that?" he said. He had run over something. He pushed on the brakes. The truck lurched to a stop. He opened the door and jumped onto the highway.

Curtiss lit a cigarette, and rearranged his legs, patiently awaiting his freedom from this road-company Whitman's embarrassing innocence.

Back Jim came, coming to the door more slowly than he'd gone, and climbed in behind the wheel. He shifted the pillow which compensated for his short legs and took a sudden, fathomless breath, and sat still and looked at his hands in his lap. Curtiss glanced sideways, wondering why they weren't moving on, and saw tears in the man's eyes. "You git behind the wheel of a truck," he was mumbling, "something little and helpless comes along and you mash it. Why are we like that?" His shoulders started to shake.

"It wasn't your fault," Curtiss said.

"No, it was an accident. I couldn't of helped it. It run out onto the road. But I still did it, son."

"Mr. Lace—have a heart," Curtiss said.

After a moment, Lace wiped his face and drove on, hating the young man.

Curtiss was surprised to see sand. Long stripes of gray sand running through the brush with blackberry vines wound through it like barbwire. He noted some houses back off the highway. Lost ruts led to the pine-hid houses; there were faded signs on the shingle roofs: Balsam Pillows. "What is a balsam pillow?" he asked.

Jim always gave people a second chance. He looked at Curtiss and smiled in a friendly fashion. "You tie up pine needles, ferns, sprucetails, Curtiss, and pack them into a rough cloth pillow and sew an embroidery squirrel or a flag on it. Smells good. Foresty. The old folks make them in town now but there ain't any market anymore. My, they stink."

"What stinks? The pillows?"

"No, the old folks. They get their clothes all pitched up." They passed another of the disused houses.

"Hell of a place," Curtiss murmured.

"You should see the ones got people living in them. That burnt-out wreck there if you're interested used to belong to an old German pillow-maker named Dietche."

Curtiss lifted his head.

"He lives back of Myron's now," Jim continued, and at last they dropped down onto the valley.

"Tell me about him."

"His son John's the black sheep around here—went to jail years back. Come out on parole. Some say he's run back here—but why he'd come back here where he was born and reared beats me. I don't think it's so."

"Huh," Curtiss said, amused.

"I remember John well. We was good friends. The circus come to Malone once and John loved circuses. He was the easiest fellow to get along with in the world—and he didn't have to be—some overpatriotic fellows burned him and his Pa out of that house back there and chased them into the hills back of Myron's. That's how he lost his eye. You can't help a war. Well, once over to the circus at Malone John took care of the six-bit tent—funny women and such. Hair on their br—tits—and all."

"I saw that in Florida," Curtiss said. "It was all wax stuff though."

"That's the diseases. We get the diseases all the time. This was the live oriental sexual freaks—"

"Oh."

"Yeah. Very rare. John was eighteen—"

"What about that eye?"

"Well, didn't I say? It got burned out in the fire."

"Got you. Go on."

"Nineteen-nineteen: he was about eight. Well, one day years later, I went out to see him about somethin'—a girl or other—I used to drive on the back roads shootin' rabbits from the car and occasionally I'd find John face down in the dust mumbling to himself, flies and spiders partying on the meat he was bringing home. It was just too long a walk from town."

"How'd he make a living?" Curtiss interrupted.

"Natural mechanic—kind of a born talent for fixing machines. You could only get him workin' for a week, fore he'd disappear to get liquored up. But he fed his Pa, on and off; give him credit for that."

"What about you were saying—something the freaks, Jim?"

"He slept with them! We never knew with which—but Lord how dull life must have been to him to do that. Then one day as I say, I went over to see him, and he was gone. *Gone.* Didn't even tell his Pa where."

"No kidding—he slept with the freaks?"

"Yeah. No kidding." Lace was all for kicking the kid into the road. Nothing really interested him except horror of one kind or the other. John's eye. The freaks.

(It was just that Curtiss lived in the cellar of the house of love, and Jim lived in the attic.)

Jim had never realized the crippling strength of the spell the young Dietche had cast on him, on Orilla Ano Devereux, and on a lot of the other young who, no longer young, still remembered Dietche as something particularly unique, and who spoke of him in ribald awe. The rotten, freshly killed Frank Daville had admired Dietche, for example, and he was never going to get over it now. Jim Lace had only wanted to demonstrate this affection for Dietche; but he was finished talking. Whether it was the horrors or just Curtiss's unsympathetic tone of voice, he was feeling embarrassed again. The young man was as uncommunicative as a post. Because Curtiss was alive, however, Jim tried twice to attach himself to him—and twice slipped off. He wouldn't try again.

Still, the young man was there, living and breathing, like anybody else.

The engine rose to a scream on the back stretch. The big man in the helmet settled his head on a pillow. The head preceded the car by a few inches. The man closed his eyes. His head hit the wall a fraction of a second before the bumpers and together they bored a hole through the wood.

Josie's heavy face sagged as he removed his helmet; he shook out his blond hair and rode past the stands with his arm raised. The lack of enthusiasm killed him. "Nevah seen such poor sports," he complained to his driver. "Why do you care, Josie?" Henry deLancy asked wearily, dropped the cracker at a faucet, and drove to the trailer where he lived with his wife and the little girl. Josie lit a cigarette after he'd drunk and flung his helmet on the ground. He picked it up and flung it down again. What was the matter with them up there? They all seemed dead. Josie was the only one of all the sunflowers who kept his sunflower fresh, the only one of all the bedouins who had a real audience sense. He threw the cigarette away.

It certainly wasn't Josie's fault. He couldn't know that Frank Daville had broken his neck the night before in an automobile wreck. He hadn't heard the announcement about Howard Lace. And he didn't know who John Dietche was. Death was his trade, but he had no idea what proportion of death there was there that day in those stands, nor how serious a thing it could be to people.

Halfway up the grandstand, Orilla turned to a man behind her. "Do you know who I saw in a field on my wedding day?" she asked.

The man took his eye off the enormous silver and blue bus the mechanics were drawing into place down below. "Orilla, you been spreading that story for days now," he said.

A pocket of loafers nearby, friends of Jim Lace, made the noise of the voice between the legs at her. "We know that story, Orilla. Jim told us what you was saying. And it's a lie." Dietche could have led those old kids into hell had he wanted to. Only they'd been waiting so long for something like him, they were the first to disbelieve in his return.

In general, it was depressing to hear about John. The old ones felt guilty for burning him and his father out long ago on that infamous collective lark. Then John had developed into a lark himself, a drunken buffoon who mocked their efforts to stay righteous and sober. He'd always bragged that he'd escape; they were secretly relieved when he did and the day they heard of his arrest they were both justified and sorry. And now was he out and around here? Probably not. Orilla was a famous liar. Why in God's name would he return here? It was rubbing salt in an unhealable wound. "I don't want to believe it," said one woman knitting for a baby still in her gut. "Have him around they'll be trouble." People leaving their seats walked on her knitting bag.

"Won't rain," said one old peasant who barely spoke English.

"Troopers'll pick him up if it is true," someone else said.

The people sat thinking about Howard Lace, and about Dietche, and about Frank Daville who had rolled his car onto his neck, so everything seemed to come together when Josie smashed his head through the wall, and they picked up and went home. It wasn't Josie's fault.

"There's the bridge," Jim said and nodded at a long red tray of iron that took the road in its arms down at the end of the valley. They soon crossed it in a clatter of loose planks and found themselves on the stained outskirts of the town. Red houses ran along the winding river below them, poor and neat, and then they were into town proper with the high school, and the flag bleeding on an enormous flagpole opposite the fresh-granite Catholic church. The church turned Curtiss's head. He watched it spin slowly away in the rear window. The sight refreshed him. The granite recalled vespers on his knees at school, obliterated in incense, and the rustling white silk vestments of the passing priest, the smoking censer, and darkness, worshipping himself.

They parked at a sidewalk raised high off the ground because of the great snows that had filled the streets. Lace got out.

Curtiss looked over the town. A drugstore, a shoe store, an insurance office, an A & P, an alley leading down. It was so real, he thought, they could have made a movie of it right there. A movie house, a bar, and then a bank at the edge of a small silver bridge in the middle of the view. The smell of ground coffee and post office and then a strain of skunk passed through his head. Some were smells he recalled from other towns; the skunk was real.

Jim came into close-up and began speaking. Curtiss stirred, breaking the mold of stillness that had formed around him. His seat was wet. He got out of the car. Jim told him he was lucky that Carmichael hadn't shut down, Carmichael's excuse being that he was taking inventory. Curtiss nodded and walked to the store. "Good luck," Jim said. Curtiss turned. "Oh—thanks, Jim," he said.

"You're welcome," Jim said miserably.

The way Curtiss disappeared into Carmichael's, Jim knew that the young man had forgotten him forever. As far as the boy was concerned, Jim was nothing—zero—space. Jim slammed himself into his truck and drove quickly to the fairgrounds, where everybody he knew was.

Inside Carmichael's Curtiss bought eight work shirts and a pair of brown boots and four pairs of blue jeans, leaving Myron $31 in debt to Carmichael. He left the store and carried his bundles across the street and down the steep alley.

The shallow water filtered loudly over the stones lining the belly of the river. He could smell the coolness under the bridge. The sweat on his back grew cold. He took out a cigarette. The concrete ceiling cupped the noises of the stream and of his match raking down the yellow box in his hand.

While the young man smoked and watched the water passing over the bed of slippery rocks, he remembered John Dietche. He began smoking too fast, thinking about the fight, so he sat on a round stone and put his elbows on his knees and stared into the stream. Soon he was outside the hour; soon he was shut out from the pressure of the sky, becoming part of the flow of the water, forgetting everything.

The river ran two inches over the red and green stones, forming small pools in the sand where spiders nervously walked the gelatin surface and rowing bugs sculled out angles. Curtiss dissolved. 'Gee,' he thought in a few moments of complete entrancement. The gee-moment, which only came in those rare handfuls of seconds when he could be drawn by the irresistible pull of stillness out of his barricades; until what was mortal in him betrayed this pleasant sort of suicide by becoming sore on the cold stone. He looked around furtively and got off the rock and unwrapped his parcels.

He pulled the pins and shook a new shirt open. The sleeves and waist fell free and with them a piece of tissue paper; with great care he undid all the buttons. He took off. his tattered white shirt and pulled the new shirt over his white arms and shoulders, feeling the freshness of the cloth. He changed into the new boots and tied the old broken aristocrats by their laces and stowed them, with the old shirt, in the shoe box and reknotted the string. He did all the shirt buttons up including the one at the neck, tucked the tail neatly into his jeans, retightened his belt, and after holding his arms out to admire the shirt and looking down his chest to see the row of pale lettered buttons, picked up all the parcels, and came out from under the bridge.

He hiked up the alley and went down the main street, passing store after store, contented and relaxed, pretending he was a young man just like himself in an empty town. Then he heard the cars coming.

Startled, he walked more quickly, to get away before he was discovered.

Jim Lace pulled up outside the grandstand, leaned out the window, and said to a man in a black coat, "What's the matter, Sam? Why's everybody going?"

"Well, Jim," Sam said.

"Show no good?" Jim asked cheerfully, losing on Sam's face the sense of desertion the young man'd given him. Sam would never walk away from a man the way Curtiss had. The crowds swallowed the truck.

"Your brother is dying," Sam said.

One thing at a time, Jim thought. "My brother dying, Sam? Who told you he was dying?"

"It got around. The doctor's with him now."

"I'm glad the doctor's with him. He'll need a doctor. Which doctor is it?"

"What'll you do, Jim?"

"Well," Jim said, taking deep breaths as the news bit into him. "I don't know, Sam."

Sam slapped the truck. "See you back at the house?" he asked.

"O.K." Jim said.

'I had a feeling something like this was going to happen today,' Jim thought, watching the people coming out the entrance to the track towards him. 'They all look so cross,' he thought. He opened the door and left the truck and walked with them and started talking to them, trying to cheer them up. "*Jim,*" they said, shocked. "Well, don't look so sad," he told them. Then, realizing what he was doing, remembering what had happened, he tried to get back to the empty truck, but he found himself caught and carried along in the current of the crowd. He stood stock still. They all flowed around him, staring back into his face as they went.

Dietche's bad eye couldn't blink because the muscles of the lid were burnt; it stared at the emptying stands. The two men sat in a car and the boss came over and leaned in on the window and asked what in hell they thought was going on.

"My friend can tell you, Dan," drawled the spade-bearded man behind the wheel of the car.

"Howjedo, Dan," Dietche said.

"What's going on?"

"They've had bad news, Dan," Dietche said. "The rajah's going to die—that's the fellow the man mentioned dying on the mike. He owns a lot of the farms. They love him. It might be hard for you to understand how they feel. You know, I don't see why you bring your big jazzy circus—"

Dan just wanted to hear who was to blame. "If I lay my hands on that skunk announcer," he interrupted, "I'll break every bone in his body."

"Don't see what difference it makes. They all paid," Dietche said.

"Damn bastard," Dan said. "The hell with it, Will. We're getting out of here. They can see you ride when we come back in September."

"We lose the relief collection at the intermission," Will explained, the beard slicing the air as he spoke. "We thought they was all leaving for drinks and hot dogs, y'see. They're all goin' *home*." Will pointed at a brass disk with a racing car pressed out on it nailed to the dash. "We can't get no insurance—we sell them tokens now if they was anybody around to buy them—and pool the cash for hospitalization. Dan takes his cut of course."

Some kids wandered across the track towards the yellow car which Will had borrowed from another daredevil to take Dietche around in.

"Can we go someplace else?" Dietche asked, pulling his hat over his eyes.

The car lurched away, passing the carcass of the bus. "That the thing you jump?" Dietche asked.

"You can see it day after tomorrow night if you like."

"I'll catch you when you come through in September, Jess."

"Call me Will, don't forget?" Will smiled mostly with his eyes which hung close together behind a large nose.

"You sure do like changin' your name," Dietche said.

"Well, Dutch, it was Dan's idea this time. We had a visit this morning from the town fathers wanting to know if Dan carried any convicts on the payroll. And since I'm known as an ex-convict by my other name, Dan didn't want to hurt anybody's feelings, so he changed me."

"Town fathers?" Dietche murmured. Putting one and one together, knowing that he was safe with these worthless people, safe from the law, and safe from temptation. It was the kind of life he'd be most attracted to if ever he decided to live on the outside; it was such a wretched life compared to his. "Do you hurt yourself jumping over that bus?" he asked.

Will was a big guy and frightened of everything. "I don't reckon I'll live long," he said with false cheer.

Dietche slapped him on the back of the neck. "My it's good t'see you again!"

"Easy there, John, I got a boil comin' there som'ers."

"How'd you...why you're covered with them!" Dietche exclaimed.

"Sleepin' in the car," Will explained.

"You're not too well paid, are you?"

"No."

"I'm broke myself."

Will looked at him. "I ain't askin' you for nothin', boy."

They drove past large vans men were filling with ramps, motorcycles, and the smashed wall, and moved on out of the loading area to a string of trailers by the river. A woman in a sun suit came from a large white trailer with a garbage pail.

"That's the woman takes care of your daughter. Mrs. deLancy," Will said.

"How come you got such a dirty job, Will?" Dietche asked. They both watched Mrs. deLancy's long, bare, pale legs go out of sight.

"It pays the best of all the rides," Will answered.

"Why'd you grow that silly beard?"

"Because I got no chin," the daredevil said, knowing by the man's tone of voice that Dietche was after something and that it would be best to tell the truth if he could.

Dietche faced him, leaning his right arm on the counter of the dashboard. "Did you—now tell me, Will—did you tell Dan: 'Listen, Dan, ever since I was a little feeb I wanted to jump over a Greyhound bus; all my life, Dan, I've been waitin' for you to come along; so you let me hop over that bus or else, see?' No, Jess, you didn't. You got down on your knees and you said, 'Please, mister, anything. Anything.' "

"My name's Will James after the fellow who wrote *Smoky*. You remember *Smoky*—I read it to you—"

"What do you get paid, Will?"

Why was John so high on his horse? "Why you askin', sonny?"

"Don't wander!"

"What do you care what I get paid?"

"How much do you get paid?"

"John, ain't you sweet-tempered today?"

"You just come last, Will, that's all. Last come, last served. Will, you don't really have the guts to do that big ride. But you're broke, stud; you got to. There's nothin' left for you."

Quietly, Will asked John why he was so het up.

"Well you ain't concentratin'," Dietche said and called out, "Why don't you tell me the truth?" He didn't want Will just to say it.

"I guess I told the truth," the bewildered man replied. "I wanted the dough like anybody would. It's easy work. They don't care what you was. I'm gettin' out."

Dietche reached his arm across and took hold of Will's door handle. "Why do you risk your precious life for fifty dollars?" he asked. He didn't think Will's life was so precious, but he knew Will did. Will was a scared rabbit, and Will liked to be around people. Maybe that was it. But if you just said that right out, it didn't sound right. That was what Dietche was after; neither of them knew it for sure.

"I get fifty dollars and a nice percentage," Will replied, concentrating as best he could. He'd say whatever John wanted him to, if he could just get a steer. It was like going up to a tree and shouting 'You a tree?' and kicking it for not saying so. Will didn't know what he was. He was.

"What's the percentage?" Dietche asked.

"Five."

"What's the break?"

"Sixty-forty of the total admission."

"Who gets the forty?"

Will gently caressed the point of his beard. "We do," he said.

"How many men you split with?"

"Eight."

"What's the average take?"

"John, it comes to about ten bucks extra a night if that's what you're tryin' to find out. It ain't much but it's better'n farming."

"Aren't you ashamed?"

"I guess I don't want to argue," Will said. "I ain't you, and that's it." He laughed uneasily, and his little eyes followed Mrs. deLancy back up the steps of her trailer.

"Don't you see you're lyin' to me, Will?"

"No!"

"It ain't the money," Dietche said. "It ain't the easy work or that they don't care who you were. You told me years ago you'd make hundreds plumbin' when you come out."

There was no question of liking the work; the first ride or two Will felt pretty new. Now he hated it. "The plumbers don't want me."

Dietche spoke again, quietly. "Where's the man who did the bus ride before you?"

"He died."

"How?"

"He didn't get off the ramp right."

Dietche looked at his cellmate sadly. "It's awful what a man has to do to live. You're so chicken of heights and speed, havin' to do this. Just 'cause you can't get along by yourself."

"How much livin' you get on your farm, sport? Them farm women are some pickin's, I guess. Boy."

"No, they ain't, boy," Dietche replied and waved his hand in emphasis. He was going to tell Will how well it worked. How he'd beat the odds. Until Will asked him what appeared to be an innocuous question and Dietche began to list a little.

"How would you support Louise if you had to all of a sudden—say she went blind?" the bearded man said.

"Don't care."

"Maybe you ought to think a little more about it."

"You're somebody to talk."

"I can talk. I got a paying job and I'm living in the open."

"Long's you keep changin' your name and growin' beards."

"I can quit when I like, Johnny—"

"You can die when you like too," Dietche said. He could have had it like Will very easily. He recognized the point. Could have had the big sloppy fat life. It was also that Will had to force himself to do the ride that disgusted Dietche. Had to overcome his natural terror. And it was tearing him apart. And why? Because he had to be around people. Because he was *obliged* to. For some reason, perhaps feeling the guilty twinge of so much innocence, Dietche cared more about what a man should do with himself than Will—or Cowboy—or Jess—or 70164—whatever was left of the man who, underneath his borrowed names, was nothing more than a capacity for pain; and he wanted, in the innocent's way, to make Will ashamed of himself, which he couldn't. If Dietche didn't care, he wouldn't have run so far. "You got a party goin' tonight?" he asked.

"To Avalon. You comin'."

"Oh yeah." They got out of the car. Dietche pulled his hat over his face and danced behind a semi.

Will didn't go off passing judgments around. Why couldn't the lean, cockeyed son of a bitch take life as it come? Every so often Dutch'd get this way in prison. He was usually as careless as any of them until somebody touched him on his crime and he'd get righteous and start looking down on his buddies. Will didn't know what the hell Dietche was after—ever. He asked if he'd like a job with the daredevils and got the horse laugh. Will shook his head. They didn't seem to be friends any more. "Friends don't act like judges, John," he said.

"I ain't judgin' you, boy," Dietche said. "No. You go ahead and do what you want." He suddenly asked Will what he meant by that question about the money for the girl. Money was nothing to Dietche; it had cost him to much. Will replied that Louise needed clothes and food like anybody else. Dietche asked if Mrs. Long Legs didn't care for her.

"Sure," Will replied.

"Well, O.K."

"You just wanted to see what she looks like, don't you?"

"That's it," Dietche said.

"Dewey Newbold's crazy about her. Him and Mrs. deLancy share the honors. Mr. deLancy hates the kid as much as he hates his wife and Dewey, but he's Catholic and he's holdin' on. I don't like her."

"What's all this jabber about money?"

"Nothin'."

"Then why'd you bring it up?"

"Everybody's got to have some feelin's about their children."

"Can't feel for somethin' you never seen, can you? Boy!"

"No, I guess you're right," Will said. He felt helpless. "Don't worry, Dutch."

"No, no. I ain't worried. They told her I come, I reckon."

"Why're you so upset?" Will asked, scratching his beard, which had become itchy in the sun.

Dietche laughed and hit Will again on the back of the neck. "I just don't want my old buddy to get killed on that damn bus. Wish you could have it as good as me," he said. "What's the matter? Oh Lordy—did I hit that boil again?" Dietche exclaimed.

The big bearded man bent way over, his hand clasped to the back of his neck. And then he stood up, saw Dietche watching him, and bit his lip to stifle the tears.

Before they went inside deLancy's trailer he told Will that nothing would change his opinion that Will was a slave to do the job he did and added that the reason was due to the fact that Jess was ashamed of what he was; that Will-Cowboy had lost his self-respect; all of which 70164 began to deny with vehemence—but Dietche had gone inside to meet his little girl, whom he. had never seen before.

She wasn't there, however. She had already left for Avalon.

Curtiss was back up on the great hill—below him lay the red bridge he'd crossed once each way now.

It was five o'clock. One by one the cars returning from the fairgrounds zoomed past, but did not pick him up. He had stood for an hour, hand up, thumb out, waiting for someone to be so kind.

At last one car seemed to be stopping and he stood neatly and smiled. There was only one person in the car. When it went past he picked up a rock and flung it. Feeee.

Curtiss froze.

Feeeeee, the thing mewed again, gathering Curtiss's attention.

He looked quickly around. A whole white car was there in back of him. On its forehead a chrome plated siren and red light. Two moons sat behind the windshield.

'Done nothing' Curtiss thought.

Feeeeee, the horn said once again.

He went quickly to them. Down rolled the window and a fey voice asked what he meant by throwing rocks at cars.

"Nobody'll give me a lift," Curtiss told them, shaking.

They asked where he was from.

"New York."

"Well then, you certainly ought to know better'n to throw rocks at cars. What's your name?"

"Curtiss Lake."

"Get in, Curtiss."

When he was safe on the back seat and moving, he thanked them. They said nothing. Three quarters of an hour later they left him at the fork where Myron's road joined the state highway and went on, as silently as they'd come.

At supper, Curtiss told them how much the new clothes had cost. "There's a letter for you," Myron told him, "come special delivery."

"Where is it?"

"Postmaster's bringing it out tomorrow. He's comin' to a party I'm giving."

"Oh?" Curtiss asked, wondering why in hell Myron was giving a party. He repeated what Lace had said about Dietche, so Myron had to let him in on the reason for the party. He told him Dietche was paroled and that Myron didn't want people knowing he was employing an ex-convict. Somebody said they saw Dietche here and Myron wanted to prove he wasn't. To Curtiss it seemed a reasonable prejudice.

After supper they went as usual to the barn. Curtiss undid the clasps over the cows; they necked their stanchions apart and backed out free. The sharp, unmusical smash came again and again as the harps opened. Hooves splashed in the flowing gutters and eventually the last of the herd squeezed out into the evening air. "You won't forget you owe me thirty-one dollars now," Myron said. "Carmichael called me."

"No sir," Curtiss sighed.

He liked to be able to leave places when he wanted. Escape was now cut off.

"Good night," Myron said.

"Hey, how about that pill."

"Oh yes."

Dietche followed the road by moonlight. He wouldn't have used the headlights anyway, had there been any on the car.

The cold night air rushed over them through the vacant windshield. On both doors was a huge white spot and inside the spot a big black number six.

For a long time the road curved in and out of briar-strangled stone walls and dark woods. They were traveling the back roads. Until, at last, they drove into a deserted barn and stopped. He shut off the engine, and in the dark silence, they heard the dim radar of disturbed bats. Dietche unfastened the wire holding the door shut and stepped out, liquor and suspense making his thin heart twang in his chest. "Come on," he said. She did not hear, transfixed by the bats. "Come on, honey," he insisted.

She slid out and together they walked away.

Myron's darkened house floated past and he led her off the black crust into the clover field. The soft leaves tickled her bare legs and forced her to smile. He led her inadequately, as if it were not she but himself he was leading. Once he stumbled and fell and she waited, smoothing her skirt and puffing her hair with her hand, while he got to his feet.

He had found her wandering yawning, bored, sleepless, around the hotel in Avalon. People were playing crap in the toilet, arm-wrestling full-length in the hall, and locking and unlocking each other in other rooms. It was no place for her. "Want to go home with me?" he'd said, pushing his hat back and squinting down at her as best as he could in the smoky neon. She turned away from him then. Later, however, she caught him wandering through the hotel rooms exactly as she had, and she went to him. He couldn't see clearly at all then. "Hi," he said surprised.

"You're my Dad," she said, exhausted with the noise.

"Yeah." And then, in his drunkenness, he repeated his mistake, and she gave in.

"Am I going to sleep there?" she asked, staring into the bare white cell.

"Where is everything?" Dietche asked bewildered. (Myron had cleaned the place out for the party.) The corps of bottles, the cot, his suit, the Sterno stove, the hundreds of coils of string he'd collected, were gone.

He found the stuff under a strip of rotten canvas in the back. "Goin' to get a lock someday," he said unsteadily as he brought his possessions back into the room. He unfolded the cot under the window. He threw a bundle of undershirts on it for a pillow.

She looked at him.

"What's the matter?" he protested.

Reluctantly, she took her clothes off and let Dietche hang them on a hanger for her, the hanger he used for his prison suit. She lay down in her slip on the blanket and he covered her with the suit.

"Where will you sleep?" she asked.

"Back at the hotel," he said and took out a package of corned beef sandwiches, curved from his pocket, and divided them with her. She took a couple of bites out of politeness and lay back, not looking out the top of the window at the star-crazed sky about to dawn, but at the closer, more secure ceiling just above her. In the moonlight she looked like a statue of a pleasant child fallen backwards in a garden.

He threw the crusts and paper in a pig bucket just outside the door, replaced the lid quietly so as not to wake the dark house across the clover field, and sat down against the wall to wait for her to go to sleep.

After a moment he got up.

"Hey," he said hoarsely, bending over her.

Her dark eyes shifted to his face. "Hey," the seven-year-old replied.

"Why don't you go to sleep?"

"I'm thinking of going home."

'Thank God,' he thought somewhere. "That ain't no life for you," he protested.

"No?" she asked.

"No," he said and put his lips to her forehead. Her forehead cooled his brain. He stood up, clear-headed for a moment. "I'll be back tomorrow," he said. "If I don't make it, you go over and tell the lady who you are. She's got a soft heart. Hear?"

"I think I ought to go back now."

"We'll talk about it tomorrow." Quietly he left the cabin, his blood secretly drawing him back to the party. Anyhow he had to return the car.

As he drove back he realized he was a fool to bring her there. He didn't care for her. It was a foolish, childish thing to have done, and he knew she felt so too. He cursed himself.

CHAPTER SIX

The ulterior motive was the only motive the guests had for going there. Myron knew they wouldn't have accepted his invitation so readily just to come out and see him.

Until they discovered something for themselves, or by accident Dietche should come back earlier than he expected, he was master of the situation. At the same time he was master, he was at their mercy. Like a forgotten date on a calendar, the unexpected lay waiting for him. Not on his own land, though, he figured. Out beyond—on the borders.

Covering the foreground went his wife, the most unaffected liar of them all, because she could believe anything she wanted.

After lunch Curtiss had gone upstairs to reopen once again the heavy red copy of *War and Peace* he lugged around with him on all his travels and never finished, and Cora cleared the lunch dishes.

Two o'clock.

The screen door banged, and banged again. Cora set a table under a tree on the lawn, and came again with a tray of glasses. The wind played the glasses against each other, disturbing the young man in the window above who was staring over the valley, the fat red book in his lap opened to pages two and three. In the bathroom down at the other end of the hall from Curtiss's room Myron scraped his chin with a brass razor that had belonged to his father. He removed his sideburns and foliage at his throat. Cora now brought a new cake into the world, spread a layer of hot chocolate over it with a knife, and laid it to cool in the pantry.

Outside, the glasses continued to clink in the wind and the chunk of ice melted in the lemonade pitcher.

Surrounding the *Ile de* Greenhalgh—the house, the sloping, dusty hill above it which held the empty chicken house, the trough, two barns, and a silo—surrounding the indigestible core of this whole doubtful, fence-scarred organism were acres and acres of hay the color of weak yolk, and across the broken highway twenty thousand corn plants which ran up to the river stopped, and then ran on again to the edge of the distant foothills. Although crop and herd lay out of Myron's mind, although he worked automatically now, corn and hay and cows were the power behind his mean throne; and on certain meditationary days, standing in the fields, boots plugged in the earth, Myron could feel the weakness strive up to him, as if he, of all people, bore the secret of life. He was ricketed by the connection. The failure of the land caused the slow erosion of the soul. Loss, loss, loss.

He wiped the components of his razor, replaced the newly dried blade on the mossy spindle, and screwed cap and handle together and lay the old tool back in its place behind the mirror. The sink plug came ripped from its socket; water, lather, and hair whirled out the orifice. His little black eyes coasted the area cleared by the blade, followed by his hands and a few drops of cold water. He went into his bedroom and changed his overalls for black wool trousers and a white shirt. The boots then socked the floor; a stench rose. He laced on a pair of town shoes, stood up, arranged his boots by the bed leg, and laid his hand on his wife's comb, listening to a car slow down and turn into the driveway. Back in the bathroom, he rinsed his hair in Lucky Tiger, snaked the blackness over his skull, split it in two, and turned the ends back. He looked quickly at his face again; clean, combed, reeking of hair goo, pleasurably convinced of his homely beauty, he descended the stairs.

Myron broke open the car. A man, a woman, and a little boy got out. Right away, before he had demanded something to eat even, little Jack asked in an innocent voice who lived in the white cabin by the woods. Nobody lived there, Cora said, patting his head, which also smelled of Lucky Tiger, and guided Mrs. Brunet onto the lawn. "Nice day," she said. "Yes," the other wife replied. Cora brought up current affairs of which she knew nothing. Mrs. Brunet, of course, knew everything, it turned out, as she revolved her large head to keep track of her short, wartime skirt, her husband who drifted with Myron and Jack up towards the barns, and to watch for John Dietche. "If it doesn't rain this summer," the older woman said, before commenting on Cora's dress, "it will be a trial. What does Myron say, Cora?"

"He doesn't say much, Mrs. Brunet."

Mrs. Brunet nodded and glanced at the next note in her head; Cora replied that it was really a very old dress and together they went into the house to bring out some chairs.

He couldn't see any reason why John Dietche should be there. But Myron looked strange, and the rumor had made him famous. "Wish I *could* afford more help," Myron said, speaking of the city boy, and how hard it was for them to do all the work themselves. "It's a big place," Brunet said. His face was torn like an old pair of boots in a dump. "What's that white house for, Myron?" Brunet asked.

"Used to be a cistern with a roof onto it," Myron replied. "When the water dried up I floored over the mouth—made a little shed out of the thing." It was almost as if he'd built it for someone, Brunet said. "Like to see it?" Myron said.

Brunet shrugged and his lips shut down slowly over his teeth. "No," he said.

"Let's join the women," Myron said. They went down to the lawn.

Myron let his wife do most of the talking. He stayed in the background, watching Brunet and Hugh Plunkett and his son Roger, who were all watching—all watching for John.

Roger lifted the wicker chair the old man lived in out of the back of the delivery truck. "Mrs. Greenhalgh, it is a privilege to visit you and your husband," the father said while his dim eye cast through the guests to the refreshment table and hooked the pitcher, full, he prayed, of liquor. "Punch, Roger!" he said while his son was speaking to the gracious woman before them. "Yes, Pa I'll go for some in a sec," Roger said. "I'm fine," he told Cora.

Myron felt so light. If John came back, which way would he come? he wondered. His wife was having a good time. He envied her. She moved from topical branch to branch; there were no crashes; the subjects could support the weight. The weather, the weather, the weather. Frank Daville. Cooking. The conversation was liberating to the talk-starved Cora; fatiguing for Mrs. Brunet; stupefying to Brunet who kept up a fixed smile like a laundry rope under a heavy wash. Embroidery became the topic. Cora's tongue leaped.

E. R. Sage, postmaster, lifted a glass of lemonade, his magnified eyes swimming in his rimless glasses, looking for John Dietche.

Upstairs, Curtiss read us MAIL on Sage's windshield, shut *War and Peace,* and went downstairs.

Sage turned to Myron and said, "Where's John?"

Myron's face drained. He tried to smile, "Who?" he asked. He dropped his hands, shaking, into his pockets. A series of unbearable changes rang through his nerves.

Sage moved his glasses. "Little Johnny Brunet—where is he Cora?"

"Oh, little Jack," Cora said. "Up the barn—some where—" she said. Sage noticed nothing. He needed new glasses.

Everyone was there then, and the party proceeded. Alcohol was not necessary to make these people run properly, although it was necessary to make the Plunketts run properly, and they subdued their disappointment with the punch as best as they could. All remained as they had first come, aloof, watchful, and at least once during the afternoon remarked privately on Cora's excessive exuberance. Curtiss came on. They noticed his fine-boned face, his skinny length, his cross mouth. He took the letter from Sage, thanked him quietly and retired.

"I don't remember anything like it," old Hugh said, tickling the backs of his hands. "Worse'n it was last year. Look at that corn."

"Ain't you glad we're in the grocery business, Pa," Roger said, cleaning his golden spectacles on an old handkerchief, hooking the baboon limbs over his ears, and squinting into the cornfields as he had been told.

"We'll go soon," the old man whispered.

"I'd like to speak with Mrs. Greenhalgh some," the son said. "Do."

He reached down and touched his father's shoulder with his fingertips. "We'll go in a jiffy Pa."

"Sure," Hugh croaked. "You chat with Mrs. Greenhalgh and leave me settin' dry as a bone. God, what terrible punch that is. We got anything in the truck?"

"I'll only be a minute. Just want to chat some."

"Any booze in the truck?"

"It wouldn't look right, Pa. We'll go soon. You want to find out about John, don't you?"

"Chat. Chat. Chat. Jim Lace told everybody Myron denied he was here."

"Myron could be lying."

"You sure want to chat."

"No I want to see John too."

"You won't find John in that dress of hers."

"Pa set *quiet* now."

"I'm parched."

"Set."

"I'll set," the old man mumbled, watching the grass where Roger's feet had been. Cora's feet appeared there. "Oh thank you,

Mrs. Greenhalgh, more delicious lemonade, thank you," the old man croaked in horror. He took the glass from her hand and put it to his lips, and when her back was turned, poured it on the lawn.

Everybody Myron had invited was a champion gossiper, especially the Plunketts who held down a crossroads and a switchboard in a distant, more populated valley.

To the postmaster she was a woman with a kind of waxy glow; not his type; but he was frequently obliged to look down her dress. Roger, coming up to them at the lemonade table, was obliged to as well. "You oughtn't to buy your groceries at the A & P. You come to our store Mrs. Greenhalgh," Roger said.

"My husband does the shopping," she said. "Ask him." She wished for things to say. "Have a cookie, Roger?" she said.

Two hours passed. None of them had been out to Myron's before. Cora kept them going. Cora the bold. It was only her energy that kept ennui from eating into their deeper curiosity, which would have satisfied Myron. None of them were friends. The weather, the weather. Pigeons. Pigs. He was about to tell her to slow down when a terrible congulant to their drifting attention rose. They'd all heard the news. They didn't know how it happened. They walked away a bit, leaving the old man alone under a tree in his chair, but Hugh caught them. He wanted to hear. "Roger can tell you to home, Hugh," Sage called thoughtfully. He put away his glasses, two octagons of ice, and there was nothing left of his face.

But the old man insisted and Roger had to carry him over and set the weightless contents in the center of the circle.

Why the letter had been sent special delivery Curtiss had no idea. "My dear Curtiss. ..." The letterhead indicated a cheap motel on the outskirts of Cairo. The other letters he'd had bore similar letterheads with other addresses. There was no date .... J.J. had simply marked the hour. Six P.M. Cocktail time. "I didn't get the job," the letter continued. Curtiss was not surprised. The man was over fifty. "... I didn't get the job. They must have seen the roots of my hair were silver. Forgot to have it redyed. Your Aunt Grace wrote and said she is never coming back to me." Curtiss was hurt by that. He didn't know why. He read on:

> ... So there it is kid. She is in Chicago, however. Here is a letter her sister Polly sent me which Grace wrote her. I will never understand that destructive bitch. Can you picture Polly getting her scissors and cutting out Grace's address before she mailed it on to me? What kind of a woman is that? Out here in this stinking motel, nobody to talk to but a lot of stinking coalminers. They got a dandy strike going—watching them kick each other silly gives me something to do. I tell you I'm going to find her! That letter came from out here in Illinois. It won't be hard to find a stupid beautiful woman like that. You know why Polly goes to all the trouble to torture me? Why she keeps telling Grace I'm bad for her? You know why? Because Polly wants me. You didn't know that did you? Ain't I something.

Curtiss turned to the blue, scented leaf of stationery in his other hand. It left his fingers smelling Grace's soft, giving perfume the rest of the day; he didn't wash that hand that night, and it helped him to sleep. The letter was badly creased. J.J.'d crumpled it in anger.

> Dearest Sister,
> The ride out was a fright. I didn't get the job, but never mind, wasn't it fun to try. You asked me if I would look for J.J. when I got out here. How typical of you to offer and help me to hold to a very necessary decision. Rest assured, I could handle it if we did meet, which I trust

will never happen, dearest. It was decided we were no longer happy in each other's company, isn't that right?

I don't know if I agree with you that he's weak—he is very bad for me. Of course I'm still fond of J.J. What a terrible night that was. I've never seen bear so cross. I am still not sure your presence was absolutely necessary. I was getting along swell telling him myself. I mean he wouldn't have broken quite so many things if you'd stayed home. Certainly we could have picked a better time than the night Curtiss came home from school, poor lamb. Have you heard anything from him? None of us are very good about writing, except you. Write soon.

G.

A postscript had been unintentionally censored on the other side when Polly scissored out the letterhead.

p.s. Could you lend——dollars?

Curtiss returned to his uncle's letter. They were like three lost elephants, his relatives, looking for each other's tails. He thought of them as elephants because they seemed so vulnerable. There was a time, not more than twenty-four hours ago, when he could not think of them so generously. But today his drawers were full of new clothes and the night before, thanks to Myron, he had slept like a top. He finished J.J.'s letter.

Kid, look up, keep your chin out. Send me anything you want me to sign. Kid, look up, keep your chin out. I said that. So long. Please *write*?

JJ

Curtiss looked thoughtfully out the window. How, when time after time they broke apart, did J.J. and Grace always turn, eventually, back towards each other? Why did she *pretend* to be looking for work in Chicago? She knew J.J. was out there somewhere. That was all. They had patroled the bars of the nation, on and off, for years, pretending not to be looking for each other.

While Curtiss thought about them this way his usual disgust slackened, and, hey presto, he was sorry for them. But he never moved his hand to ink or paper. He figured he had nothing to write, which was true. He shut the two letters away in a drawer with a confident bang and went downstairs, and after a while he began to mistrust them again and to become distant in his pity. He could go all the way from disgust to pity and back in one bound, without ever passing through understanding. It was as if he had a special pass.

It was too late for understanding. His confidence had been shaken early on. His weapons as they were developing were silence, detachment, and treachery of an emotional kind which might make it forever unwise for people to get involved with him.

He looked at the stamp a moment in the kitchen before throwing the envelope away. The little boy drew him in, unconsciously. And whose house was that? Why in the world did J.J. send him the letter special delivery? He knew. But why had J.J. *had* to?

As he stepped across the kitchen he heard voices softening through the walls. He threw the envelope in the garbage can.

The postmaster paused and sipped his lemonade. Curtiss rejoined the circle.

"Howard's house was stuffed with people. I went upstairs—it was quiet as a church. I knew Howard was in the big bedroom but I had to go to the john. That's when I found Jimmy. It was his room, I guess, 'cause he was lying there on his back staring up at the ceiling. The walls were plastered with girls. I didn't know that he mighten be sick, too. 'Hello, Ernie,' he said. 'What am I going to do?' 'Oh is that you, Jim?' I asked. He looked at me and turned his face to the wall. I backed out and closed the door. It was a little boy's room."

The company warmth drew the sting of the story: how wonderful just people are, Cora thought, edging closer.

"Father Hannen was by his side as I came in the sick room. Howard's head was clear as a bell. I asked him if he'd be up and about soon. He asked if Jimmy was with me. He couldn't move his head for some reason. I said no—"

Myron wished Sage would get to the economics. He cleared his throat and looked down past his arms, listening and occasionally taking a look out for a man walking down the road.

"—then in a terribly frightened voice, Howard asked me if it was true John Dietche had returned."

His nerves jangling, Myron made himself look dead into Sage's eyes. Sage dropped his gaze. "Howard asked Father Hannen if he'd roast for burning out old man Dietche back in 1919. Father Hannen laughed. Then suddenly Howard took to jumpin' about, sayin' he was all clogged up. I called the doctors quick. They were making coffee downstairs in the kitchen."

Myron interrupted. "Did Howard say who would run the mill and the store?"

"Let him go on!" the old man lashed out from the wicker chair.

"He said that Kean had bought the business *long* before. Nobody knew that. Then I yelled for the doctor—"

Looking fiercely at the old man, Brunet asked, "What will Kean do? What's his policy going to be?"

Roger touched his father: the old man was wiggling with impatience. "I want to hear how he died!" the old man groaned.

Sage said, "As a matter of fact I don't know what's going to happen, policy-wise, Brunet. Somebody telephoned to Plattsburg to find out if Kean'd let Jim run the show. Kean didn't understand what they meant. You know, Kean's a nice fellow, Brunet. I wouldn't worry if I was you."

"You'd worry if it was rain ran your post office, Mr. Sage," Brunet said and turned his leather face to the fields. The story was over as far as he was concerned. The postmaster had no real news.

Held in the magic ring of guests, Cora would not lift her voice to stop what her conscience told her was an evil thing: Hugh was begging for details. As hostess, she should have stopped it. The harsh, observant Mrs. Brunet had noticed this social helplessness about Cora—how hungry she was for company—how she clung to everything that was said—how nosy she was. You ought to make your man take you out more, she thought.

"That's all," Sage said.

"Ernie, tell me how he died. How'd he take it?" Hugh said, embarrassed.

"Story's over," Sage said with an indulgent smile and walked away from the circle.

"Yes," said Cora weakly.

Myron took the men up to the barns, leaving Hugh, who had fallen asleep in the anticlimax, under an elm. Cora took Mrs. Brunet into the kitchen in order to show her Dietche wasn't there either.

The men looked in the stalls. The bull was sanding his pen with his nose.

"Nice clean stalls, Myron," Sage remarked, and as they all continued up the hill, Brunet asked the young man, "Lot of work?"

"Yep," Curtiss replied.

What if they found him? Myron had no idea what. Nor they. Given they knew he was on the run, they still wouldn't turn him in immediately. Perhaps one of them might drop a hint to the troopers one day. There was a deep urge to find him, and it had little to do with what he had done. His name still rankled, as an ancient rival's name rankles on in the memory of a jealous lover.

"Why are you taking us up here?" Brunet's voice licked out, wondering why Myron was so easily playing into their hands, and if therefore Dietche was there; but Myron pretended not to hear—loving the mystery as much as they—and led them past the small barn, across the top of the hill to the mouth of the larger barn. Down below at the edge of the clover field was the small white house, where he would take them next.

Myron asked how much they thought he'd get for the whole farm. To find this out was the expressed reason he was taking them around.

"Where'll you go Myron?" Sage asked.

"Ain't goin' necessarily," Myron said.

Brunet looked over the tractor parked between the lofts. "Ten thousand dollars for the whole lot. But you're mortgaged."

Myron nodded.

"You can't go," Sage said.

Why did they all scrape so to him? Brunet wondered. What was there about the little man that made them all, himself included, walk just a fraction behind him? Why this distance, this rare attractiveness that kept them from being natural with Myron?

He led them down into the clover to the small white cabin, feeling more strongly than ever—as time passed and the odds rose in his favor—his own invincibility. They came closer and closer to the solitary white cell, and the closer he came the more he wanted to tell them. He kept his dark face at the ground, grinning, and stopped near the cabin and let the three men, Curtiss, Sage, and Brunet pass one by one through his gaze, towards the steps to the broken screen door. He imagined Brunet and Sage trembled as they went. Perhaps, he thought in a moment of high fancy, they were afraid Dietche was in there. Sage's large feet bent the steps; he was about to go in, but he stopped, his hand on the screen door pushing it slightly open. He turned.

"Yes, John-Paul?" Myron had said. "Myron," Brunet said. He wanted to confess to him. "Myron why are we out here?" he asked. "What the hell are we doing out here?"

Above them on the steps, the postmaster swore. (He hadn't seen inside—the screen was too finely meshed, the sun was on another facet of the cabin, and the little interior window faced the dark woods on the other side. No light penetrated within, and she made no noise as she slept.) "Brunet," the postmaster warned, coming back down the steps.

"I don't know why you're here, John-Paul," Myron was saying quietly. "I thought you might help me fix an estimate for my farm."

Brunet decided that he'd only make a bigger fool out of himself if the game went on. Angry and defeated he walked away. The postmaster came down the steps, wanting to ask what the matter was. Myron brought up the rear, herding them in his mind.

Brunet stopped. He turned in the knee-length clover. He took Sage's heavy arm and pointed at Curtiss. "That's him," he said. "Jim was right."

"Who?" the postmaster demanded, wishing they'd get back on the lawn where his ventilated shoes wouldn't take up the dust.

"That's who it was," Brunet said with a look at Myron.

"Don't tell," the postmaster said.

"Aw, what the hell, Ernie!" Sage protested. "It's silly!"

Sage nervously adjusted his glasses.

Brunet said, "Sage and me thought we'd find John Dietche here. Isn't that right?"

"Yes," the postmaster, the only man with a tie on, said dismally.

Myron gasped, "John Dietche?"

"Guess we owe you an apology. Orilla Ano said she saw him here a week or so ago. I guess it was Curtiss."

Curtiss accepted the role with pleasure. "Call me John," he said. "Some of my best friends are called John."

"*Is* your name John?" Brunet asked later, who couldn't laugh at anything except violent jokes.

"No. Curtiss is my name. Who is John?" replied the young man glumly. And so he found his place in this world at last. He was John Dietche. The postmaster had slapped him on the back. They all laughed nervously on the way to the lawn—no one touched Myron and began seeking polite ways of getting away.

Meanwhile Cora had shown Mrs. Brunet over the house—Curtiss's untidy bedroom, the kitchen, the unused living room. On the way back to town, Mrs. Brunet was going to have to tell her husband she'd seen nothing suspicious. Orilla must have been lying: there wasn't a trace of Dietche in the house. They all gathered on the lawn again, plain people on the plain grass.

Myron was beginning to feel exhausted and, as he handed Mrs. Brunet a last glass of now warm lemonade, he saw something awful coming through the clover from the cabin. What the hell was that? he wondered.

"Who's that, Myron?" Brunet asked.

Myron's eyes narrowed, focusing with difficulty on the girl's face. The jaws were lean and she was thin and walked like a wand.

Well there it was. 'The damn fool,' Myron thought. The parachute which had been about to drop him so gently to the earth had suddenly flown off his shoulders. He began to fall with sickening velocity. And all he could do was stand mute while the hired man's daughter came closer and closer the wind taking the pink skirt of her pinafore. The sensation in Myron's stomach was nauseating.

"Huh," he heard Curtiss grunt.

"Well," he heard his wife chirp blandly. "Now there is a *charming* little girl!" and ran to the tiny couple as they stepped across the gravel driveway onto the lawn. "Hello there, Jack," she said. "I see you got yourself a girl friend."

"Her name is Louise," Jack said. "She's from the daredevils that come yesterday. I found her sleeping in that cabin of yours, Myron."

"Ain't you the Prince Charming, Jack," Myron replied faintly.

Cora turned to Myron with a helpless look.

"She's been lent us," Myron said and continued with an attempt at carelessness. "Come last night late. Jack must of woke her up." All Brunet and Sage needed to be convinced was to keep looking at Louise's pleasant face. She was called Louise, she lived with the daredevils, and her last name was deLancy, Louise told them and then shut up, sensing something wrong. They were all, except Brunet, surprised Myron knew people like daredevils; Brunet believed it with a vengeance. Myron ignored her to begin a conversation about the corn.

Cora knelt and tied her shoelace and told her to go play with Jack.

But Sage had squatted beside her. "Hello there," he said.

The girl let go of Jack's hand to face the threat by herself. "Hi you," she said, her small, perfect eyes sinking into him.

"Are you a daredevil too?" Sage asked.

"No," she said.

"What's she—French?"

"No, she's American," Cora replied. "She's from New Jersey."

"I seen that face before," the postmaster said. It now hung on his post office wall.

"No, you haven't," Myron said.

"Can I eat?" The little voice was measured and even, like her father's, from disdain.

"Didn't she have lunch?" Mrs. Brunet said.

"Yes ma'am," Louise said. These people weren't any of them on her side, so the answer was yes to anything.

Cora brought her a plateful of cake and cookies. Jack ran after her into the house with a glass of lemonade—she said she'd eat indoors—when a black car zoomed down, rocking in the bumps of the road, running, without a sound, into the soft clover, and stopped; but before it stopped, a man had got out and was already walking in slow motion towards Dietche's cabin. "Louise!" he called.

'Oh no,' Myron thought, and waved across the driveway, shouting that no one lived there. That he had the little girl.

"Farmer says she's over there, Dewey," the driver called out the window.

The car backed out of the clover and ran quietly up onto the driveway.

Louise came around the house. "Dewey!" she cried as a tall man with a toothbrush moustache walked out of the clover onto the lawn. She flew into his arms and hung, legs up, like a package in a Christmas tree. The other man got out from behind the wheel.

Myron's guests had drawn together in the background as if they were going to be photographed. Little Jack watched somberly from his father's hand as Dewey opened the back door for her.

"Get in Sugar," Dewey said.

Their trousers were the color of the evening sky—the driver's pale orange, Dewey's bright magenta. On their small feet they wore sky-blue suede shoes. They were people Myron could not have believed existed. He'd never seen the kids in town dress like that and he'd never seen it in the movies. They were white Negroes. 'Go on,' he thought. 'Go away,' he called in his thoughts to the effeminate specters, whose faces were as fresh and innocent as newborn puppies. He couldn't bear to look at such people. 'Go on,' he thought desperately.

"We'll be going now," the tall one called Dewey drawled at the car door. "The show is movin' south? Thank them for meals, Louise."

"Thank you for the meals," Louise said.

"Good-by, dear," Cora said, her hand at her mouth.

The car backed out onto the highway and stopped.

Dewey leaned his head out the window and began to say something to Myron. It looked like it was going to be something about John. "Don't mention it!" Myron cried, running right at the car. "Good-by! Good-by!" he said in his high voice. Startled, Dewey closed his mouth and pulled his head into the car. He asked Louise if Myron was drunk.

What had happened? Myron wondered, unrelieved, watching them go. What was in that car? Those men with voices and clothes like that. They'd got him. Dietche was never coming back. Myron had lost. The sudden presence of the outside world had bumped Myron. The swift motion into his farm and out again had a terrible effect on him. He felt how little he was, how bound down to a small, insignificant bit of dust he was. The idea stalked his closed-in mind. Somebody would have to pay for all this. Somebody would pay. Who dared risk all this? Who dared bring that girl here? "Well, Curtiss," he said, demanding a little companionship in his agony, "that was a funny thing, wasn't it? Did you think those fellows'd come for her? Did you ever see people dressed like that?" Curtiss warmed himself cautiously on his boss's upturned face and said nothing. Myron went off to say good-by to the Plunketts. "Good-by, Hugh," he said, peering into the gloom above the tailgate where the old bird sat in his chair.

"So long, Myron. See you in the movies," Hugh said. "Did you say you had a nice time, Roger?"

"Shore," Roger said, buckling the chains on the gate. "Al'ays have a nice time here. You come to our store now, Myron."

"I will, I will." Myron followed the truck into the highway, "You bring down your prices." He slapped the roof distractedly. The old man waved from the back as they drove off.

E. R. Sage buttoned his coat round his stomach. "You going?" Myron asked him.

"Oh yes. Post office been closed two days. Got to get set for Monday morning." And so he went. Later Myron couldn't remember any of them going.

Brunet, however, stayed on a little longer. "What they say in town, Myron, is that considering how hard you work, why ain't you doing better?"

"I don't see how it's anybody's business. Who's *they?*" Myron asked.

"Sparks and Greenley—oil truck drivers."

"They don't know anything about farming."

"They tell me that in the winter they see your lights first on in the morning when they start, and last out when they drive the trucks home at night. They say you deserve more than you get. You plough at night, too, don't you?"

"You got to work hard."

The sun was going down. Brunet rebaited and tried one more cast. "What they admire is that you do it all by yourself."

"I got help," Myron said.

"Course the boy is some help—"

"Curtiss's worth two." Myron went to Mrs. Brunet and opened the door of the car for her.

Eavesdropping from beside a nearby tree, Curtiss shone at Myron's false compliment. Curtiss had a responsibility now, which was not a responsibility at all, but which merely seemed so, just as the jacket on a pill appears to be the pill because it holds the shape of the thing in the eye. Curtiss was the figment of the imagination of people he did not know, impersonating a man he had to pretend he'd never heard of. As long as he wasn't himself to them, he could be anybody to these people; he knew he certainly didn't mean a damn thing as Curtiss Lake. As long as they didn't require him to be himself, but Orilla's mistake, he could enjoy their company. He felt a slight affection for Myron for having got him this disguise. Curtiss was probably going into the theater.

Brunet realized Orilla could have been mistaken, but suspicion, like need, is relentless in dissatisfied people. "Know what kind of trees these are, son?" he asked.

"Elms," Curtiss replied.

Cora and Myron stood outside the car door, watching. Inside little Jack and his mother waited.

"Why elms? Why here? No elms for a hundred miles. And how'd they grow in such orderly lines?" Brunet asked.

"Myron's father put them in to hold the earth down. So Myron told me."

Brunet drew his finger along a thin crack in the foundations of the house. "Roots are doing that," he said and took a linen hat from under his chair. "Myron too proud to say he's got other help 'sides you?"

Curtiss said he was the only help there, and at last Brunet went to his car, thinking that unless Myron was a demon he was a hell of a liar. There was just too much to *do*. When they shook hands, he felt something uncanny in Myron's touch. Brunet had been a dragon in the Ku Klux Klan and had learned enough there to appreciate the secrets that lie in the dark as well as the light, and had developed a taste for them. He drove off, wondering if he wasn't reading more into it than the facts warranted. But he *felt* there was something uncommon in the little man with black button eyes and the shiny black hair.

It was all over.

"Oh, Myron, I'm going to miss that Louise, you know. She was so sweet," she said.

"I just hope the father comes back," he said.

"He's got to come back," Curtiss said.

"Back *here?*" Myron asked, with the first touch of cynicism he'd ever felt in his life. He watched the Brunets disappear on a turn at the end of the road, and his mind colored magenta. "You say you saw lots of them daredevils in town? Did they talk about John?"

"I didn't stick around long enough—" Again, before Curtiss had finished speaking, Myron left him, and went into his house, unbuttoning his good shirt. He had to keep moving. That evening he went with Curtiss to get the cows; he couldn't stand still; he did not want to be alone.

Night held the farm. With a new dawn, it would be released. The order was unchangeable: the sun retired, the moon came out, the stars went on and then would fade. There were, however, despairing rebels to order out walking that night, disturbing the peace.

He had sat five hours in a hotel room waiting to get back to Myron's. And you just don't sit five hours doing nothing unless you're a special religious type or sleepy. He'd ordered a number of drinks and by the time they let him out he had a little difficulty in navigating the stairs.

When Dewey Newbold found the kid missing, his pals held the hired man in the chair, but Dietche, glad to be relieved of the responsibility, had told Dewey where she was before Dewey had his leather jacket off. "Go get her, Dewey," he said. When Dewey returned to Avalon with Louise that afternoon, Will the Cowboy drove the hired man back.

The stillness of the evening might have moved a poet had there been any in that place that evening: but not during the ten minutes of hell in front of Myron's that yanked Curtiss to his window in the clapboard palace. Not in that ten minutes of human disarray could nature's beauty hold its spell when onto the stage blundered the wheeling, unannounced figure of the hired man, drunk as a lord. Dietche broke his bottle in front of the house and kicked the glass across the highway. Clink! Clink!

"You love that child. Waaaal, Dewey—" he muttered. He faced the moonlit road, a long, jointed brandy shaking a fist at an idea miles away. "Take her!" he cried.

By the time the words came, squeezed out between bitter gratitude to Dewey and a shuddering reluctance to return to his ten times now more lonely cell by the woods, there wasn't much meaning left in them, especially to Curtiss so high up overhead.

Dietche jerked around and faced the house. The moon caught the burned eye. Curtiss's flesh crawled.

"I'm back, boys!" he cried. "Everything going ahead now!" Angry at having to return, angry at the fear which had exiled him there. Anger which tasted like joy because he had gotten away with it. "You lily-livered John—why'd you want the tot in the first place?" He kicked the road as if trying to get a band going, bam bam bam, and shouted, "And could've had the wife. Oh Mrs. deLancy, you are the cat's whiskers. Ain't it the truth? You know Marcovitch—my Jewish friend?" His voice snarled up through the trees. "Have mercy on his soul! I hope he rots!" He gave a convulsive shudder. "Let go," he said as if to somebody on his back. Before he finished laughing the road came and struck him in the face.

Curtiss thought he'd passed out, but presently music came from the corpse. The young man called his name from the window.

The singing stopped.

"Dietche!" the young man called again.

"What?" the voice replied.

"Get off the road."

"Why should I? Nothing coming."

"Come on, get off the road."

Curtiss was half into his trousers when he looked out again and found the road empty.

It was all over. Louise had come and gone like a sparrow flying in and out of a living room by mistake. It wasn't Louise for herself he'd wanted. It was her and all the people she lived with. It was what they all were capable of. As he sat in the puke-smelling room of the hotel in Avalon, he decided that his carrying her off was the last act of sabotage he could possibly commit against himself. With Louise gone, he figured, there was nothing left to tempt him beyond himself.

The broken screen door opened and slammed. "Hey!" the voice came from far away in the night. The door slammed again, a whiplike snap in the distance, and then he collapsed, missing the cot, in the corner of his little room like a scarecrow thrown inside when the snow starts to fly.

Long after the form had become silent again and everybody else was asleep, Myron lay awake, looking down his bare arm at the small cabin, a square cube of white against the distant black trees.

CHAPTER SEVEN

Monday Myron bore down in a cold, savage inflexible way, ostensibly because he felt Dietche owed him for the little girl. But it was more than that. That was the excuse.

He was frightened. He thought Dietche was thinking of leaving him.

And the conflict would continue to exist even though the fear that Dietche would escape was groundless—if things went on in a fairly normal way, Dietche would never escape.

What if that secret exchange of promises months before hadn't occurred—what if there wasn't this breakable seal holding them together—would Myron have been as occupied as he was with Dietche—would he have derived such odd joy from a simple cash relationship? Probably.

Why was it Myron couldn't see the one important thing about Dietche that would have allowed them all to live in peace? Why couldn't Myron understand that Dietche would never go? Why did Myron drive him so hard, why did he make war on the hired man?

War, because he was drawn, relentlessly, not only to keep the pact they'd made, but the man that had come to make it. Drawn to a double vacuum—not only to that of words, but to that within the man. The man was the object he began to seek now, not the thrill of having him there—he couldn't take any more lawn parties. It was almost as if Myron wanted Dietche in the same way Myron could imagine things; which was impossible, because men are not born of other men's brains.

War, because he was partially blind—Myron could not see that Dietche wanted to live here. Myron could not understand (and therefore stepped on) anything that was not in motion.

War, because Myron lived in fear now, fear which brought him closer to the object. And that experience, in turn, made him more afraid.

He did not see that he might destroy Dietche. Being what he was, the hired man could no more nourish Myron than his sandy fields. You cannot kill earth, however.

There was no absolute, no single governing idea or fault, no specific filament to lift apart on the forceps from the entire muscle—Myron simply was for a time and then would be dust. Only in motion through time lay the evidence, because he would leave nothing behind, and foresaw nothing ahead; he had set out on no voyages of discovery, inherited no maps, had no ambition to be anything one would find in the classified directory or on any monument. He patroled existence as naturally, and finally, as a fish the sea.

Curtiss was amused whenever he fell upon the conflict, his view blurred now by a slight friendship with Myron and the slight pity he felt for Dietche ever since he saw him perform on the road beneath his window while the young man sat smelling his fingers, in the whorls of which still lingered traces of his aunt's perfume. Curtiss seldom saw Dietche those days—he could afford a little pity, despite the scar in his mouth which, when he touched it with his tongue (it had become a kind of talisman) reduced his interest in Dietche to zero. If Curtiss—if any of them had known what was really going on—Curtiss would probably have left already.

He didn't see much of the hired man those days because they all had different jobs. Life seemed about average, and he would be moving on soon.

The milking was almost done by the time Dietche got in the barn that morning. The squat aluminum milkers, like steel, marine, yet sympathetic creatures, were drawing away under the last three cows.

Curtiss closed a lever on the pipe leading to the air pump and drew off the long hose which ran down under the cow into the milker. The four black sockets sagged on the cow's udder as the air returned and came away easily when he pulled; draping the hose around his neck, he poured the warm contents of the milker into a can on the alley, turned to dip the suckers in a pail of antiseptic, and saw Dietche down in the doorway, interrupting the morning light. He sneaked into the herd. Myron's small boots moved below the belly of the adjoining cow. "Myron," Curtiss whispered, "he's up."

Myron's head appeared over the top of the cow and saw Dietche walking towards them, the sun urging him gently along from behind.

He stopped when he got to them and shoved the brown hat onto the back of his head. The flesh around the extinguished eye was colored and swollen. Through his good eye, crusted with sleep and dirt, Myron and Curtiss looked terribly healthy and wide-awake. He told Myron he'd have a few more puffs of breakfast and then he'd get to work. Said unless he had a few more puffs he'd fall down. His voice was light and careless as usual.

"You're late," Myron said and carried an empty milker around to a full cow.

"I bet I am," Dietche replied.

Curtiss popped on his four pistils and stood up empty-handed and lit a cigarette. Myron was letting him handle a milker for the first time. The responsibility—as far as this particular young man was concerned—was quite powerful—was a formal sort of affection. Being so necessary, he naturally, being the kind of person he was, became a little pissy; passing the hired man on his way out for a drink of water (Dietche had had to sit down for a moment to keep from throwing up) he said, "Let's go, huh, John?"

"What did you say, Curtiss?" Dietche asked, staring after him.

"Nothing," the young man replied.

"You best not," Dietche replied.

Myron ordered Curtiss out of the stalls to harness the horse for the manure wagon and he put Dietche onto a heifer too tiny to carry the suckers. Dietche laid his head on the warm flank and closed his eyes. He had to drag on her a while before she'd give. She didn't take to it and struck out. "Har!" he cried. She hit his ankle. The thin film over his temper parted and he punched her.

Myron returned to the departing herd. "Where you been, John?" he asked.

"Here'n there," Dietche replied amiably. "Got to the party about six Saturday... down to Avalon. More liquor'n you could shake a stick at.... I ain't been that drunk for years... after a while everybody in that hotel turned... blue." He yanked away with his fore-fingers, the milk going blip blip in the pail, his good eye closed, the other a pale freckled egg.

Myron was fascinated. "Lots of wimmen I guess, John," he suggested.

"Oh yes," Dietche said, opening his eye at Myron and then spitting in the gutter. "There was 'bout twenty, twenty-five people all told in this little room. 'Bout twelve midnight some sport thought he'd be funny and yelled fire. I was standing in the doorway—'cause I can't stand little crowded rooms—and course everybody come stompin' over me. Later I went back in to see Mrs. deLancy who was taking care of Louise—Louise y'know is my daughter—"

"Go on."

"She was real nice lookin', Mrs. deLancy. We got sort of close. Then her husband rears out of the deep and give me a lot of sass and I'm on my way back to the door again, my head in my hands. Drank just a little more. On the way... I met little Louise. She didn't say much. She knew who I was. Eventually we come back here. Then I went back to the party and really started havin' a good time. Sunday I just sat around the hotel. I guess they come for her? Well there you are. That was the big weekend. Never again."

Myron told him he was a fool to go so far into the bottle. The cops might have seen him. Dietche reminded him that maybe he knew just a little bit more about that than Myron. Myron said he wouldn't let him go again.

"I won't go again," Dietche said.

"Say, why'd you put her on to us?"

"Wanted to show her I had a place of my own she could come to."

"That's my cabin, John."

Dietche shook his head, smiling listlessly, his eyes still shut, his head against the cow's flank.

Myron rubbed his ear like a little boy. "I told you not to go anywhere without telling me," he said.

The heifer was dry. Dietche set the pail across the gutter on the alley. "I told you where I was going, Myron," he said patiently. "Nobody seen me all weekend that knew me. All the boys is grown up. Howard Lace's dead."

"I know that."

"Well, O.K."

In a rare moment of complete objectivity—he was in a childish mood—Myron asked, "Why did you ever come back here?" Dietche let the heifer go. "Why'd I come back, Myron?" he asked. "Why'd I come back here?" He couldn't answer that. It was like being asked why he was born.

"You could've escaped with them fellers—you could of gone away forever," Myron said.

Dietche tried to smile. "And leave you, Myron dear?"

"Aren't you scared?"

"Of what?"

"Of the police—of bein' caught?"

"I ain't scared of the police. You don't stay scared of them long when you've been in jail. Tell you I come back because I didn't like all them people at that party. Not enough room t'swing a cat in. I appreciate quiet. How's that? You're awful nosy."

"Just wanted to know what's on your mind is all."

"That's funny. Nothin'."

"You ain't goin' to run, are you?"

"Nope," Dietche said patiently. Nothing on his mind except maybe Louise. You fall down, you get up, and that's the way it goes. No regrets. Pay the tab and go on. Just don't cheat. Trouble was he didn't know *Myron's* plans.

Myron was so sure Dietche loved his daughter and wanted to escape—Myron was almost enjoying the feeling—suddenly he had a thought that he might take the little girl in, and maybe Dietche would stay forever. They'd have to figure out how to handle those characters in that black car. Thought was as far as the idea got, because when he suggested it the hired man, Dietche laughed at him. So in the back of Myron's mind the lean rack of bones continued running away from him—it was to become a nightmare—and on his conscience, of all places, the one fact of immediate importance remained.

Dietche's expressed fear of small crowded rooms lingered in Myron's memory of the story of the party. He decided to put him to work in the henhouse.

"Where's John?" Myron asked.

"Don't know," Curtiss said, ladling manure onto the wagon in the stalls.

Myron put his shovel aside.

Coming part way up the hill he saw the body stretched out comfortably in the shade of the trough. The faucet was running. "Hey!" Myron called with a nervous giggle that came to live in his throat from then on. He stood over the hired man, hands thrust in his bib. "Get up."

"Gimme two more minutes, Myron," Dietche said, but Myron was filling a cup of water, which he poured on Dietche's face.

"Thanks," Dietche said, crawling to his feet, shaking water out of his eyes. "Just havin' a little nap. God, don't you ever drink, Myron."

Myron made his quick, half-smile, which seemed almost an apology. "You don't want to sleep on the job, John."

"No sir."

It was then that Myron told him he was going to spend some time in the henhouse.

"I figured it out," Dietche told him, sitting where he had been waiting for them to come up from lunch, smoking, his hat drawn over his nose, the back of his red head against the barn wall. "You can't afford hens," he said. However, a little while later, Dietche left the tool room pushing a wheelbarrow containing a shovel, a broom, and a putty knife, up towards the little black henhouse on top of the hill.

She lifted the curtain on the pantry window. What was Dietche doing up there? Myron had not told her anything about it. It was taking the hired man the longest time to get the wheelbarrow up the hill. She frowned. Was Myron going to have chickens?

"What do you think about so much?" Myron asked trying to sound offhand that evening as he and Curtiss stopped to speak with Dietche at the trough. The herd floated away behind them like a dragon with its fire out.

"I only been thinking how long it's been since there was chickens in that chicken house," Dietche replied.

"Told you," answered Myron. "We had a batch before the war—"

"I don't suppose you got somethin' you'd ruther have me do more in the open?" Dietche interrupted.

"That's what you been thinking."

"Yep," Dietche knew from Myron's tone, or from the way Myron held his head, that he'd be in the henhouse tomorrow, the day after, and the day after that until it was clean as a whistle.

Curtiss put his cigarette out. He asked when they would be cutting the hay.

"August," Myron replied. "If the tractor don't break to pieces before."

"What's the matter with the tractor?" Dietche asked.

"Don't go. Gasket blew."

"You sure?"

"Yes."

"Want me to fix it for you, Myron?"

"Curtiss," Myron said.

The young man was watching the stars. "Sir?"

"Feed the horses."

They divided up, Curtiss going down to the stables, the hired man and Myron climbing to the top of the hill.

Myron poked his flashlight into the henhouse. He was shocked and pleased to see what little progress the hired man had made. "What have you been doing?" he asked. A patch a few inches square lay cut in the thick crust in the center of the floor. Myron's eyes smarted. He pulled his head out. Dietche was describing how difficult it was to get down in such a tiny space—in the heat—without having to crawl out for air every five minutes. He took the flashlight, pointed it on the roosts. They were beautifully cleaned, with a layer of dust on them as if he'd sanded them. "Done them," he said. If Dietche kept at it at this rate the place'd be ready in a week, Myron thought. Dietche put out the light.

"When you putting your hens in, Myron? Soon? You'll need a run, won't you? Why don't I start sinking a few post holes out here—?"

"Ain't going to have none," Myron replied.

"Oh?" Dietche queried. "You don't want to let your hens run loose. Let them out, they'll get all muscle."

"Ain't going to have no hens, John."

Dietche paused. "I'm workin' in this stinkin' box for nothin'?"

"I wouldn't say that."

"You ain't having no hens?"

"Nope. Got you in there for your own good. Hee hee hee." Myron's hopeless laugh was the noise of his nerves—his nerves were paying the bill. He had to tread so delicately, otherwise Dietche would run.

"You're kidding."

"Yeah," Myron said. "Oh yeah."

"You're so *corny*, Myron."

"Am I. Well—just don't bring any more of your relatives around here, hear?"

"My relatives?"

"That Louise."

"Louise—that baby girl?"

"We almost got caught, John."

"How? No."

"Them fellers come to get her—?"

"Yeah—"

"Well I had people here, friends of mine, on Sunday, see. What if them feller's mentioned your name?"

"Why'd you have people here—what if I'd come back early?"

"You got to listen to me, John. You do what I say else you'll be in trouble. You trust me."

"I'm your man, boss. But you got to do the sensible thing—you got to protect me—"

"They thought you was out here. I showed them they wasn't nobody around but me and the wife and the boy."

"Lucky as hell I stayed in town all day."

"Yeah, that's why you can't go no more."

"That's fine. Now what about them hens? Are you or aren't you? I mean is there any point in me killin' myself for nothin'?"

"I think we might just have them hens, John."

So long as Myron didn't exactly know what he was doing, didn't plot Dietche's destruction deliberately—as long as Myron acted half thinking his way along—it was obvious what he was up to. You set a man a task, knowing he isn't hot on it, and you don't let him off. You drive and drive him. Well, no birds are all that important. Dietche felt that if Myron could joke about not getting the hens in such a crude way, in such a heartless tone of voice, there was something crude and cruel on his mind. In other words, the little devil was getting mysterious again. Dietche was too tired to think any more about it that night. Maybe he deserved it. Maybe Myron was right. He shouldn't have brought Louise. It'd work out. There just had to be peace and quiet between them all. But he was feeling a little eccentric that evening himself. He felt the need of an ace in his hand. Of some release. "Boss, you're some joker," he said.

"Hee hee," Myron said as they walked down from the trough.

Dietche put his hand on Myron's shoulder. "Hee hee."

"Hee hee," Myron said, grinning and blushing slightly from the familiarity.

"Yeah. You like jokes, boss?"

"Don't mind a little fun."

They were passing the cow stalls when Myron found the putty knife in the circle of light from the flashlight. He bent down and picked it up. "How'd this get down here?"

"I threw it—it's all bent," Dietche explained. He thought: if Myron would just leave him alone, just let him go home so he could use his last atom of energy on the walk, and not on anger. Myron was saying, "You spoilt the knife. I'll have to find you something better than this." When suddenly the moonlight—as Myron switched off the flashlight—struck something bright at the base of Myron's finger. "What are you looking at?" Myron asked.

"I never seen that before," Dietche said.

Above them hung the fat white moon. They sounded like conspirators. "That's my wedding ring," Myron said and slowly hid his hand in his pocket.

"You never wore it before, did you?" Dietche asked, puzzled.

It was Cora's ring, but it did not fit her, she had got so fat. Myron found it that morning in a drawer and just put it on. It was weakness to wear jewelry. His father had often warned him that gold brings thieves. His father told him to hide everything because whatever you have brings somebody who won't have it. But Myron was getting pleasure from the ring. He found it absorbed some of the pressure on his nerves. He also found he liked it shining on his hand, and that he had liked it when Dietche noticed it.

The more he drove Dietche, the more of this sort of thing he'd need. One day he'd be planting flowers in the dead beds about the house again, be deciding to put on another ring, be painting the trees....

The hired man was speaking of something else. "What year is that car of yours, Myron?"

"Thirty-four."

Dietche turned into the clover.

Myron stopped. "John." He wanted to talk some more.

"Hello."

"What was you up for?"

"Stealing. I was innocent though," Dietche said in his light, plain voice, and walked away.

Myron murmured something about not believing him and continued on to his house. As he was getting into bed, he decided to change the hiding place of the ignition key. He did not know that had Dietche wanted he could start the car without a key—any car, for that matter. But Dietche didn't take Myron seriously enough for that.

Around midnight, Dietche went to the big barn, and half an hour later walked out with the tractor's broken gasket and went directly to Myron's garage. The main house swelled out dark and still across the drive. He went cautiously, avoiding the gravel.

Inside the garage stood the beige sedan, the tank full of gas. Myron kept the car in good condition—with a little luck, Dietche could have made Buffalo in it. He felt his way to the hood. He knelt, unwrapped a greasy towel on the sand, revealing a wrench, a screwdriver, and a rubber-headed hammer.

It took him five minutes to fold up the hood. He didn't make a sound.

Working swiftly and silently, he lifted away the cylinder head and was delicately pulling the gasket over the spindles when his elbow knocked the hammer into the engine. Dietche's face shut with anger; his hand reached down inside and took the hammer. He waited. Nothing happened outside.

He laid the gasket which he'd taken from the tractor on the car block and refitted the head and screwed the bolts back down the spindles. He couldn't see a thing. Setting the wrench onto one nut after another, he tightened the head to what his intuition told him was the correct pressure for that kind of engine. The right tool would have been a needle wrench; he'd sold his with the rest of his tools years ago for two gallons of gin. He screwed in the spark plugs, pressed on their leads, adjusted the radiator hose and oil and air filters and, with great care, lifted down the halfhoods and clamped them tight. The car was as before, except for the broken tractor gasket he'd put in, which would keep the car running a short while, but not long.

He rolled up the tools, crept outside and made his way back up the hill.

The moonlight lay on the low pastures and fields as on a thick sea, like white oil. He looked in the trough—and it was suddenly full of silver. He passed the small barn and in a moment disappeared between the two great doors of the big barn where the tractor stood, its engine in half. Below the two horses were awake and heard him and lifted and dropped their mailed feet.

More swiftly, and with less caution than in the garage, Dietche lined the tractor cylinders with the gasket he'd brought from the car, replaced the head and all the organs, and twisted the crank. Nothing happened. He twisted it again. The engine fired. "Well," he said, sliding his hand along the shaking thorax to find his way to the seat. "Won't run forever," he said brightly, beginning to feel really delighted. They nosed into the night air.

Once past the small barn, he shut off the engine. The elephantine tires declined tonelessly past the trough, the stalls of the big barn, through the gate, crunched onto the driveway, and then veered off and straddled the path towards Myron's back door, Dietche's foot bouncing up and down on the brakes. Then he yanked the brake handle and jumped to the grass, opened the screen door and latched it to the side of the house. Turning, he bowed before the waiting tractor and spun the nose, climbed back into the seat and let the brake off. The tractor bumped gently into the doorway.

He compressed the clutch, shifted into gear, and with a furtive look at the dark window above, shoved the throttle forward as far as it would go and hooked it. The engine roared. And then he let out the clutch.

The tractor heaved forward, held firmly in place by its nose in the door, and then, as the screaming rose, it began to slip back and forth in the troughs the wheels were digging in the lawn. The cylinders began to misfire.

Dietche was on his way to his cabin when Myron's light went on. "I fixed it for him," he said, squatting down on his steps to see what would happen, grinning.

Curtiss sat up in bed, half asleep.

"Some devil," Myron muttered, going downstairs naked but for his shoes. Exhaust fumes and the smell of burnt oil blew into the kitchen. The house was shaking.

"Fire," Cora said dimly, remaining in bed.

Myron stopped astonished, seeing his tractor trying to get in the pantry. He realized immediately who had repaired it and that it was probably his own fault Dietche behaved this way. He ran into the living room, hitting his shin on the radio.

"Damn," he swore, rubbing himself.

He found the front door locked. He was trapped. "Where's the key to the front door?" he called from the bottom of the stairs. She couldn't hear a word he said.

"Mother!" he cried. "Where's the key to the front door?"

Getting no answer he ran back into the pantry, stood on the eyewheels, and started climbing over the hood of the tractor. The hood was red-hot and the little wheels coated in oil. His bare feet slipped, his underarms dropped on the radiator cap. "Ow!" he cried, stroking his burnt flesh, and pursing his lips in pain.

Curtiss meanwhile crept along the hall and through a crack in the bedroom wall saw Mrs. Greenhalgh sitting up in bed rubbing her eyes. Her nightdress had fallen around her waist. He tiptoed back to his room.

Far across the clover, Dietche watched the kitchen window open and a naked leg emerge with a shoe dangling on the end of it. Then the shoe fell off. For some reason that killed the hired man. He gripped his ribs laughing.

Myron could hear Dietche. He felt around the cold grass for his shoe, all the time watching the darkened, distant white cottage, knowing how Dietche had done it, and made a note to call the garage in the morning.

He climbed hurriedly up on the tractor. "Damn!" he cried as his bare ass hit the cold iron seat. "What's the matter, dear?" she called out the window.

He shifted into reverse and backed away from the house, naked outdoors for the first time in his life. He twisted the wheel and headed up the path as a car's headlights swung across his white body from a curve of the main road. Myron's eyes glittered like a lizard's and then the lights left him and the car passed, leaking feminine laughter out its windows. "Oh Lord God Almighty!" Myron cried, lisping the words because his teeth were upstairs, embarrassed, enraged, so enraged his arms were stiff on the wheel. He steered the machine through the gate, seeing the tail lights disappear down the road out of the corner of his eye.

The tractor stalled halfway up the slope near the trough. He set the brake and jumped off and walked back down through the gate like an angry spook, his private parts banging about like sin. There was a flock of those damn girls working at the A & P; it would undoubtedly be them out till dawn screwing on a working day. "Them Italians," he muttered when he returned to bed, waving aside her protests concerning the grease on his thighs and feet.

"Shut up. Shut up," he said, and lay down and burned until he fell asleep.

Oddly enough, things were a little more relaxed around there after that. At least it seemed so to Dietche. Myron let up a little.

The next morning, back in the henhouse, he laughed all day long, loud, so Myron could hear him. Myron let him laugh. It was good for him. Myron was baffled by Dietche's behavior with the tractor. It was so pointless. Dietche was behaving like a child. It brought out the father in Myron.

On the morning of Dietche's fifth day in the henhouse a friend of his, on whom Dietche had said he never wanted to lay eyes again, left New York for Myron's. His name was Roland Marcovitch. It was he, and a man named Crosetti, who had sent

Dietche up on false charges. It was he who made those two telephone calls the month before.

Except for the hard stuff in the corners, the henhouse episode was almost over. He had worked slowly and patiently on the six-foot-square floor, paying his methodical penance, and as he dragged the long hoe across the shit, he thought, 'If only he'd of tarpapered the floor,' which was about all his brain had use for in the way of thought those last hours.

The wind dropped; he crawled out for air.

Five minutes passed, which was all the respite he allowed himself, and then pulled himself back inside the little heated box, grasped the hoe at the neck and knelt to finish the southwest corner, hoping Myron could find work for him outside that afternoon. That's what he hoped every morning. He didn't like to ask any more.

He nearly wept when his head hit the roof, because once in prison he was caught trading a straight edge he'd taken from the barber shop for three cartons of cigarettes, and to teach him a lesson, they put him in the Hole for a week. No, not the Hole, but into the door of the Hole. He was too tall for it. 'Jesus', he thought over and over again, listening to somebody going nuts in the black room he was the door to, 'if *he* flips in there—' But he came out of it; because he was innocent of the crime they'd convicted him of. Thinner, nevertheless, and very afraid of tight places.

The hoe went quicker, scratching up a pile of dung between his sore knees.

He was working fast, so fast he worked himself right into a corner. The handle of the hoe jammed into the wall, throwing him off balance. He landed with his head in the junction of the ceiling and the floor, and was held in place by the hoe.

"John," Myron said, looking in the door.

A few grunts came from the hot interior, asking Myron to get out of the doorway, he was blocking the air.

"Are you sick?" Myron asked.

The voice came again, shaking like a dog when it removes itself from a stream. "Get me out," it said, not loudly enough.

"Can't you get up?" Myron asked.

"Naw."

"What's the trouble?"

The long legs scratched out, tearing the black paper off the walls.

Myron asked again what the trouble was.

"Earache."

"You best get up," Myron said.

"G'wan, Myron," Dietche whispered. "Get."

"Thought you said you had earache."

"Get."

Myron heard the legs rattle again as he went down the hill.

Dietche called on the past and it came to him like a nurse. He remembered learning that the more relaxed he made himself in the door to the Hole, the less would seem the confinement. He relaxed. He reduced his breathing, which wasn't hard since there wasn't anything but dirt to breathe, and concentrated on the nail of the little finger which was lying six inches from his eye. He put everything he had onto it. It wasn't much to look at, he thought, as fingernails go. It wasn't going to be his eccentric sense of humor that saved him. That, like the instinct for survival, was desperate and anarchistic. By experience Dietche was a builder, not a dynamiter: by experience, not by nature, he was a smiler. It was, he thought, about the most interesting fingernail he'd ever seen. There.

The haze before his eyes diminished. He grew smaller. He backed out. He brushed himself off and walked unsteadily down to the trough and drank.

That afternoon, he complained. "Myron, you remember when we had that little do in the fields last month. You remember what I told you? Did I say I'd kill you?"

"All I remember is I told you to git that henhouse ready. If you don't I'll turn you in."

"I don't care."

"We'll see."

"I don't care, Myron. I jes' don't care," he muttered, walking backwards up the hill waving his finger to and fro. He backed into the trough. "You go ahead and call the troopers. You tell 'em John Dietche's here and he don't KEER!"

"You g'wan," Myron called up to him, laughing. Their voices carried easily back and forth. There was no wind.

"Myron you ring up the troopers and won't I tell *them* something. We'll all go south for the winter, boy. Nice stone beaches, everybody eats together."

"They won't believe you," Myron said.

"I believe you, Myron," Dietche said, standing high up on the rise. "Say!"

"What?"

"Why am I goin' in here again? You ain't goin' to have no hens."

"We'll see."

Dietche's glance fell on the young man who had just left the house and had joined Myron at the gate; he thought he saw something that looked like dirt on the boy's face. He looked harder. The young man turned away and stared at something—a bird— and when he returned his face to Dietche it was the same old gray expression again. "Why'n't you put him in here?" Dietche called at the door to the henhouse.

"What's he say?" Curtiss asked quietly.

"Don't know," Myron said.

"What's the matter with him?" Curtiss asked.

"He's on the drink this morning," Myron said.

"It's awful early," Curtiss said.

"Yeah," Myron said.

When Dietche saw Myron and Curtiss cross the highway below on their way into the fields, he crawled out and sat in back of the henhouse, facing the mountain. A few hours later Myron found him there asleep, his ragged face tilted down against the wall, his mouth open, his hat off. Gently, Myron shook him. "Johnny."

The head slipped further down and the hands fell on their wrists on the stubble ground.

"Johnny," Myron said. He hated him. He was so far away, and Myron was going through so much. During the hot, sleep-less nights he'd wake Cora and make her sing songs or recite nursery rhymes until he went to sleep. And furthermore Dietche had played that silly joke on him for which Myron had forgiven him. "John!" he said harshly, and Dietche woke up.

The cows crossed the side of the hill ahead of Curtiss and stopped, watching Dietche duck his head in the trough.

Funny thing, Myron sometimes believed they would be get-ting hens after all. "Sure I'm goin' to have pullets, John. Now why don't you go back in there. There ain't much more." It was the morning of the sixth day.

"And I say you ain't goin' to have no pullets and I say let me help with the cultivation or anything."

"You'll do as I tell you. There's nothing else at the moment anyhow."

"I'll run," the hired man said.

"I'll know it."

"Yes, you will."

"G'wan now, Johnny."

Dietche's eyes burned red with fatigue. He spoke slowly. "What's eatin' you?"

"What did you say?" Myron asked, looking quickly at Curtiss, out of earshot, at the end of the runway.

Dietche cleared his throat. "What's eatin' you, I said." And flung his hat on the cement.

Curtiss walked hurriedly out the back door.

Myron smiled. "Go on up there, John. Please."

Dietche swept up his hat. "Stop fooling, Myron. I'd *go*."

"When are you going?"

"Before I'm dead, by God."

"How will I know when you're going? You wouldn't dare tell me."

"That's up to me, ain't it?"

Myron frowned. Dietche's threat itched in his skull. He could not stand it spoken out like that. He stepped into the milkroom and turned both faucets on. "You can quit if you like. Let Curtiss finish it."

"I'd go *now*," the hired man said.

Myron came to the door and said in a low, piteous voice, "Why don't you then?"

"I'd go now," Dietche continued, screwing up his good eye at the little farmer, "seein' what a difficult feller you turned out to be. Only I got to *stay*. If I can persuade you to be nicer," he mumbled.

"You just behave yourself."

Dietche didn't speak for a moment. He worked up what on a clean, healthy human face would have been a smile. The little black-eyed doll-man stood still in the doorway above him, his toecaps sticking out over the edge of the steps, his brown face and his neat black hair and his flat, lusterless, wrinkle-framed eyes pointed down at the tall, mangy piece of bone and vellum which was fingering its hat and nervously brushing off its neatly patched khaki shirt which kept a semblance of dignity about the man which was not needed because all the dignity needed was in Dietche's face. Dietche was like something that drifted upright. And when Dietche said, his broken face lifting up, "You know what I'd do if I was me?" he grinned weakly.

"I don't, but my wife's got word to call the troopers the second I yell out," Myron said quickly.

Dietche shrugged. "It ain't important." He went outside and up the hill to the henhouse, confused and weak, having lost the thread of what it was all about. Myron was right. Somebody had to be boss.

Myron watched below from the gate, not leaning on anything, his hands tucked in the bib of his faded coveralls and his flat black eyes taking the sun as he looked up at the henhouse wondering if they hadn't gone too far.

Curtiss was in the big lofts pitching hay.

Dietche turned slowly back and forth inside the henhouse. Occasionally a panfull of feathers and crud would fly out into the wheelbarrow parked beside the doorway. Myron heard the dropping screen crash.

He was about to turn away to work a few moments later when he realized nothing was going on up there now. "John?" he called. "John?" he called again, going up.

Cora thumbed the mail-order catalogue while she waited for her bread to bake. 'I'll have ten Reds, and ten of them,' she thought, her feet swamped in pretend hens and herself in her cotton dress feeding them pretend corn.

She heard Myron's shrill cry through her meditation and her expression changed to one of gratitude.

Myron was yelling for Curtiss.

Curtiss put the hired man on his hip and retrieved the hat which had fallen to the ground. They carried him down the hill into the clover with Myron at the feet.

Looking out from the lace of the kitchen window, Cora experienced a feeling of disgust equal in its strength to her rapidly growing need for lots of hens. 'Drunk,' she thought. 'He's too kind to him.'

Myron watched his victim's expression as they bumped easily along towards the cabin. The face was not in repose now but in a kind of dried-up state, like a bird that's been hanging dead a long time in the telephone wires.

On the way back Curtiss asked why Dietche drank so much.

"Excuse me—what did you say?" Myron asked gently.

"I just wondered why John drinks so much."

"That ain't drink."

"Oh no?"

"No—he's sick and we got to take care of him."

"What's he got?"

"Don't know, but we got to take care of him, Curtiss."

CHAPTER EIGHT

He peeked through the crack in the door and smiled. He seemed on the point of tears. "John."

Dietche turned his head in surprise as the visitor strode into the cabin. He apologized as he came and with manic impulsiveness took a cellophane envelope of white powder from his billfold, asking—everything came in a rush—Dietche to dust the powder on his dinner that evening.

"Why don't you do it yourself?" Dietche asked.

Roland waved his hand, smearing the question—to him, ideas, words, seemed material—clay and paint—that afternoon. "I—" he said, then stopped. "You won't help me?"

"No," Dietche replied.

"Are you going to stay here the rest of your life?" Roland asked, changing the subject. Dietche didn't answer and Roland collapsed on a stool beside the door and the light hit the cot again. His eyes, occult, plump, lying on either side of a full, curving nose, stared outside as if he were trapped. Roland had grown heavier. His face was made of different sorts of curves, like fruit. The eyes moved. They saw a bird land on the huge blue roof of his car, thinking it was water. It was burning metal and the bird flew away. Roland Marcovitch sighed, and as the sigh expired, the flies seemed to sing louder around his sweet-smelling body. Roland became uncomfortably aware of them and got up. It was a small room. They followed him easily.

"How's Crosetti?" Dietche asked.

"I don't know. I am penniless."

"Well, if you're penniless, how come that big car out there?"

"I stole it," Roland said, with exasperation. Then he burst out, "I always meant to pay you!"

"I bet you did," Dietche said.

"I tried," Marcovitch suffered.

"It don't matter."

"It does matter," Roland said, wiping his head with his handkerchief. He had lost his hair. "I am morally ruined," he added.

"Excuse me, what did you say?"

"I am morally ruined," he repeated, taking off his coat. He had no idea of how he appeared to others. Dietche had felt like laughing ever since he came. The facts from which he spun his insufferable guilt were these: seven years ago Dietche lived in the same hotel on the Jersey side of the river, and one night as usual was sitting in the bar with his newly married wife when Roland, whom they had known a little while, came running in, took Dietche into the toilet, and offered him fifty thousand dollars to go to prison for ten years in his place. Roland was in a hurry. Dietche didn't want to do it, so Roland put what he'd managed to get out of the jewelry store in Dietche's room and disappeared. And soon the police arrived.

The frame-up hit him so hard—like an auto accident which includes a lot of innocent bystanders in its wake—so hard it killed everything in him, including his love for his wife—except unlike an auto accident, it didn't happen all at once. When later he heard that she died in childbirth it was a consolation: dead, she was not going to run off with anybody. When, much later, he came out on parole, he was stillborn. During the years in what is misnamed stir, even the hope for revenge died.

He went upstate toward the hills he'd come from, ignoring his obligations to the parole authorities.

While he lay under Myron's blanket listening to the man who had betrayed him walk up and down among the buzzing flies, Dietche compared his little girl to the dead, almost feature-less wife, whom Roland had brought to mind.

The gangster had spotted Curtiss, "How much do these people know?"

"Very little."

"Why did you come back here in the first place—where you were born? What about the police?"

"You're more nervous'n ever."

Roland was known as the umbrella man, because they said it was always raining in one way or another wherever he was. He sat down and leaned his bald head into the screen door. He sighed.

"I'm not happy."

"You married?"

"No."

"Why don't you get married?"

"Now? What an idea!" Roland said, soft breakers smashing strongly in him. "Me—Roland Marcovitch—taking some young girl—dragging her through a life of cheap rooms? You know how I feel about it. I would love to. But no. It's too late." There was a light froth on his lips, left by the breakers. "God, I'm tired of traveling. You know that I never stayed in the same place more than a week? I've been to Mexico a hundred times since I saw you last."

It sounded like he'd enjoyed it. Dietche wondered what Myron would make of Roland when he came. A middle-aged figure from the weak heart of Europe—possibly a man, a fragment, some living thing which had been a man once, who escaped the sleek whip which had made a stripe across all Europe, slaughtering his relatives, burning towns, dismembering cities, destroying charts and minds—how deeply Roland regretted the loss of his town, the only place he could remember feeling confident and Jewish at the same time as the same thing. How he despaired of losing the one address he cherished, where he could always go back if he failed, if he succeeded. And now he had failed—in

Portugal, in South America. And there was no town anymore to go back to. He degenerated further. Nothing meant anything if there was no town, no family, no mother, no father, nor brothers. Self-driven, alone, afraid, unbalanced—a warm, desperate figure in a worn suit with a bulge in the sharkskin under the right arm where he sometimes carried death, like a second heart. "Well," he said, looking at his watch. "I must convince you."

"Do you keep any of her stuff?" Dietche asked.

"Yes."

"You sell it and send the money, hear?"

"I'm not going back," Marcovitch murmured. "Why am I here? I'm supposed to provide you with revenge for the mess I've made of your life."

"Not interested."

Marcovitch smiled. "I have an agile mind. I will persuade you."

"Look—" Dietche began slowly. He hadn't any strength. "Let me say something serious—"

Roland pulled at his trousers. "Come. Tell."

"You don't have to fool around with poison."

The sad eyes traveled to the figure under the blanket. "You must provide me with expiation," he said flatly.

"Depends on what it means."

"Payment for sins."

"I don't blame you anymore. I took my chances."

"You did not. You had no choice. I framed you!"

"Nobody's got to live in New Jersey."

"I framed you. You were an innocent lamb led to slaughter. You hate me!"

"I just don't care anymore. It's been so long."

The round man twisted his round hands together. "You hate me! Of course you hate me! Why not?" he cried. "My God, what did I do to you? Think!"

"Rolly honey," Dietche whispered.

"Don't Rolly honey me. Look inside your heart! Did your parents never tell you we butchered Jesus Christ?"

"Sure, but that particular killing was a long time ago—"

Roland released himself and slapped his knee irritably.

"Don't say you like me, dear." He bent his head and looked out the door.

"I never said I like you. Look, what I wanted to say was, would you like to take care of my little girl?"

Marcovitch turned violently on the stool. "What?"

"I asked if you'd like my little girl."

"Louise?" Roland bit his thumb. He rose off the stool. "I'm going for a walk. Hneeee Jesus," he moaned.

Dietche asked what the matter was.

"What's the matter?" Roland protested. "What's the matter? Idiot!"

"Keep her as long as you want, Rolly. And if you don't like it—well—we'll think of something else." It was the same tic that made him pick up bits of string. Now he wanted someone to pick up this loose, wandering little girl. It was just a thought. Roland might want to do something for her—more than those pastel beauts in the daredevil crowd did. "Keep her as long as you can stand it. Maybe you can send her to one of them boarding schools. Pay the bills by mail. They'll never know who you are."

"No!" Marcovitch barked, cornered, frightening himself.

"Think of the kid," Dietche continued. "You know what she does? She lives with them carnival people. They don't want her. Try it. Six months."

"Would you help?"

"In a little while."

"What if it didn't work? What if she didn't like me? I'd have to bring her here?"

It was getting too complicated, Dietche thought.

"Be sensible," Marcovitch said dully.

"I am," Dietche said and asked for water. Roland filled a glass from a pail. His hand shook and some of the liquid spilled on the floor. Dietche asked him to wipe it up. "You always liked kids, didn't you?" he said, amused.

Marcovitch beamed helplessly. A daughter. A little life to care for.

Dietche closed his eyes. He didn't really care either way. Suddenly he grew cold again: Myron was outside the door, blocking the light. "Door's open," Dietche murmured.

"Come for the tray," Myron said through the screen. "Can't find Curtiss."

"Come in. Like you to meet a friend of mine."

"Wall I'm terribly busy," Myron said coming in, cross-faced and curious. Dietche pulled an uneaten tray from under the cot. "This is Myron. Myron, this is Roland." He wished they'd all leave.

"Howjedo," said Myron.

"Hello, Myron," Roland said.

Myron looked him over slowly—the fat, tear-shaped body, the nylon shirt, the necktie, the large feet. "You know what's wrong with John?" he asked.

"Another glass of water please," Dietche said from the cot.

Marcovitch shrugged and turned away. "It's jaundice."

"Jaundice?" Myron said, taking the glass. A man like this Roland was quite something to find in your back yard.

"Did he used to get sick before?"

"I know very little about him—we met over a game of cards."

"Don't stay too long," Myron said, suddenly annoyed now by the Jew, and took the tray and went out.

It was a minute or two before they spoke again. Roland rubbed his eyes. Myron—something—possibly the break in continuity when Myron came in—had depressed him terribly. The former reminded him of someone he'd seen in the newsreels. "It isn't that I don't like children," he said wearily. "It isn't that I don't want your little girl. But I *framed* you, John—"

Dietche asked him to speak louder.

"Louise isn't any solution," Marcovitch continued. "It's stupid."

"All right."

"I must *die*."

"I can't work up interest in anything today."

"That's what I have to get at! Look—the child is out. There is only one more thing that could convince you of my uselessness— might stir you—" He paused, but decided not to play the trump yet. He lifted his chin and looked out the door. "In this world of blind confusion—John?" he said, turning to the head which lay on the pillow like a plate. John was asleep.

Roland got up and shook him. "How could you," he said, hurt.

Dietche asked what was wrong.

"You weren't listening."

"Well where were we? Oh yeah. You goin' to take the kid?"

"Ah," Roland said in despair and folded his arms. "Look this evening—"

But Dietche was shaking his head. "I wouldn't kill you for a million dollars."

"Please!"

Dietche grinned. "No."

"Why not? Oh why *not?*"

"Are you kidding? I'd kill you if you had cancer or something."

"Cancer. Cancer," Roland said. The word had music in it. He was happy again. It just came over him, like a burst of sunshine. All at once he had never enjoyed an afternoon more. It couldn't be possible Dietche had forgot. That he no longer felt like punishing Roland. That he had forgiven him. That would be all right, though, he thought. Roland felt that if you can forgive a man you can kill him. Indifference is the stake in the beast's heart. "Can you think of any reason why I should live?" he asked.

"Say—if you went back to Europe you'd have to be an honest man—I hear there's nothing to steal there anymore. That'd pinch, wouldn't it?"

To lie still in the earth, he thought—a broken vessel of fear and dread, a man who had sealed his fate with a wretched, emotional self-consciousness of purpose that had all the elements of grand opera. "John," he said sharply, looking at his stolen watch again. "If a man killed someone dear to you, you'd hate him, yes?"

"Yes."

"Hate would overwhelm you."

"Maybe. Water."

"Listen to me!"

"Please—I'm awful thirsty."

"So if," Roland continued, dipping the glass in the pail, "I—"

"Don't spit in my water, Roland. Don't you know about germs?"

"Yes. Yes, I do. Sorry. I'm sorry." He put his hand on Dietche's arm. "Now look." He kneeled beside the cot. "Listen—"

"Listenin'," Dietche said and drank.

"If a man commits a murder, he must be killed."

"Yeah. If he gets caught. It's the law."

"But what if he hasn't been caught?"

"He'll get caught."

"So you are interested."

"All right."

"You were so indifferent a moment ago."

"Well does this have anythin' to do with me?"

"Not yet. Now, what if the thief gets away with it—but you saw him do it. Would you kill him yourself?"

"No. I mean if I read in the papers about somebody killing somebody and the headshrinkers spring him, well, I get sore. But if it was me that killed somebody, hell, I'd squirm, I guess. I don't think you have to kill. Lot of them kids in with me just got scared. Well you get scared and kill, you ought to burn. I mean you can't suck the tit all your life."

"I've killed," Roland said.

"What?"

"I've killed—at last."

"You've started that now?"

"I had to. I had no choice."

"When?"

"On a caper."

"What?"

"A job."

"Why don't you say a job? Are you trying to impress me?"

"A job. A job."

"What did you kill, Roland?" Dietche said patiently.

"An old woman."

"So?" Dietche said. He guessed he believed him. "So what," he said.

Marcovitch stared at Dietche. "So what?" he said and then shut his wet mouth. "Well," he continued looking sideways at the floor. He gathered his courage. "Yes," he said, "and I killed a child." He attempted a careless shrug.

"You're off your rocker," Dietche said.

"No I am not."

"You're foolin' me."

"No, I am not fooling you," Roland said with disgust.

"When did you do it?"

"Last week."

"How?"

"With an axe."

"Bull."

"It's true!"

"You wouldn't kill a fly."

"No? Put yourself in my place. You've gone into a house at night and you've filled a case full of jewels and silver and on your way out the brat wakes up and there's an axe—Boy Scout axe—on his bed and a cop happens to be outside."

"Whyn't you run?"

"A man who has been stealing for a long time is in no condition to do any running—can you imagine me running? I was paralyzed. What did I do. I take the axe and I raise it over my head and I—are you watching? So watch!" Roland got off the floor. He could not see Dietche's face, his raised arms obscuring his view. "Watch. A little boy—but he should cry out—" He brought his arm down in a quick movement. "And I was free." He held up his coat and pointed to dark stains on the sleeves. "Look."

"You're crazy."

"No I'm not. No I'm not." Marcovitch walked slowly to the window again. He appeared to be staring at an object in the fields now—a vision of light which lay inside, in his alert, screwed-up mind.

"Did you have to kill a little boy?" Dietche said politely.

"It was the reasonable thing to do. You don't believe me?"

"Roland, I'm beat. You're a nice guy. Go away."

He turned and stood over Dietche, smiling, perspiring, his eyes wide, ripe, ready to fall, his hands on his hips. "How well do you know me?"

"Go away."

"I'm a man."

Dietche glanced up at him, annoyed.

"A man needs love," Roland continued. "No man is an island."

"Shit."

"What happened in that hotel—after you went up? Your wife stayed on."

"That's right," Dietche said and asked for another glass of water.

"Well," Roland said and shook his hips suggestively.

"Well what."

"Hmm*mmm*," Roland said.

"That isn't very funny," Dietche said.

"No."

"Cut it out. You? She was a young girl."

"Why not?" Marcovitch asked.

" 'Cause she was mine."

"Ah. Well. You were going to be away a long time," he barked, and then his voice broke and became sweet and low. "Please forgive me—I—kn-know better. Who are you? What do you know?"

"It don't jibe."

He held his hand out at Dietche. "How can you be sure?"

"That's right."

Marcovitch's knees pressed the edge of the cot.

"Oh-h-h-ho. Look! Look at me! The insect is in focus."

"I *knew* her."

"You must be very sure of yourself. I wouldn't be so sure," Roland cried, and strode away and turned, and the flies turned, and shouted, "you think you take a virgin and it seems she's yours forever! Well." His voice dropped to a whisper. "Don't think for a moment I believe anything so stupid as that. Don't imagine I haven't seen the sadness of this world. You silly knight on a horse!"

"Oh you seen sadness all right. You cry when the sun goes down."

Marcovitch turned away from Dietche and shouted, "I am so sorry for you sometimes!"

"All right."

Roland blazed with indignation. What was the matter with him? "Will you never believe I made love to your wife?"

Dietche began coughing. "Will you get out of here?"

"Why do you shout? You hurt yourself."

"Because I wish you'd shut up."

"Do you doubt her?"

"No."

"She lived a year after you went away. That's a long time for any woman to wait—not that this woman waited a *year.*" There was a pause. "Think!"

"Yeah, think—that's the fun of it. Wait a minute—you hold on there—"

"Shall I tell you what happened? She lasted three months. A lonely woman. She said you'd understand. Do you understand? Do you really think it matters to them?"

"Maybe. But you're still a liar!" At the same time he shouted, or tried to shout, he wondered why the hell he was angry. (It's the facts that surprise). But still the anchorite said again, "You're a liar!"

"Well, it can't be proved now of course—perhaps the bellhop would testify—the maids—the dinners for two—"

"In that hotel?"

"Think."

"What in hell do you gain by all this chatter?" Dietche asked.

"My death," Roland replied.

"Why don't you just shoot yourself?"

"Here." Roland held up the packet of tropical poison, delighted. "Look. Your revenge."

"My what?" Dietche said.

Roland looked alarmed. "Why do you go back? We come so far! What's the matter with you—can't you understand anything?" he said.

"Rolly, you're a liar."

"I am not!" he cried. "What I say is the truth! How do you know? Who are you, you neurotic fellow?"

"I know my wife never laid you," Dietche said.

"Wasn't it possible?"

"Yes it was possible."

"I framed you. Not anybody else."

Dietche didn't say anything for a minute. He was beginning to buy it. "All right," he said.

"Doesn't it make sense?" Marcovitch asked. "Why didn't I frame somebody else?"

"Maybe because you wanted me out of the way."

"So there."

"But my wife didn't care for you."

"No—but she had to eat—she needed clothes for herself and the baby coming. She was getting big, naa? So who am I to give money away?"

"Yeah."

"Who am I to give money away, I said."

"Yeah, I heard you."

"Well, John," he said, shaking his head, his eyes tiredly, forever on guard, "there you are."

"You tellin' the truth?" Dietche asked, and you don't ask a liar if he's telling the truth unless you believe him.

"Could she work pregnant?" Roland asked. He stopped at the door. How he wished he had done it. He stammered on, guiltlessly. "She was wonderful."

"You damn foreigners," was all Dietche said.

"You know me now, don't you," Roland murmured. The curtain was coming down. It wasn't a smile on the man's face, was it, Roland thought, walking out down the steps. The hired man was choking with rage and defeat, wasn't he? What did I do to him, he wondered in some remote, rational corner of his mind—wherever the warnings are stored. Dietche must be angry, must be profoundly disgusted with him, Roland figured, walking away through the clover, whistling a sad tune.

He waddled down the highway from the farm until he came to a broken gate. He walked through it into a field and sat down under an apple tree. He didn't know what would happen now. He only knew that Dietche believed him. And then, without expecting to, quite precipitately, he fell sound asleep.

The waste matter from his food was going into his blood and tissue because the bladder was blocked. Where skin closely overlay his bones a shade of yellow appeared—on his temples, elbows, knuckles—and then it entered his eyes. He looked like tallow. The disease, and Roland, had weakened him, and he drowsed again.

The farm drew away from the sun and the change in light brought relief to the fields. For the birds the coming of cool was always curious; they commented briefly on it and woke Dietche. He felt weaker.

Marcovitch had been right to think he could get at Dietche through his feelings, but the visitor was wrong to assume they were feelings like his own. The hired man was not like him. He was a man for whom time was in the hands of the clock; for whom emotion was not a mysterious power, but a co-operating influence as plain in operation as the sides of a triangle; for whom people were material objects from which he expected nothing except respect. Wrongly imagining him to be of the more subtle world he knew—of music and science and love and death—Marcovitch had tried to get at Dietche through anxiety which, with good reason, he believed, existed in all men. But Dietche had not been touched in a long time.

The stakes were not what Roland hoped they were, stakes of pride, ego, frustration. That day Dietche had simply learned that he was right. It was almost as if you saw something underneath the surface of a painting and removed it only to find exactly the identical painting underneath.

Obsessions like Roland's live in certain people like a virus: but to those free, disappointed, cheerful men who do not make war on themselves, there are none.

So it wasn't despair or anger that Dietche experienced that afternoon, feelings which Roland hoped would help Dietche kill him. Dietche didn't want to kill him. He didn't care enough to kill anything. He was merely surprised.

To those betrayed men who have got over it entirely, there are memories and a certain minor wisdom from having passed through an interesting life. They have no spite, no regrets, no corrosive sense of a past injury, no self-hatred dipped in self-accusings, poisoning the heart and mind. *Feuilles mortes. Keine angst.* He was no longer aware of himself except in his shaving mirror or when the sun drew his shadow on the ground.

'Je suis,' the hired man thought, reciting his grammer. *'Tu es. Il est. Je viens à Paris. Je viens à la France. Je mange. Je suis*—He stopped. 'I wonder if he's telling the truth,' he wondered. 'Oh, Helen,' he thought ruefully. Meaning 'Oh, John.'

The feeling of dismay might last, but that would be all. No man is free from anything, including evil, unless he's never committed evil.

A car door slammed on the road and woke Roland. For a moment, he could not remember where he was. He lay on his side, his arms and legs broken about like a swastika. Life crawled around him on hundreds of black legs. He imagined them little people drawing threads over him, tying him to the earth. Tying his body to the earth, because he had a definite sense that his body was something else. A blade of grass swung down over-loaded with a ladybug and bumped his chin.

Roland opened his eyes. A man was calling him from the road. Above him the branches of the apple tree looked like defects in the sky. The branches were dead—but the sky, oh that sky, he thought. And an ant crossed his palm with love. Roland was flooded with joy.

"Hey!"

Roland raised his head, breaking the threads. He stood, clearing them off his suit, and walked down to the gate. He felt the earth give beneath his shoes.

"Where did you come from?" the man asked, his face scarlet in the dying sun.

"I parked to take a nap," Roland lied.

"Looked s'if you dropped out of the sky. Where you goin'?"

"New York."

"You know the way out?"

"Oh yes."

"Been a nice day."

"It has."

"The reason I woke you up was you'd catch cold on the ground."

"Thank you."

"Where you been?"

"Avalon."

"Lot of salesmen go by Avalon. Not all of them come back this way."

"Thanks for waking me up," Roland said, walking away.

"That's all right," the man said and watched him go, disappointed not to have made more of the conversation.

Marcovitch headed towards the farmhouse to arrange dinner.

"You awake?" Myron said as he and Roland carried in the trays.

"I'm awake," Dietche said dimly.

"Your friend's goin' to eat with you—he said he'd pay," Myron said. The screen door slammed and he was gone.

"Roland," Dietche began, "did you figure on dyin' here?"

"No," Roland replied, laying his tray beside Dietche's on the floor and then squinting at a road map he'd brought from the car. "The poison will begin to take effect—unless I get a flat tire—at Fort Ticonderoga." He lifted a finger from a red dot and folded the map. "It looks like heart trouble. There is nothing to worry about." He picked up Dietche's hand, folded the fingers around the cellophane packet, and went outside to the car. He turned on the ignition and tapped the glass window of the gas gauge to unstick the needle. He had enough gas. He crossed the road and sat on the remains of a stone fence and watched the sun drop towards the hills beyond the river. He wanted it all. The spreading orange stain on the sky made him sad—then morose—then cheerful, and, finally, bored. He wondered how anyone could feel bored, though, facing death.

Inside the cabin, Dietche's thoughts were vaguely fixed on his dead wife again, trying to remember what she looked like. He heard Roland coming back; with an effortless motion, his wife slipped and fell away. Only space remained in his mind, among the other spaces.

Roland stepped over the trays and sat on the edge of the bed. The hand was empty.

"John," he said. "John," he said again. He clapped his hands. Slowly the dark red skull turned on the pillow. "You going?" he asked Roland.

"You did what I asked?" Roland said.

"You promise to go after you eat?"

"You did what I asked?"

"You know, I don't care about you and my wife," Dietche said. "You could have saved all that."

Roland didn't believe him. "If you haven't helped me, I'll stay here until you do."

"I know you will."

"So did you do what I asked?"

Dietche said: "Yes." His lips did not move when he spoke. The adam's apple moved like a mouse under his skin. The empty, wire-haired hand lay on his chest, practically covering it. "Boy, you are somethin'."

"I am," Marcovitch said, his hands circling his watery knees. "Which tray is mine?" he asked. The drops on his head caught the sunset.

Dietche didn't hear him.

"I asked which tray is mine," Roland said again.

The sun was about to disappear now, in that annihilating moment of suspense just before a gun goes off, or when a flying bird reaches for the branch.

The moon was out already, gauzed in and unlit above some clouds.

Dietche's hand fell on one of the trays. He lifted a plate and put it on his chest; then he stuffed up his pillow behind his head.

Setting his tray on his lap, Marcovitch took a fork and put it into the beans and brought them towards his mouth. Before he put them in, he closed his eyes. He looked as if he were being kissed.

By the time he finished the beans, his hands were steady again. "Coffee?" he asked, setting the tray down. His plate shone.

Dietche hadn't eaten much. "No coffee," he said.

Finally, Roland put down his cup and wiped his mouth on his sleeves. "I am dying," he said.

"How does it feel?"

"I feel like a new man." Like a great weight, care had lifted off his shoulders. He had hoped to feel less guilty, however. Perhaps it wouldn't come all at once. "How do you feel?" he asked.

"I feel lousy."

"But you've forgiven me at last," Roland said, putting on his coat.

"Yeah; you goin'?"

"I'm going."

"Well, good-bye, Rolly." Roland extended his hand. Dietche reached up and took it and dropped it. "See you."

With relief, Dietche listened to the screen door close. Roland always gave him plenty of kicks.

The car started.

Dietche pulled the other arm from under the blanket as the car drove away. He pulled a boot out from under the bed and dropped the unopened packet of poison in it and shoved it back under the bed.

But he could not take Roland for long stretches. It was such a chore to get rid of him.

The highway wound along the edge of the lake. The band of numbers turned in the speedometer, illuminating the wet face as it passed through town after town, scaring children and old people.

Reason—memory—downright fear rose in him over and over again, asking him to stop. Sheldon—Crown Point—with each town, Fort Ticonderoga came closer. At any place along the way he could have had his stomach pumped out. He drove at thirty-five, at the edge of giving in. But it was a broad, safe edge. He wasn't showing off.

By the time he made Ticonderoga, he was in high spirits. When he thought about Dietche, he no longer felt his terrible guilt. Drugstores asked him to stop and have his stomach pumped out. A police car in an alley, like a crib, entreated him. A young woman smiled without quite looking at him as she went through his headlights at a stop light. He wasn't doing it for them.

The voyage led past iron street lamps and large square homes and then he was way out of town where the stars were noticeable again. Nothing was happening quite yet. He drove off the road and waited. It was past the hour. He couldn't just wait for it, though. He pulled into the road again, sighing. Other cars ran past him in moments of light, careening toward homes, friends, enemies. He rolled up the windows for the flight into the unknown where none of them were going, where none of them existed.

Twenty miles below Ticonderoga he drove savagely into a neat, ploughed field, behind a wall of bushes hiding the road. He walked away from the car and sat helplessly on the earth. His watch said ten-thirty. The stars flashed just over his head, fresh jewels scattered out of a broken sack. He didn't want them. Foreign hills climbed like children around the bedded horizon. Roland had known all the shapes of the mountains in his own country. They were one big happy family. He'd never felt lost and deserted in Czechoslovakia.

It was cold. He turned up the collar of his jacket. He didn't dare look at his watch again. He didn't feel tired, sleepy, or drowsy—any of the things the Chinaman'd promised him. He couldn't believe it. He just couldn't believe it. He thought he was going to die that night. Here he was all prepared like a bride, resigned and happy, and then nothing. And at that late point, the first peace he had known in years began going all to pot. Dietche hadn't done what he was supposed to. Fear struck Marcovitch's heart. 'I've been jewed,' he thought. Colors came to his tormented mind. Blues and golds. He saw the side of a fish fill his sight glowing hot gold, and then a pair of wings as he got up and stumbled across the furrows to the car and opened the glove compartment and brought out two things, one of which was a small box of cartridges, three of which he inserted in the virgin chambers of a revolver; and then, with one arm holding the open door for support because his knees were going, he struck the barrel into his ear and pulled the trigger.

CHAPTER NINE

Myron couldn't expect anything of the clouds overhead, and kept his head down, dividing his time among his cows, the fields, and the hired man.

But by the end of that week the clouds were annoying him which meant he *had* been watching them. Never changing their high, feminine, careless interconnection—never coming down to earth—every morning more of the streaks, light and stratospheric, then every evening covering the sunset like bandages on a fresh running wound and then, as he undressed in the window, pure white gauze over the moon.

In the white cell beyond the barns, lay a weak, puzzled Dietche. 'He's come here four, five times a day, for a week now,' he thought. 'He don't say nothin' except he wishes I was better. You'd think he'd let me rot.'

By the middle of the second week of Dietche's illness, Myron turned on Curtiss, unable to bear the strain. "You get that tray out of there now or by God you go home tomorrow," he burst out one morning. "I can't go in there all the time."

"Take it easy," Curtiss suggested and walked in front of the horse. The reins snapped. The horse sprang forward, surprised. Curtiss yelled. "You move, sonny," Myron said, going on smoothly, the iron wheels twisting across the highway and down into the field, carrying the boss towards the bridge where the corn was now growing that they had planted nearly two months ago. Curtiss got up from the road and brushed off his seat. "Damn him," he said. Above him the thickening clouds; behind them the July sun.

"Who is it? Who's there?" Dietche said.

"It's me, Curtiss."

"What was I saying?"

The young man stood holding the half-eaten tray at the screen door, watching him sideways. "You were talking about prison."

"Forget it. How's old Myron?"

The young man stood beyond the radius of Dietche's sight. "He's O.K."

"What was that shoutin' I heard between you a minute ago?"

"There wasn't any shouting."

"Reckon my ears are too good."

Curtiss put out his foot at the screen door. "So long."

"Say, Curtiss—if Myron pulls anything, you let me know. Don't keep it a secret."

"It isn't any secret."

"What ain't?"

On the way through the woods to get two cows that had not made it for milking that morning, Curtiss stumbled from fatigue and sat a moment on the hillside and looked out across the valley. They had been cultivating half the night to get the ground turned in case those clouds were going to come down. You could see the difference he and Myron had made on the potato fields. The earth was yellow-brown where they had turned up the soil under the stars, a perfect square in the gray-green surface of the valley. It was satisfying to see the landscape change because of what he and Myron did to it.

Thirsty, he made his way to the spring, and in a moment he was kneeling, charming himself in the pool in the woods.

Myron appeared in the trees, moving in and out for a look at Curtiss.

"Hey!" he called.

Curtiss jumped up.

"Come over here!" Myron called.

Curtiss ran back to the path. Myron gave him hell for loafing and said he was going to fire him. They went up into the high pasture.

The threat appeared to be forgotten, for sentimental reasons, when they discovered one of the cows had calved early. The corpse lay under a sourberry bush, covered with bruises from its mother's tongue. Myron took it by the new heels and went into the woods, and when he came out, they walked silently down behind the two cows, one of which still had the afterbirth, and Myron told Curtiss he should stay on until the end of the summer. Myron had recalled his thirty-one dollars because of the calf.

While Curtiss was locking the cows in their stanchions that evening, Cora reminded Myron about his promise to give her some hens. "We'll have to see," he said, alarmed, and took his cap off the icebox and escaped to Dietche.

"You promised me," she said. "You got that henhouse ready," she said as Curtiss came in. Myron had gone.

"John," Myron said, "when do you figger you'll be up? It's gettin on to August—"

But Dietche was asleep.

Dietche was awake at that time the next evening, however.

"Here's your supper, Johnny. How're you feeling?"

"Johnny ain't hungry."

"D'you want any pills or anything?" Myron asked him softly.

"You're a lit-tle late asking that."

Myron sat down on the stool by the door. "What'll I bring—asp'rin—soda?"

"You hold on to your pills—you'll be sick one day."

"Never been sick a day in my life."

Dietche opened his eyes. "What day is it?"

"Tuesday?"

"The boy quit yet?"

"I don't know what you mean. The boy is doing fine."

"You don't know what I mean."

Myron folded his arms and sat up straight, embarrassed, "No. We'll be cuttin' the corn soon."

"Ain't you never goin' to throw away that sausage?" Dietche asked, referring to what was on the tray on the floor. "I ain't never goin' to eat it, Myron. Chickens'd eat it. Say, you ever going to get them chickens?"

"Start cutting the hay in three weeks. Dammit, it'll be burned up by then if them clouds don't break. Corn's shot," Myron said.

Dietche would never forget him. Dainty as a flower, his little blue cap on his shiny black head, his faded blue legs crossed like related L-squares, the heavy boot on the crossing leg hanging aslant off the thin ankle, arms folded, the elbows bare, and the dark, serious face staring shyly at the floor. Myron had been sitting that way for half an hour now.

"Ain't you got nothing better to do?" Dietche asked, nervously.

Myron didn't reply.

"Cows in?"

"Comin' down now," Myron said. "What do you do all day in here?"

"I *think*."

"What do you think about?"

"I think about how to pay you back."

"Pay me back for what?"

"Don't you know?" Dietche asked again.

"No," Myron said quite honestly.

Dietche thought Myron was telling him to forget it. Dietche'd figured Myron for a tough guy, and he'd stepped out of line with the little girl. He didn't exactly like being treated that way, but he didn't have much choice. "Look, boss—let's have it out," he said. "You got me—but in the future don't hit so hard. O.K.?"

"John—you do such foolish things. You want to hide out here—and still you want to go on and do just as you please—"

"That's true, boss. But you don't have to run me into the ground."

Myron smiled. "I don't know what you mean."

"Makin' me work in the henhouse for one."

"But I need that. I need that henhouse, John."

"You goin' to get hens?"

"*Yes.*"

"Well, O.K. if you say so."

"Why do you say you're thinking about how to pay me back?" Myron asked.

"Don't you know?" Dietche asked.

"No," Myron said, quite honestly, and got up and left, hearing Cora call him.

Dietche sighed and with effort pulled himself over on his side. There had been moments when he didn't know if he'd take the poison from surrender to the rotten condition of his body or from just plain boredom. Now something new had been added, which increased the attraction of the packet of white powder in his shoe.

"Good morning," the blue-legged, dignified little man said the next day as Dietche woke.

The sausage had gone. There were three fried eggs. "How're you feelin' this morning?"

"Worse," Dietche said, frightened by the eggs.

"Honest?" Myron asked.

"I feel awful," Dietche said. "C'mere quick. I got a terrible ache in my throat. It's burnin'." He propped himself on one elbow. "Look Myron!"

Myron ran forward, wanting to help, not knowing what to do. The hired man swung with all his might, missed, and fell on his shoulder. "Close," he whispered. Myron backed, astonished to the door.

"Water!" Dietche cried, halfway out of the cot. "Oh my head!"

"John—if you try that agin, I'll call the police—"

"Myron—please!"

"Here—here," Myron said, running the glass to the man.

"Go way now," Dietche said, drinking.

"One day it'll be you that does the goin' away, Mr. Dietche. One more trick like that and I swear to God—"

"Myron—I'm goin' to get well now," Dietche whispered, staring at the gently banging door.

Myron, of course, had to go back in eventually. He knew by the fact that Dietche was asking for more food that he must be getting better. He couldn't bear the idea of the hired man gold-bricking. He had to see him.

"You'll call the troopers if I raise my hand, won't you?" Dietche said.

Myron backed off. "You goin' to start somethin' again?"

"Maybe," Dietche said.

"I'll thrash you," Myron said.

"You'd call the cops?"

"I would."

"What if I was to kill you, Myron?"

"It'd be hard now—" Myron fished in his overalls. Dietche turned his head on the pillow.

A blade shone in the daylight surrounding Myron's fist.

"I see," Dietche said. "You got full pockits." He grew silent. "You're a thinker, too, Myron."

The knife disappeared and Myron folded his arms. "Yes," he said. "I am."

"Myron," Dietche announced, frowning, and then couldn't go on.

"Yes?" Myron asked.

Cora began canning the corn Myron and Curtiss were picking. The crop twice filled the truck sent to take it in. Until the sand came up, Myron's father used to fill ten trucks.

August came and Myron began digging for a new silo. He didn't ask himself if he needed a new silo. The half-empty red cylinder bound to the big barn was enough. It was as if it was Myron he was trying to grow.

"Hello," Dietche called to show him he was awake. He thought it was Myron.

"How are you feeling?" she asked.

"Not so good as you'd expect," he said. "You get your chickens yet?"

"No," she said with dignity.

"Think you'd ever get them?"

"What do you think?"

"Well, that's how it is, ain't it?" he said.

"That's how what is?"

"I guess so," he said.

She went, a little irritated, leaving behind a trace of desire in him and the tray on the stool.

The next footsteps brought Curtiss. He carried in the dinner and breakfast the next day. "You're gettin' thin," Dietche said as the young man withdrew in the morning. "Where's Myron?"

Curtiss said, wondering if he was getting thinner, that Myron wasn't coming in any more. He had too much to do. The regime proved itself on the boy. His shallow attachment to the boss dried; he wrote J.J. a postcard and began *War and Peace* again—there was another book he used to read with more interest, but he hadn't the energy for it now. He wished that Dietche would recover, almost as much as Myron. Dietche appeared to be the key to everyone's happiness except the woman's. She had her own way of getting by.

One day—they were waiting for Dietche to come out—there was a kind of music in the air. Cora's jars, sealing on the stove, were steaming, rattling in the big pan. She couldn't hear the music. Most of lunch hour Myron spent by himself pulling weeds out of the beds about the house. He sported two rings now and a turnip. His pockets sagged. The knife and the watch pulled him off balance unless he kept a hand out when kneeling in the beds.

Curtiss ambled out the back door. He stopped. "Hey," he said.

Myron jumped up. "What?"

"It's so quiet," Curtiss said.

Myron looked up at the sky. The clouds were coming down—they had reached the point where their shadows covered the farm.

"It's always quiet," Myron said.

Anticipation, the soul of music, hung between every moment.

The wind blew the clouds slowly across the valley floor.

The dark, cold pines creaked in the mountains, the river bled to death, a crow yelled, winding up the string tighter and tighter. Across the clover, Dietche still lay, his face drawn into an expression of deep concentration.

Why didn't he come out of there? Twice Myron set down his tools and marched inside and then came out again. Once, interrupting a repair job on a joint in the great empty lofts in the big barn, he went down to the house, lifted the receiver, and actually turned the crank. But the minute he heard the operator's voice, he hung up. He couldn't turn him in.

That evening the boss sat two hours before the kitchen window, staring across at the cabin, wondering what the game was.

Dietche was *well*. At last, exhausted, he turned his gaze away from the square across the dark clover and went upstairs and made ready for bed.

Dietche watched the lights go out in the main house. He sat up: for a second he had seen her, in the upstairs window, brushing her hair.

CHAPTER TEN

Myron was on the road when the tall, gaunt wreck tapped down the steps on his cane bone legs, drank in the sun, stretched a little too optimistically and sat down suddenly out of sight in the clover. Myron went over to find him.

Dietche's hand played with the ants in the grass while waiting for his strength to return. From under his hat brim he watched Myron coming.

"How are you?" Myron asked.

"I'm well now." He snapped an ant off his finger and looked up, squinting. "How're you?"

"You goin' to work soon?"

"How about today?"

"You can wash the separator and then help Mrs. Greenhalgh in the kitchen."

"Oh—" Dietche said. "Oh, that'll be fine." He made to get up. "Here y'are, let's have your hand."

"No sir," Myron said, backing away.

Dietche stood by himself. His knees were the weak link. He leaned forward and touched the dirt with the tips of his fingers to balance himself, then straightened up. He put it on a little. "There," he said, going through the clover. "All by myself. Look here—I got a note from my little girl." He took the letter from his pocket. "It says she ain't comin' up for the fair but to thank you all for—"

"I read it," Myron said and hastened on ahead. Dietche fell further and further behind, featherlegged and half-blind in the sun.

Myron went into the milkroom. Curtiss was turning the crank. The hum rose and increased until it was a low scream and the milk, pulled apart inside the big blue case of the separator, began dividing out the slender, flat aluminum tubes white and yellow, milk and cream falling into separate pails, causing a fragile suds in each. Curtiss was turning too fast. Myron told him to slow down. "It's almost done now," the young man argued.

"Slower, I say. You got lots more to come yet. When you're through find your way out to the corn. Mr. Dietche'll clean up here." Myron left immediately.

Dietche came in and held a dipper under the milk stream and swung it to his mouth. "Oh that's good." He drank again and wiped his beard on his sleeve. "When you're done, give me the high sign, Curtiss, hear? I'm going to dry out."

"O.K.," Curtiss said, watching him creep outside helping himself down the runway with his hands. He wondered if he should have been more cordial. Dietche was white except for the beard and his one green eye and the blind blue blank and their setting, the two oval, hay-colored fields. His skin was like a rodent's belly after so many days in bed. He was clammy. He smelled of bed.

He leaned on the barn wall outside, his fogged head turned up into the light. The dying hum of the separator mixed in his ear with a bunch of bees hanging on the eaves above his head. The sun leaked into him, dried the skin, and went in deeper, blazing his sluggish blood. His lungs began to stir. He coughed, feeling quiet, dirty, alone, mean, and pestered with the notion that he just had to shake Myron loose of him once and for all. He pushed off the wall and entered the wet room which Curtiss had vacated. Myron was just one of those motherly types of keeper who get anxious if you cross them. When he had dried the parts of the separator with a clean cheesecloth and carefully rebuilt the machine, he went slowly, carelessly, deliberately, and not without a certain suspense in his heart, to the kitchen.

"If you've come for a drink of liquor, Mr. Dietche, you won't find none here," she said. God, he was dirty, she thought.

"Ain't you well?" he said, standing at the screen door behind which she was swatting flies and watching him out of the corner of her eye.

"You bin sick from drinkin'," she said. She didn't know him well at all. The only way she could talk to him was as if he was a colored man.

"Myron said I was to help you."

"He did?"

"Yes, ma'am, he did. Would you mind openin' the door?"

She let down the bridge and hurried away inside.

"Mrs. Greenhalgh," he said, splitting peas into a dish. "I guess we ain't goin' to have them hens after all."

"Not right now," she replied from below. Fans of soapy water appeared behind her brush on the floor.

"Why do you think Myron made me do all that work for nothin'?" he asked.

"Don't think he made you do all that work for nothin'—don't think so at all," she said. "Think he intended to have chickens but things piled up. I don't mind."

" 'Course you don't mind. Don't make any difference to you."

"One day," she said.

"One day what?"

"One day'll come—" she redipped the brush, "when we'll all be better off."

"Shore," he said. "When do you reckon that'll be?"

"*When,*" she said and got up and carried the pail outside and dumped it on the grass.

All at once the cuckoo lurched out of his house above the sink and opened his bill. Cora wiped her hands and fastened the catch.

"It don't cuck," Dietche said.

"Myron don't like the sound," she replied.

"I can fix it back to cuck if you like."

"Don't you go foolin' with it, Mr. Dietche—he wants it quiet around here he'll have it."

"Please yourself," Dietche said; he had done the peas and asked if he might use Myron's razor, he was out of blades.

"Where is Myron?" she asked.

"Wrappin' corn with the boy," he said.

She went into the living room and lifted one of the the blinds. She couldn't see them.

"Well?" he said.

"If you be quick," she said. "Git on upstairs. I'll bring some hot water." She didn't want a man lookin' like the wrath of God workin' on her property. That's why she let him go up, if Myron came. "That'll be fine," he said.

"Ma'am," she said.

"Oh stick it," he said under his breath going up and smiled. "Ma'am."

She filled a pan, lit the stove, and set the water on the flames.

Upstairs, a pale man hiding in a briar patch looked out at Dietche from the bathroom mirror. 'Boy,' he thought, 'we none of us gettin' any prettier.' He rolled up his sleeves. She came in with the pan. He put in the plug.

She was pouring the boiling water slowly into the sink

"I'm not accustomed to the luxury of such hot water for shavin'," he said and closed the door behind her.

She didn't reply.

"I'm in love with you," he said.

The steam rose out of the basin.

"Did you hear me?" He stroked his beard and waited and grinned an awful paper grin.

"Mr. Dietche," she said, turning at last.

"You're not a beauty queen," he said, surveying her various pieces with his one polite green eye while the other seemed to be looking over her head, "but for a country girl you're preserved right well, I must say."

"You'll just have to get out of the way, I'm afraid."

"Let me call you Cora—I call you Cora in my little bed at night."

"Will you open that door or do I have to call for Myron?"

"You best call for Myron, Cora, cause I'm not leavin' you. Ever."

"Myron."

"You best call."

"Myron!"

"Mrs. Green—Cora."

"What?'

"Cora," he said, advancing on her. "C'mere."

"Oh Lord," she said and struck his hand with the pan.

"Ow!" he cried.

"What's the matter?"

"Hot!"

"Well," she protested.

"This is my bare hand, lady. You know it burns."

"What'd you expect?" she asked, looking at the hand out of the corner of her eye.

He stepped from the door. "See you."

"I won't say anything," she said, opening it, "this time."

But she did not go down the stairs—she went down to the window at the end of the hall. Far across the road, in the slowly collapsing cornfields, two men moved in and out of sight carrying balls of twine and scythes. She turned: the thin silhouette was standing at the other end of the dark corridor in the electric-lit bathroom door. She drifted sideways into Curtiss's room.

He walked slowly into the hall. To Cora his footsteps were leaves blowing down towards her. "Don't come in here," she said.

He hesitated on the threshold. "This your room?" he asked.

"Curtiss's. Whose room did you think it was?" she said, clearing her throat.

"Myron's."

"Myron and me sleep in the other room."

"Oh," he replied. "How is that, Mrs. Greenhalgh? How's that work out, you and Myron sleeping together?"

She figured the best way to get free would be to keep still and wait until he went away.

"Cora, I love you," he said.

She sighed, still holding the pan, standing in Curtiss's west window, looking down the road.

He drifted over to Curtiss's dresser, leaving the door free. "What's this?" he asked, picking up a cigar cutter.

"You leave them things be," she said. "Don't talk so loud."

"The house's empty—just you and me. Look," he said, "the other side makes your face bigger." He stuck out his tongue in the enlarging glass of a traveling mirror. "I love you," he said, and put the mirror down.

"*Stop,*" she said.

"My," he said, opening the top drawer of Curtiss's dresser, "lookit all them work shirts, Mrs. Greenhalgh." Dietche didn't know why she stayed. "And look at this—this interestin' old book." He picked up a ragged, torn paper-backed volume and read the title page. "You want to read this book—you want to have a look at what happened to Friendly Flossie some day, Cora," he advised. He pulled open the next drawer. "Do you think Curtiss wants to be a farmer? He's got all the equipment—shirts, jeans, Friendly Flossie—here, you want to read a few pages of this book?" He came to her.

"You get out of this room this minute," she whispered. "They're coming back!"

Dietche looked out the window. "No, they ain't," he said.

"You close them drawers and git washed and git downstairs."

"No," he said.

"I'm going," she said. But the door closed in front of her.

"Mrs. Greenhalgh," he said quietly. "You ain't no fool. But you're awful blind's to what's going on around here."

What was he saying? What was he going to say? She wondered, as suspicious as her husband of thought. "You don't sound very happy with things around here, Mr. Dietche," she said. "What seems to be the trouble? Is your pay too low?"

"Mrs. Greenhalgh, I don't get no pay," he said.

That made an impression. She didn't believe that he didn't have *any* money. "Well, salary's up to you and Myron, ain't it?" She pulled open the door and went out of the room. You could almost hear the reel unwind in Dietche as she went.

He paused—he wondered if this was what it would be like to murder someone. So cold, so easy. It might be that Cora was the straw that would break Myron's reluctance to call the police— it might just be that Myron was close to her. No, that wasn't it. Something was wrong. She wouldn't have stuck him so long up there unless it meant she was attracted to him. Cora was only another one of his tools, like Dietche and Curtiss. If Dietche could make her his—if he could get her on his side he'd have something on Myron. It was probably a lover she wanted. Well, that wasn't hard. I mean, he thought, it was just a question of being hard.

Across his one-track mind lay the curious aspect of the prey. It struck him as odd that a woman of over thirty should behave so strangely if all she was after was a bit of the golden rivet. And if she was so long on principle why couldn't she get downstairs? A chain is as strong as its weakest link and where was that? Where it usually is, he figured, hearing her go into her bedroom. "Mrs. Greenhalgh," he called through the dark upper jaw of the empty house.

"Yes," answered the frail's voice.

Dietche wandered down the hall. She was looking—she was always looking out windows—out the bedroom window at the empty henhouse up on the hill. She could see hens around it like toy sailboats on a pond. He couldn't see them.

'I'm really not like this,' she thought. She wasn't going to stand for him much longer. Something was driving her—her revulsion at Dietche's filthy, cockeyed face—his dangerous power: did he know something about them? Because there *was* something about them, there *is* something about everybody nobody knows, and then along comes some person who can see it.... And he wasn't all that nosy, she thought.

A lot of the time she didn't even know he was there—that afternoon she kept running into the hired man upstairs, she recalled later.

Had he caught her at the right moment—the moment when the burden of life simply must be set down a moment? Did she feel life settling on to crush her now that the hens were denied, the hens which she had set heart on, the parcel-sized egg-laying white lives denied? The moment before the sun hits the edge of the world; before the hammer strikes the gong; the moment when anything can happen and frequently doesn't. She looked out the window. A dark roof of cloud lay over the whole valley. The air was close to the ground, hot and dopey.

The box under the mattressless bed caught his eye as he came in. A heavy round brass padlock, shaped like a heart, hung through the tongue. "What's that?" he asked.

"That's our strongbox," she said.

"Cora," he said, stretching out his arms. "Come."

Her large bosom began heaving slightly in its plain red dress. "You best leave this farm." It was cool outside.

"Come to me."

"You best go."

"I love you," he said.

She sighed and shook her head.

He moved.

"No," she said, "don't do that," she said, even though his grip was feeble as the tongue of a dog.

"Cora," he said, trying not to laugh at the expression on her face.

It began to rain as she went downstairs thinking about her white chickens, her childhood days, her mother and father, and the mattress which was airing out in back.

It fell just right—plentiful, unhurried. Out in the fields, the corn crowns shook and toppled because, hidden in a confusion of leaves and stalks, Myron was drawing his scythe into their yellow ankles. It was dismal in the cornfield in the rain but the rain was soft and merciful. Myron preferred it that way. It soothed him. He didn't mind the water down his back. He liked the cool air and the new browns and greens brought out by the low-key radiance of the wet sky.

Up in the main barn, the young man slammed the hatches shut, dropped off the ladder into the hay, walked spring-legged to the barrier, and jumped over into the runway and then pulled on a fireman's raincoat and went up to close the sluice below the spring.

Dietche was back in the bathroom. He left the door open and talked to her, thinking it was her crying below in the kitchen, but it was a faucet in the sink which needed a new washer.

When she had put the mattress indoors, her direction was Myron's left ear. She went across the road under a sheet of wrapping paper. She found him. She bent her large, red, wet head, keeping an eye out for Curtiss in the dark mysterious jungle ahead. But Curtiss was on his way up the mountain.

It took her about a minute to tell Myron and to plead with him to fire him.

Myron put down the ball of twine with which he was wrapping a bundle of the long, greasy shucks and started back towards the house.

Dietche dried his face—he decided to use the scissors first—the beard was too much for the razor. He was taking the scissors out of the medicine cabinet over the sink when Myron came up the stairs, wet from the fields. He hadn't expected Myron.

"What's this she's been telling me?"

Dietche said that she couldn't have told him much. In Myron's eyes Dietche could see the sun coming out in the bathroom window behind them just before Myron drove his little fist up into Dietche's neck. The hired man fell, dropping the scissors, which stuck in the floor. The free blade pointed up so that the instrument resembled a high-kicking dancer. "We'll have a little lecture now," Myron droned, his foot ready to boot Dietche if he reached for the scissors, "same's I give two other fellers a few years back. You just hold still and then you'll know everything and you can go back to work. She don't enjoy *love*." He pronounced it as if it were a four-letter word. "You'll never get her to sleep with you lessen you force it and you aren't strong enough. She don't like it, 'cause we decided not have no kids. She never gets her pleasure." Myron swallowed, embarrassedly. "I don't trust no gadgets, y'see."

Dietche could hear, but it would be a long time before he could speak. He sat in the doorway, holding his throat, watching the scissors dance.

"So you best look for somethin' else to satisfy yourself with. How did you manage in prison—palm of your hand, I 'magine? I'm tellin' you this for your own good, John."

"You get yours, Myron?"

"And one more thing—listen," the boss went on, "you come here and asked for work and shelter. Now I don't figure this is anything more than the fault of your illness, that's how tolerant and 'maginative I am. I need you for the work." Myron took the knife from his pocket and opened the blade as he went downstairs.

Cora said she'd rather not have Dietche around any more, but Myron went by saying everything was fixed.

"But My—he might come after me again—"

"Well, it won't be the first time, although I thought they'd of let up on you by now. It's your duty, mind, t'see he don't get upstairs. I can't watch him all the time myself. They all want to get upstairs. It's because you're so attractive. When you're older they'll stop. Be vigilant." He stopped and went back to the foot of the stairs. "C'mon, John. Come down out of there now."

Myron went outside.

She frowned. He wasn't she.

Dietche got to his feet. He'd failed. All he'd figured out about the bit of wrapping paper in the succotash—about her bein' the key—well, he thought, with a shrug, he'd have to find another way out of this. He put the scissors in the medicine chest and picked up his hat off the floor and went downstairs.

"Where is he?" he asked simply.

She could not hear him.

"Why don't you just apologize, Mr. Dietche?" she asked.

He bent in front of her and made a face. "You're a stupid woman, Mrs. Greenhalgh," he said.

"What?" she asked tired.

"You're a fool!" He hit the table.

"What?" she demanded.

"Go to hell," his lips said and he went outside. Myron was standing a little to one side off the path. She'd let him down. She'd just been teasing him. It hurt his dignity.

Myron removed his cap and put it in his pocket. It fell out. He hadn't put it in far enough.

Dietche walked out as if he was on his way to mail a letter, thinking in his light-headed careless way if maybe Myron didn't *like* him fooling around with her.

When Dietche got so close Myron could read the trademark on the hired man's shirt buttons, something informed Myron that this man was not human and that Myron Greenhalgh had to be saved from him. That if anything happened to Myron Greenhalgh because of this silent, uncaring, this evil, empty man, this dirty, unshaven—fear gripped Myron the closer the inaccessible man came. Dietche passed him, his head lowered, not realizing what Myron was thinking.

Not realizing until after he'd passed him in his earthless tread and the knife flashed. The point of the blade entered him and stuck in one of his ribs. He felt the pain and the tug as Myron, terrified, jerked the knife free and almost flung it into the hayfield behind the house, he was so shocked; but then folded it up carefully and put it in his pocket and went into the house. Dietche gasped and held his side, feeling the blood spread through his shirt. He tore the shirt off.

It wasn't a bad cut. He looked at the screen door.

It wasn't a bad cut. But it had come from behind and it could have gone in deeper and that made it a very strange cut to Dietche. He went slowly, terrified, to the faucet on the trough.

He bathed the rib in running water until the bleeding stopped, his eyes fastened on the screen door below. There are two kinds of killers—sudden and slow.

Perhaps he wouldn't ever try again. But how could he be sure? 'What the hell am I going to do now?' Dietche wondered. He looked about to see if Curtiss was around. He was all alone. He leaned against the trough, in the sun, watching the house, putting his shirt on again and doing the buttons.

"Myron," Cora began. She found she almost cared for him in a sexual way—she hadn't seen the little moment outside the door—being able to take care of him. He wouldn't say what the matter was. She thought it had to do with her.

"Yes?" he replied, his hand gripping hers to his side, spitting what was left of his lunch into the sink and wiping his mouth. Then he let go of her.

"This was delivered this morning. I was afraid to give it to you until you were in a good mood, 'cause it was bad news."

"Read it to me," he said, his hands shaking under the towel.

"Dear Myron," she began.

"I've been looking over Howard Lace's accounts and I find you are in arrears of three thousand dollars.

"Come into the office, and we'll talk over a loan. Otherwise I may have to foreclose on you."

"This was comin'," Myron said.

"Don't delay coming in, Myron. Do it before you start cutting your hay.

"We are opening the big mill again and I am going to see about building some tourist camps around here. Things are going forward in this town like never before.

"I'll be writing you again anyway. I don't like you far flung farmers to lose touch with the community. Have you seen the new bowling alleys back of Seward's drugstore? Take a look on your way in.

"Sincerely,
"Jack C. Kean"

"Well," Myron said, "he's got a big mouth, don't he?"

She put the letter in a drawer in the table.

"Seems to be in a terrible hurry," Myron said.

She asked him what he was going to do.

"Nothin'," he replied. "I bet you there are letters all over the district like that one. They'll set. I'll set too. If I jes' set like the rest, he can't do nothin'. He'll have to get all them others and he can't afford it."

She took advantage of his apparent good humor to revive the question of hens.

"You'll get 'em my dear," he said. "Not jes' now. Generally speakin' life goes on here as it al'ys had—Dietche and Jack C. *Kean* regardless. We got the hayin' to do next couple of weeks, 'n the heifers'll freshen so we'll have some milk comin' too. Mebbe if things work out we'll git down to the Fair next month. What'd you think of that?"

"That'd be grand, My."

"As I say, life goes on. Mr. Dietche is still what he is and we'll have to keep him a secret. He's savin' us a lot of money."

"When's he goin'?"

"As I say, we got the hayin' to do and that'll require everybody's co-operation. You know what I mean. I mean we won't talk about him again."

"Yes I do," she said.

Later, while Curtiss and Cora sat around the table after dinner, Myron tried to get something on the radio. All he could get was news.

"Wiggle the aerial," she said.

Myron came in from the living room. "Battry's dead," he said and sat down and thumbed through his breed book, putting on a large pair of spectacles to do so.

No matter how he tried, the only way the young man could make it with these silent people was by working hard every single day as Dietche did, and he was getting awfully tired of that.

CHAPTER ELEVEN

"You'd say you et about seven last night?" Dietche asked, stopping in the woods and setting down a clothful of tools slowly. His side was not quite healed yet.

"Unless the clock is wrong," Curtiss replied. "And my watch."

"The clock and your watch will do. If I was to be invited for dinner and I sat against the wall say, where would Myron be?'

"You'd be sitting on him."

"I would," Dietche said without humor. The top of his mind was watching the first touch of fall in the woods. "Myron a big eater?" he asked, letting go of a red-tinted maple leaf.

"Not too big."

Dietche's walk had lost its careless, drifting gait. He went stiffly up on the path.

Roger Plunkett had been delivering the groceries each week, which saved Myron facing the Italian girls at the supermarket in Cannonville. The only sacrifice was not getting to his P.O. box, but he never had any mail anyway, just circulars. Nevertheless, he had to go to town at last to get the mowing teeth sharpened, and while he was away he had given Dietche and Curtiss the job of breaking down the shack in the upper pasture. He wanted the wood.

As they approached the small gray eminence beside the stream, Dietche told him a little of the story. Curtiss began to laugh in his harsh, nervous way. "Oh no. No," Dietche said. "Don't do that." The hired man was in a funny mood. "She was pretty, y'see. I was twelve. She was a fool to put up with it so long. Not too bright. But she liked it. She had a lot of trouble later. We paid, of course." He was in a sad mood, it would have seemed. You wouldn't have expected it of him. But he was going to kill Myron. He unrolled the cloth and picked up a crowbar. Until he killed Myron or Myron killed him, he was free—but he was going to have to lose that freedom. That was one of the thoughts that made him sad. And then he felt, too, somewhere, that it couldn't work. But he couldn't help himself. "They'd all stand in the woods around here and one by one they'd go in to her. They all seemed to know who was next. Never had no fights."

"Huh."

"Then Myron came up and put her in jail. We all got away, drunk as lords."

Curtiss rolled up his sleeves. "Huh."

"Yes, huh. By God, I wish I had some whisky. You got any?"

He was worried about something: that much Curtiss's feelers brought within the walls. "Me? No. I don't drink, you know," Curtiss said.

"No?" Deitche smiled and put his foot in Curtiss's hand and climbed up onto the roof and looked about to see where to begin. He put his fingers under the rotten tar paper. In five minutes he had the roofing stripped clean. "Start the boards," he said, pointing the bar at the eaves: the young man leaned back and hit up. Nothing happened. "Here—take the crowbar."

Hot air rose from the room as the roof opened. "Whew," he said, peering inside. "When I was twelve," he said, "there was a rug and a table in there and a picture of the president and the bed was painted gold ... now ...."

"Now?" Curtiss asked.

"Now there's nothin'—" Dietche tossed the last board down and jumped to the ground. They piled the wood on a dry rise above the stream.

"Walls next," Dietche said.

Myron had laid a long strip of fresh pine along the edge of the door after the raid. It had warped the door fast to the frame.

"Myron made sure nobody'd get back in," Curtiss said.

"That's Myron."

"Too bad he caught the girl," Curtiss said.

"What the hell she have to look forward to anyhow," Dietche said. "I mean she'd gone into the whorehouse soon's she got older—and that was closin' down soon enough with the mill goin' bust. No, I reckon she paid for her misdeeds." He realized he was feeling screwy. It was the sort of thing he'd expect Myron to say. He stopped talking. He was talking too much. "I ast her to marry me, you know," he continued.

"You were a little young, weren't you?"

The door creaked. What was left of the mattress lay in one corner torn with rats' tunnels, the stripes run. The rest—which had been two rooms when a curtain closed off the bed—was bare.

Dietche began knocking one wallboard loose after another. Curtiss pried them off from the outside and de-nailed them. In half an hour, the four sides of the pocket pleasure palace were nothing but Z-crossed daylight and a floor across which damp beetles lurched for cover from the sun, whereupon Curtiss looked at his watch and informed Dietche it was lunchtime.

"Wish we might finish it," Dietche complained. "Why don't you stay, Curtiss—you don't eat lunch?"

But the young man was hungry and bored and said they should go right down.

The red and white horses were harnessed and grazing near the rakes and the wagon by. the trough. Myron saw the two men coming at him and turned quickly to finish fitting the newly sharpened blade of teeth into the mowing attachment below the tractor seat. Then he went with Curtiss down to the kitchen where Cora was waiting with lunch.

Myron looked up: Dietche was standing outside the kitchen window.

"What's he want?" he asked, laying his spoon in his soup bowl. "You leave them groceries outside for him?"

"Yes."

Myron got up, but by the time he was out the back door, Dietche was walking towards his cabin.

When Myron went back inside again, Dietche set the groceries in the clover.

While she was pouring out their coffee, and Myron was screwing open a tall blue bottle of glucose sugar he'd used as sweetening since he was a small boy, Dietche appeared at the kitchen window again.

Myron grinned bravely, holding the bottle and a spoon. "What's he doin' that for again?" he asked her, filling the spoon.

"Will you please go away, John?" she asked through the window and put two spoons of ordinary sugar in her cup and passed the bowl to Curtiss. Myron screwed up the bottle and looked at the hired man. Dietche walked off to the barns.

"That's two days he's done that," Myron said, stirring, and blowing on his coffee.

"Need you more in the field—both of you—" Myron said, sitting on the tractor with the blade folded high up over his head, "but I don't want the cows breakin' their legs in the wreckage up there. So go on up and finish it if you can by tonight. It's empty ain't it?"

Curtiss told him just a bit of the mattress was left.

"Burn that damn thing. Take some kerosene and burn it, hear?"

"Yessir," Curtiss said, and went off to fetch a milk bottle to put the kerosene in.

The hired man was waiting for him on a log in the woods. "Got a cigarette?" he asked. "I'm fresh out."

"Yes," Curtiss said.

They sat and smoked, and then Curtiss remembered something and said, "Say, John," and reached into his shirt pocket. "Say, John," Dietche murmured, blowing smoke through his long, red-weeded nose. He sat with his legs crossed, one arm propped straight up on his knee with the flat of his hand resting against his temple and the cigarette smoke breaking against the brim of his hat, the cigaretteless hand resting off in a load of white fungus, and his mind's eye picturing her in Myron's old brown Dodge driving to town every week for groceries. If everything went as it had for so many years around there, they'd have dinner and go to bed and when she woke she'd find her husband wouldn't want to get up at all. It looked like heart failure, according to Roland.

"I tore this out of *Life*," Curtiss continued, passing him a scrap of shiny paper.

The field looked snow-covered because of the flash bulb. The pale face of a state trooper stared at him beside the car. The feet of the dead man protruded beneath the blanket and three arrows, superimposed on the picture, made sure the blood would not be overlooked. Dietche bent over the photo, squinting. "Yeah, you can see the blood," he said, and handed the picture back.

"Did you know him well?"

"Did I know who well?" Dietche demanded and took the picture back and glared at it. "Why for Christ sake!" he exclaimed sharply. "It's Roland!"

"Not so good, huh," Curtiss said.

He shook his head. "It's awful, ain't it?" he said. By accident he dropped the picture and the wind took it off with it into the woods.

"You want it?" Curtiss asked, standing up beside him.

"No." He was shocked. He couldn't understand how Roland could have done such a thing. It didn't help his mood. It wouldn't be long before he'd be like everybody else. "What a shame," he said.

The two of them went on up to the shack and set to work. The frame nails drew like fresh teeth. Squeaks shot out of the pasture. "By," Dietche said, "Jesus! They just don't want to come!"

Eventually, however, they came; the frames sagged and fell, the shack was down, and they went at the floor. The work required a certain kind of intimacy—passing a hammer, helping him drag the sides down—the work broke down more than the shack, without Curtiss realizing it.

They were curious to get the floor up, not that they expected to find anything, but simply because we are born curious about what is underneath things. And then his foot hit something.

The stream trickled below them. The birds unwound in the surrounding woods.

Curtiss set down his hammer. Dietche crouched on his heels and watched the young man drag a rectangular wooden box out of the damp clay under the half-broken floor boards. The bottom of the box, rotten with wet, broke as Curtiss straightened up and the contents fell out. Curtiss set the box on the floor beside Dietche, piling up beside it a length of silk which had got caught in the nails exposed on the bottom edge of the box, stooped again, and rummaged in the fallen debris—a tinted picture of Calvin Coolidge, a scrap of red carpet, rolled and tied with string, five cloudy, cracked glasses, and a railroad lantern. Dietche was stunned.

Curtiss asked if the stuff was hers.

"Yass," the hired man drawled. 'Well,' he thought, 'that's all there is left of me. Roland's gone. Helen's gone. Louise gone.' He put his hand in and touched the nightgown. "It ain't so," he whispered. "This is where I put it." He picked up the nightgown. Things ran out of it. Death. "Lord," he said, holding it in his hand. "Years ago," he said. "Years—" he mumbled, looking at the contents of his memory. He dropped the gown and told Curtiss they'd burn this stuff along with the mattress. For a moment something of value had stirred in him, and then faded, and expired. He was having a hell of a day. Somebody didn't want Myron to die, it seemed.

When they had taken the floor and the crate to the woodpile, they made the fire. He took the milk bottle and poured out the gold fluid, rescuing the lantern. Curtiss gave him a match; the hired man wiped the sulfurhead on his trousers and laid it on the gown. The flames were invisible until they got to the stuffing where they turned red and gold.

"Curtiss, would you want to meet my father—I'm goin' over there now anyhow if you want to come," Dietche said. "If Myron sees you arrivin' back alone he'll come after me—and I want to speak to my father."

Curtiss shrugged. He'd heard of the old man.

"Well I'm goin'," Dietche said, grasping the unlit lantern.

Behind them, the black fumes of the fire rose into the afternoon air, and the fleet of cows, anchored on the slopes, had turned their heads in the one direction to watch the smoke rise.

Curtiss was thinking, with typical indignation, that he hadn't even said he wanted to come, when the whiteness of the thicket was on them. They passed through quietly. Curtiss had a hard time trying to fix the birches. They did not mean snow, white paint, jumbo straws, nor neon lights to him.

Dietche grew more and more afraid that what was coming was not right and that he had no way of altering it. He felt his desire to murder Myron, whom he hated now because he feared him, grow and spread through him like the roots of a tree, roots which were strangling him. There can be no peace in a disordered world. He was not a killer. But he would not leave.

They left behind the severe beauty of the hills, and caught, in the fine, down-shedding curtain of trees on the other side, the strange contrast beyond. They descended the steep side of the mountain and came out above a large amphitheater of red stone. Dietche led him along the side of the cut onto the quarry floor. A heap of crushed stones recalling Myron's driveway lay fallen out of the mouth of a wrecked conveyor. The buckets that had carried the stone to vanished wagons were strewn about the floor, torn off the conveyor by Myron and Dietche and their pals when they were children. Then they were out of the quarry and going down a slope of wild hay. Dietche pointed to a mass of red tin cans in a clump of scrub spruce across the road.

"This was going to be the dump for a big resort here around 1900—they were going to fill them mountains with lodges and hotels," Dietche explained, thinking it would interest Curtiss. "They didn't get much built."

At the bottom of the hay slope they went under a barbed wire fence and stepped out onto the road; facing them—the sand. "Myron's land—everybody's land—quits here," Dietche said. "Beyond the sand it's wild into Canada."

Around the desert the big, inhospitable mountains lay back, as if aghast at the desolation at their feet. "That's where my father lives," Dietche said, indicating the wreck in the distance. Their feet smoked in the loose surface of the road alongside the desert.

"Lace said you were run out here because you were German."

"Indeed." Dietche stopped. "Now look here." He wiped the sweatband of his hat with a handkerchief ochered with what Curtiss thought was part of the design. He replaced the hat on his head and the handkerchief in his pocket. "We leave the road," he said.

They stepped over the wash rim into a ditch and then onto the flat waste.

The wrecked house grew as they progressed. "It's easy," Dietche mumbled, seeing nothing before him but the empty farm and her, which he didn't want but which he was being driven towards. How could he run it?

"What's easy?" Curtiss asked.

A hundred yards from the house, Dietche began calling. *"Pa!* Pa's seven foot, Curtiss. Don't be scared of him."

Curtiss said no, he wouldn't be scared.

Dietche asked him to be quiet.

"But—" Curtiss protested irritably.

"Hush. Did I ask you to come?" Dietche said.

"Yes."

They came upon a trace of a road which led them up to the calm, gray ruin. "Pa-a!" Dietche called to wake the old man if he was asleep, so he would have time to dress. "Company!" he called.

Dietche helped the young man to climb up into the house through the door, telling him they would have walked in ten years ago when there was a porch still on it. "Jesus it's small," he said suddenly quiet and calm, dropping the gunny sack over the entrance. The odd-shaped walls were filled with sunlight; the roof was propped up with bamboo poles. A low three-legged table jiggled in the middle of the uneven floor under the weight of a bottle of wine and a gasoline can. Dietche pointed to one dim corner. "That's where I slep'," he said and then cocked his head. They heard the sound of an automobile engine.

Dietche walked to the back door and raised the gunny sack. "Pa?" he called.

Facing him a short way away in the sand was the black wooden hind end of a Model T. The whole car rested on four blocks of wood. A pen with about nine seedy chickens broke the view to his right. "Pa?" he called into the brightness.

"I'll wait here," Curtiss said behind him, having had enough of the blinding glare.

"No, c'mon," Dietche said and walked out onto the sand. Reluctantly, Curtiss followed. "He's the tallest white man I ever seen," Dietche said. "We haven't met in ten years."

The engine coughed and ceased running.

"I'll wait here," Curtiss said; a meeting between father and son after ten years seemed uniquely uninteresting to him. He stopped, frowning in the glare.

The younger Dietche watched the huge bare foot press the floor several times and then fall to one side, revealing the tiny, worn silver accelerator pedal.

A long arm, sleeved in woolen underwear, fell out of the window of the car. The other arm, with which presumably he pretended to steer, hung on the wrist through the spokes of the wooden wheel. The black wool knees were jammed up against the pewter dashboard on either side of the steering post, and his head rested against the roof.

"Pa," Dietche said.

"What?"

"You're out of gas."

The massive head turned. A noise issued from the bearded lips that Dietche could never forget—his own voice, two octaves lower. The arm out the window undid the leather strap holding the door shut and bit by bit, like an elaborate folding mechanism, the old man brought himself out, until he stood his full seven feet on the sand in his black trousers and underwear, his hand on the empty window frame of the car whose only motion for years had been down, deeper and deeper into the sand. He looked at Dietche through a pair of small, pale pearl eyes like immaculate studs, hidden in the mist of old age, eyes that had waited too long. Then he lifted them a fraction of an inch. "How do you do," he said to Curtiss.

"How do you do," Curtiss replied, in the faint grip of amazement; he had never seen such a tall man in his life.

Walter walked quickly past them to the house because standing still the hot sand burned his bare feet; at the back door, he turned and waved them in.

"Ain't he tall?" Dietche said.

"He sure is, John," Curtiss said.

Dietche scratched his ear. "I don't guess he'd be crazy."

"No," Curtiss said with not too obvious skepticism.

"He's ninety-six," Dietche said.

"My," Curtiss said, passing a huge brass bed lying in the sand by the henhouse, its knobs flashing in the sun. "That's where he sleeps," Dietche said.

"Uhuh," said Curtiss.

The old man held the gunny curtain up and they passed under.

He dug up an orange crate for Curtiss. "Sit down," he said, laying a huge hand on the young man. He figured that Curtiss was from one of the big houses in the mountains beyond. It was the way Curtiss said how do you do, the straight way he sat down.

"Don't fuss so, Pa," Dietche said, watching his father act the coachman he'd been seventy years ago.

At last they were all sitting silent, and something had to be said. Walter had nothing to say.

At last Dietche asked how he was. "Oh fine," the huge image said, in a heavy German accent. "How are you?"

"I'm fine."

"Where you bin?"

"Bin to New York. I was married. Had a little girl—" Whereupon the enormous old man turned to Curtiss. Curtiss replied that he was fine. Walter asked if they would like some wine, and they accepted.

They sat and drank. Silence creates nothing. When they'd finished the wine, they folded their hands. The old man wished these people would go so he could get back to his car. But the boy had a daughter and that rang a bell in the submerged lockers ... the boy had a daughter. How in the hell had he managed that?

The wine had left a purple stain on his bearded lips. Dietche got up and wiped his father's mouth (Curtiss clearing his throat) and sat down again.

"What's the girl's name?"

Dietche told him.

The old giant cocked his head. A little pink tongue crept out between his lips and ran in again. "Has she—?" He pointed at Dietche's bad eye.

Dietche shook his head.

The old man's thoughts then altered, as dunes in the wind. "Did you tell Curtiss about prison?"

"How'd you know about that?"

"Face told me. Everybody knows about you."

"Lace," Dietche amended; and there was another long silence. "You see many folks then, Pa?"

"No one bin here for months."

"How's the hen trade?"

"Hens are dying. Run out of feed."

"No one will buy them?" Dietche asked, dejected.

"No."

"I don't believe you tried to sell them."

"I don't expect you to believe anything," the old man said, and poured carefully more wine into the two glasses, only there wasn't any wine left in the bottle. "But they are dying, John, just the same."

"Why don't you give them away?"

The old man explored the long bush at his chin with an enormous hand and watched his son. "What do you think I should do?"

"Don't know," Dietche said. "Let them go, I guess."

"If I let them go *I'd* starve. I'm just hoping someone'll come along and buy dem 'fore they're all et," he said, drank his empty glass, and put it back on the table. Dietche said he was broke. Walter laughed. Dietche laughed, and the laughs faded, fourteen tones apart. Curtiss went outside and examined the mountains for the big houses Dietche had mentioned earlier. He couldn't see any.

"You best watch out them hens don't gang up on you one night," Dietche said. "They eat anything, you know." He wished he hadn't come.

"Where is the girl?" the old man asked politely.

"What do you care?"

The old man shrugged. "It's something, dey say, to know you are going on down here after you die."

"Well," Dietche said, "there's me."

Walter did not agree, but said nothing.

Dietche knew he should go now. The old man might as well have been stuffed. It was like visiting a museum. He was nothing. Stupid, old, sitting in a childish delirium on a sand pile.

The hard thing to understand was not *how,* which was mystery enough with just that handful of ragged chickens out there, but *why* the father was still alive. That impressed Dietche that day. In prison, where he'd learned to feel men ought to be born with a little button to push when things got too rough, he had been impressed with the mere power of human endurance. But why did *he* go on? A convict made baskets and cuckoo clocks at least—this sack of worthless flesh and bone did nothing. What called for all the banners and bugles? Here was nothing. Worse than nothing. Birds fly in nothing. "Curtiss!" he called furiously through the door. Obviously, Walter had much more in common with Dietche than his voice.

The relic stood and held the gunny sack up for Curtiss to come in.

They said good-bye, and, in a moment, Curtiss and Dietche were back on the road, heading towards the boundary of the wasteland.

Walter let the gunny sack drop against the sun again and went through the back door to the car, taking the gas can off the table on the way. He wet the carburetor, poured the remainder of the gas in the tank, cranked up, folded himself in back of the shaking wheel, and started off again towards the mountains.

Two trails of dust rose off the back road. Dietche said that his Pa was pretty nothing. Curtiss thought he was an honest old bastard. He didn't seem to like Dietche very much and that was in his favor, Curtiss felt, but did not say so.

"He's crazy ain't he?" Dietche asked, sadly. "He drives that car all year round, y'know. I taught him how to repair it." He raised his hand to take a cigarette from Curtiss and found he still had the lantern with him. He flung it. The thing arched end over end and landed with a smack on its side in the sand about twenty yards away.

"It's very sad about him," Dietche said. He held up the wire at the fence for Curtiss to crawl under and Curtiss in turn held it for him.

On the way back through the birches, Dietche was going to send Curtiss on. He wanted to be by himself. But he had no ideas. All he knew was he had to kill Myron. There was nothing else for him to do, so he continued on with the young man, walking more and more slowly.

They drew up at the dead fire. "I see you all eating through the window every night."

"That's right—about seven," Curtiss said again.

"Yeah. Well what do you say to each other, Curtiss? You talk—I see your lips moving."

"Don't say much. Pass the bread. Myron's been trying to fix the radio."

Dietche took off his hat. "Boy. I bet he's crazy. Tell me something, son, would you say she ain't happy?"

"Yes, that might be true."

"Myron's O.K."

"Oh yes."

"Them two get along in there."

"Oh yes. You know that straw thing you stick on somebody's fingers so they can't get apart? Well—that's them."

"What straw thing?"

"Mexican somethings. You win them shooting." Curtiss followed a cow down with his eye. "You get two people married—"

"If Myron was dead, she would care, would she?"

"I don't think she'd marry again for some time."

"Think he would?"

"Couldn't say."

"Well look here, Curtiss—you bin around the married set—what would you say about them two? You figger they're stuck."

"Well, she ain't too pleased about not getting them hens he promised. He's not playing it right. But she won't move. When he hits her she don't mind, does she? He needs her, as they say. Boy, that's the way," Curtiss said. "Of course I got nothing on the Greenhalghs, John. They just are and I'll be glad not to be around here come October."

"Curtiss," Dietche said.

"Yes. Yes, boy." There was something in Dietche's tone that drew Curtiss's voice low.

"If there was something you wanted real bad—say you wanted to blow a trumpet on Sundays—and say Myron got in your way. What'd you do to him?"

"Huh?"

Dietche smiled dismally and said nothing.

"He's a hard man," Curtiss said, making his tense, ugly grin, wondering why Dietche turned away. "We need a trumpet around here."

"What would you *do?*" the hired man continued.

"I wouldn't do anything. I'd give up the trumpet I guess," Curtiss said.

"Yeah sure," Dietche mumbled. "They're awful close, you say." He thought: 'It'd kill him to lose her, would it? Well that's what I *figured*. If she *wanted* me.' "Yes, they're close all right," he said. "You wouldn't think so to see the way he treats her," he said. They'd been over all that now. They were silent again—Curtiss waiting patiently like a man at a fitting.

"You planning to go?"

"Can't tell you," Dietche said. The cows were standing at the bottom of the pasture, waiting to be driven through the woods.

Curtiss asked why he couldn't be told.

" 'Cause you're an honest fellow and when they ask you, you'll have to tell them what I said."

"Tell who?"

The hired man gave him the two salient points in his biography—that he had been falsely convicted of grand larceny, which Curtiss believed, and that he had jumped parole. "If they ask you now son, you got to lie. Otherwise they'll take you."

"What's all this about?" Curtiss said, thinking that he ought to go home now. "Why hasn't he called the police? I'd have if I was Myron. I wouldn't have you around."

"He needs me. I'm free, y'see," Dietche said. "I mean I don't get no pay for what I do, long as I'm hiding out here."

"You don't get any pay?" Curtiss asked.

"It's her I want," Dietche said dimly.

Curtiss brayed: "What?"

"It's her I want, Curtiss. How does that sound."

"Sounds—well, it sounds—*yeah.*"

"I want her," Dietche said, and waved his arm in a gesture of despair. "But she don't love me."

"Huh."

"I'm up the crick, Curtiss," he said. "I really am."

'Where have I heard this before?' thought Curtiss. 'One cheap flower in all this wilderness. So life is real. I mean it is.' "If you were kind to her—I don't suppose you've wasted any time, John, with flowers and stuff?"

"Flowers?" Dietche marveled. "There's plenty of flowers around."

"I just thought you'd find it easier to get what you want. Whatever it is you want. Her, I suppose. I don't know what you want."

"Curtiss, what am I going to do?" He didn't want to take a life. "She don't love me."

"You know what I'd do?" Curtiss said.

"Yes, you help me. You bin around."

"Well I'd do this," the young man said. He'd been around.

They went down into the woods behind the cattle, Curtiss carrying the tools this time.

The closer they got to the farm, where Myron was, where the glucose was, losing his head ahead of time, the more afraid Dietche became that there was nothing that would help.

They came out of the woods. Dietche spoke to him again. "Well, if I were you I'd give her something," Curtiss said. "Give her something she wants. You see you're forgetting the box of candy. You all are takers here. You take and take. When Myron wants the bread he reaches across everybody and takes it. It's handier. You are all a pile of the most obvious hogs I ever saw. I never saw a hog give another hog anything. But I'll tell you what the hogs could use. What always works—a little manners."

There wasn't much time left. They were passing down the trail towards the trough yard by then.

"What the hell," Dietche said. "Flowers and all. I told her a lot."

"How did it go?" Curtiss asked.

"They don't like it. They like to be took."

"Well, that depends on what you mean by 'took.' But 'took's' the operative word."

Dietche had given up—he heard the tractor, its teeth chattering through the hay, beyond the house.

"What'll I do?" he asked, dully.

"Give her something, I think that's best," Curtiss said.

"What have I got?" Dietche asked, his useless eye dull in the sun, the other in the shade of his hat brim, watching Curtiss. "What'll I give her? What in hell have I got to give her?"

"Boy, you're in sorry shape," Curtiss said and walked off from the trough.

Dietche knew he'd never get Curtiss like this again. In time. "What'll I give her?" he said and raised his head and grinned suddenly in the glare.

Curtiss turned and said, as if spitting, "Money."

Dietche paused. "Money?"

"You got any money?"

"Yes," Dietche said automatically.

"Well, give her a little at a time. It's the one thing they don't have around here. You know how to catch a crow? You prop a box on a stick and then you lead a long string of corn under the box. The crow eats the corn kernel by kernel until he's under the box. Then you pull the string. And she's yours. She wants those silly hens, right? Well, you just let her have those silly hens. She'll break down. You said you had some money?"

"Yes I do."

"Well?" Curtiss said and wondered why Dietche didn't register, didn't warm to the cynicism in the old young man's advice. He must want her very sincerely. "I'm not saying it'll work," Curtiss said. "But you got all the time in the world, boy. Time and money—that's the way you get into any place on earth."

"Thanks," Dietche interrupted.

"Yeah, well, it's nothing."

"You give me a good idea, Curtiss," Dietche said, relieved, walking away.

"Seeing's how you work for free around here, you couldn't know much of what money can do," the young man said.

"No, no, that's right," Dietche said. "Thanks again. I appreciate it."

Curtiss shrugged. "I'm so glad," he said.

CHAPTER TWELVE

The long twists of hay Dietche had dropped with the rake the day before were now being folded up and hoisted onto the wagon where Myron, knee-deep, packed it in with his hands and feet and the fork. It gratified him to feel the wagon fill and swell against the poles, and Dietche was his, and was, to all appearances, before which Myron was a cluck, finally subdued.

The young man had received some kind of word from his uncle—he would be going soon. That would leave just Dietche. Curtiss knew nothing, Myron believed.

John Dietche. God bless him. Occasionally he couldn't resist approaching the gaunt, trapped man in a friendly manner. "John—" he said, coming up on him eating a sandwich on a rock near a field of uncut hay further down the road; but Dietche was in the middle of a thought and rose and walked away.

Though Dietche had come within Curtiss's emotional orbit for a moment the day before, he did not return again, and continued in his typical and absolute isolation. Almost absolute, that is, since he had to trust the young man not to tell Myron anything.

When he had packed a wagon to capacity, Myron drove into the big barn and forked off the heavy combs to Curtiss and Dietche who walked them deep into the lofts, raising them layer by layer to the hatches.

Shortly after his talk with Curtiss, before they had begun packing the overflow in the small barn, Dietche looked in at the house, his plans finally arranged.

"Well," she said, "you got your voice back."

"Look here," he said. "I hear you want some chickens."

She nearly roared with laughter.

"What?" he asked. "What?" He thought for a moment she was touched. "I mean if you had the money right here in your hand, would you buy them then?"

"Myron is in charge—"

"Would you have to ask Myron?" he interrupted. "Couldn't you do it secret?"

She did not know what he meant.

"If you could spend it only on what *you* want."

"Got my ironing," she said.

He removed his hat and from behind the leather band inside took a sweaty two-dollar bill and laid it out on the ironing board. "Iron that," he said.

She had never seen a two-dollar bill before. "Wherever did you get that?" she asked, her eyes burning down on the dark-green rectangle on the white board. Paper money was always appealing to her. It was what men carried hot in their pockets. It meant power. "Where'd it come from?"

"My life insurance."

"Oh? But you're still alive."

"Pretty near."

"Are you leaving that there?" she asked, quite amazed. It had that eye on it, staring up at her.

"Yes," he said.

Her expression thinned and her hand came down quite apart from her brain and snatched the bill and curled it into her palm. She turned her back on him. After an eternity, she heard the screen door close.

With secret childish joy, she fed the money to the cuckoo and relatched the little door. Replacing a long red hair with simplicity, the joy departing, forgetting the money, she returned to the ironing board. The whole affair had taken a minute or more, but there was no minute hand in Cora. That had been one of the strikes against a quick lover like Lace.

Two days later, Dietche was coming out the barn door when he saw a blue Buick flashing its teeth on the driveway. He turned back inside. "Your folks are here," he said.

Curtiss peered around the corner.

Myron was standing on the lawn, talking to J.J., and beside J.J. in a large linen hat was—who was it?—Grace. 'She found him *again*,' Curtiss thought and walked into the sunlight, amazed.

The first thing he looked for were Grace's high eyebrows, like hoops.

"Hello kid," J.J. said in his toughguy voice.

"You've grown, J.J.," Curtiss said.

"Hello, Curty," Grace said. They kissed; she drew back to look at him. He needed sleep. His accent had altered.

"You lost weight," the silver-haired, square-jawed uncle said.

"Where you staying?" Curtiss asked.

"We're over at Lake Moran—about a hundred miles from here," J.J. said.

"Don't go, Myron," Grace said, but Myron pulled on his cap, excused himself politely and went up to the barn. What a hot, dirty little man, she thought. "Yes, we're—what a nice man," she said, "—spending a week or so at a fishing lodge that belongs to an old friend of your uncle's, Red Bird, the famous pitcher."

"Ray Boyd, honey," J.J. smiled, "is a catcher. A very good one too."

"Of course he is, darling," Grace said, "who isn't. Curty, I'd like to meet Mrs. Greenhalgh."

"Wait a minute, Grace. We just got here. Let's give Curtiss a chance."

"Certainly," she said cheerfully.

"Surprised to see us together?" J.J. asked him.

"To tell the truth—no," he said.

"That's nice," Grace said.

"I wrote you a couple of letters," J.J. said.

"Yes." 'This is called giving Curtiss a chance,' he thought.

"You never wrote."

"I wrote you a postcard, J.J."

"Oh yes. That's so."

Grace had removed her hat, and they headed towards the back door. J.J. walked with his arms around their shoulders. "Wild horses," he said.

"Waal, isn't this a surprise," Cora said watching them file through the pantry into the kitchen.

They all shook hands. "I wish I had a farm sometimes," J.J. said. "I'd settle down and I'd make it go," he said, looking through the window; he saw nothing to encourage him further for the moment. "We're going to take Curtiss to dinner in town—if you don't need him."

"No," Cora said, wondering why the man, whose face seemed to be made entirely of corners, talked so much.

Grace asked if she could see Curtiss's room. "You go right on up, Mrs. Tavener," Cora said. Poor woman, she thought. Too good for this silver man walking around her kitchen, pretending to know about farming. But he knew farming. J.J. knew everything. There was about as much information in that square head as in the encyclopedia; the only difference lay in the quality and the arrangement.

Cora was right, superficially: J.J. and Grace did not match. The roughneck with the colored hands did not match that tall, slender woman at all. They had only the deep lines on their faces and a certain look, a look of doubt, in their eyes, in common.

"I was born on a farm, Mrs. G."

"Is that so, Mr. Tavener?"

"Yeah," he continued, and they talked on—or, rather, he talked on.

Curtiss had taken his aunt upstairs.

"Oh, it's a big room," she said, holding her hat in one hand.

He changed into a white shirt. She handed him a tie and then took his hairbrush and raked her black hair. "You have a little girl's room inside the house?" she asked. "I'm filthy. Sixty miles on back roads is no joke." The hair began to shine around her slender face.

"Why ever did you come on the back roads?" he asked, dazzled.

"Well, J.J.," she said, pulling up the sleeves of her dress, smiling with mock grimness, "always likes to go a little faster than they want him to. We thought we heard a siren. He drove off the main road to hide and got very lost." She laughed. "We started out at six this morning!"

"You shouldn't let him do that—you shouldn't let him drive so fast. You could have an accident."

"I know, dear," she said patiently. "Where's the loo, Curtiss?"

"It's good to see you," he said.

"Aren't you sweet," she said. "You've changed," she added, following his finger down the hall. He watched her close the door, and just before it shut, saw her hand reach out to the water tap. He was glad she was nervous seeing him.

Then Grace returned and put on her hat in his mirror and the room diminished.

By mistake Dietche was driving the empty wagon back to the field when the three of them came out of the house. He had been thinking of something.

"Who's that?" J.J. asked quietly at Curtiss's elbow.

"Hired man," Curtiss said.

"Hi," J.J. said as Dietche rolled past them—it was always open season on people for J.J. Dietche nodded, his hat pulled down, and passed, motionless and stiff against the reinboard, as high as a stick-bound paper saint parading in one of those tropical countries. He drew the wagon onto the highway; guided right, the teams crossed its nails and clipped off to the cut fields. Dietche left behind a feeling of dignity that settled on their first impression subtly, like fine dust. Probably it was merely his silence, but as a result they spoke seriously in the car, and Curtiss soon learned that the car was all they had.

He parked the wagon—the Buick passed him—and hurried back to the house. She was outside, collecting the wash.

He extracted a second two-dollar bill from his hat.

This time she smiled, bewildered. "Why do you—" she began.

"I don't like to see people not get what they want in this life," he said. "You want a couple of hundred pullets you'll get 'em."

"Is that so," she said. "Couple *hundred?*"

"Yes ma'am," he said, looking for Myron.

"Thank you," she said.

"I got some more."

"For me?"

"Maybe. A little."

"Why don't you give it to me all at once?"

"Not goin' to give you all I got."

"Perhaps it comes from Myron's box?" she asked.

"Have a look," Dietche said after a moment.

"Don't keep the key," she laughed.

"Ask Myron to give it to you," he said.

"No."

"See, Cora, I never like to see a person sad. *I* got no use for the money. But if you don't believe me, why don't you ask Myron for the key and take a look in that box of his? See if I'm stealin'. It's pretty weird stealin' to give it to you."

"I didn't say you was stealin'. Look here," she said and noticed that he had red hair too, "you still feel bad about that day you tried foolin' around with me?"

"Well—" he said doubtfully.

"You can forget that. It was the drink, wasn't it? And this bein' the hottest time of the year, and the flesh is weak as it says in the Bible—"

"That too," he said. "And also I recalled a piece of wrappin' paper with a certain telephone number on it you put in my dinner one night a while ago."

"I don't remember anything like that. Anyhow, thank you very much for this two dollars," she said.

"Thank you," he said and walked away, disappointed by something missing in her face—a lack of conscience, of guilt—and went back down the road to the wagon.

The days of deception formed a week. The money he was giving her must have made some impression. Myron hadn't said anything about it, so she wasn't telling him.

One morning before milking, having studied every move Myron made, he stole into the house, crept upstairs at the risk of his life, and went into the bedroom. Sleep held her.

From the lining of his hat came the fifth two-spot. He closed the door—Curtiss was coming out of his room unsummoned to help Myron lock up the cows. Outside the house, the night fused. The noises of the dark thinned—a heron early out of Canada—an owl. Curtiss closed the bathroom door and Dietche went immediately to work. He'd have to get there earlier next time. The dawn came fast.

"Hssst," he said. He knelt on the bed.

"What is it?" she asked, clinging to another few moments' sleep.

"It's me," he said.

"Myron?"

He laid a hand on her shoulder. "John Dietche."

"Ow!" she said.

"Shhh," he replied gently.

Curtiss heard them beyond the wall and forgot to brush his teeth in his haste to get out of there.

"Who?" she whispered, half asleep.

"Aw, pore thing," Dietche murmured. "Look, it's only me, John Dietche. Here's two more dollars for you."

"You are crazy coming up here," she said.

One touch threw him a little. He blamed his seven years' confinement. It had been a long while since he had touched non-commercial flesh and female to boot. "Take it," he said, holding the money out, crumpling it so she could hear it.

She did not dare turn over. Her arm shivered beneath his hand. She stopped breathing. A long sigh issued from her lips. Silence.

He felt under the bedclothes. She was ice cold.

In a moment, she revived. "Fainted," she said. There was no one there in the room.

She did not dare ask him later if it had been a dream.

Riding in with a load of hay that morning, Myron asked if Dietche wanted anything in town.

"There's a fair comin', ain't there, Myron?"

"Week from Friday."

"Well, I'll wait and go then."

"You ain't going," Myron said.

"Can't I go?"

"No, sir."

"Are you going?"

"I think my wife wants to go, yes. And I want to look at this Kean feller."

"Who's he?"

Myron explained.

"Then you want to go right bad, I reckon," Dietche said.

The wagon rattled inside the small barn. Dietche jumped down and walked outside, saying he needed a drink, his sickness was acting up.

"Don't drink at the trough," Myron said. "It's hooked up to the river now."

"You take awful good care of me, Myron," Dietche complained.

"Drink down to the house," Myron said. They were using the river for everything except their own consumption, holding off on the spring until the heat was off. It wouldn't rain again.

Dietche went into the house. "Myron wants to go to the fair Friday, you know that?"

"Yes," she said.

"Well, you play sick. Curtiss'll go with his folks, he told me. Myron'll go without you anyhow, because of this hassel with Kean."

"You got—you got any money for me today?" she asked, just about dispensing with the innocent voice now. "You didn't give me any this morning."

"Yeah," he said, removing his hat. He'd forgotten on purpose. "Now you remember what I say about the fair?"

"Mr. Dietche, I can go to the fair if I want."

"If you want any more money you won't go."

"I'll see," she said.

Dietche hurried back to the barn and she fed the cuckoo the two dollars, feeling bad that she would not be permitting the poor, lovelorn, guilty hired man to sleep with her. Feeling bad about it.

He visited her for five more dawns, without trying to make progress and not giving her any money the last two times, until one morning, when Myron had gone up to the pasture after a stray, Dietche removed his trousers. "I got another two dollars for you. But you got to let me in."

She didn't answer.

"You got a lot of money now," he said, getting gently into bed. "You got about twenty dollars now. Maybe you best get it out of the clock—one of these days it'll bust open and scatter all that loot on the floor."

"Maybe I best."

"When you goin' to order them hens?"

"Soon as I get enough money." She faced the wall, her elbow thrust out behind in protection.

To his great relief, and to his joy, her foot grazed his and retreated. It was an accident.

"Oh," he said. "Waal. You get four dollars for doin' that again, ma'am."

"Go on," she said, her brain enmeshed in fear. "Go away."

"Do you mean go away, Cora?" he asked.

"Go away."

"Cora." He selected her right arm. There were no more twos in the box under the bed—only a few fives. If he didn't get some response soon, she might absorb all her husband's raw capital and he'd have only murder to fall back on. He'd start the fives tomorrow, if she couldn't think of something else. He wondered when she was going to let him make love to her because as far as he was concerned that was where everything would be just beginning, remembering what Myron had told him on the day of the knife episode.

"Your hands are cold," she said.

"Are they?" he said, apologetically. His legs were warm. He moved in until he lay almost entirely against her. She stood it as long as her nerves could bear and then turned and flipped her body into a V, the apex farthest from him. This brought her head into his neck. Her hair was newly washed and lay untied over his face.

"Go away," she said miserably.

With self-astonishing self-control, he removed himself from the bed, telling her that he might be back the next morning.

Taking a look out the window, he saw Myron walking towards the white cabin, calling his name. Myron was no longer carrying that knife, but that made no difference. He went hurriedly downstairs in his socks.

The next morning, she was not wearing a nightgown. "How come?" he asked. She said she had a husband. He asked her how it had gone. "What gone?" she asked.

"Got somethin' for you today," he said, sitting on the bed.

"Thank you," she said, sleep slowly leaving her brain.

"Don't mention it," he said. "Cora."

In the bathroom, Curtiss, accustomed now to the silence caused by the little adventure beyond the wall, brushed his teeth in his own time.

They listened to him. "I got somethin' new for you," Dietche said.

"What is it?"

"Look," he said. He had gotten in bed and was urging her gently to turn over with his leg. Her bare skin affected him. "It's a ring."

"A ring?" she said and very slowly turned, tucking her arms around herself. "That's my wedding ring," she said, disappointed.

"Is it?"

"Yes."

"I found it in the milkroom," he said.

"Myron's been wearing it."

Dietche laid the ring on the floor. "I'm figurin' on giving you something *real* nice soon," he said.

"You best go now." The wedding ring had knocked the fantasy awry.

"Naw."

"Myron'll come," she said. 'We got to stop this once and for all,' she thought.

It was, and had always been, impossible for him to get his arm under her. "Relax," he said impatiently.

She could not speak. His fingers burrowed, stumbling under her fat stomach.

"You bring me some money, John," she said. She had forgotten she was naked.

"Relax," he said coldly and knew it was time to go.

She was petrified. She did not want to be surrounded. He gave in and drew away—soon it would grow light and the black blanket of darkness which made them and their activity anonymous would fade. And he feared Myron. But it was not the change in light, nor the fact he hadn't brought her any money that cooled her that morning as much as the change in his tone. Not so much the passing of the night nor the cash—gradually, slowly, it was all becoming a simple matter of the voice. It was not in her experience to assess the various shapes and guises of tenderness. Nor was he being so consciously artful, either. But the true sounds of love are made right along with love itself, when the heat is on, whether love is false or not.

"Now," he said the next morning—a string of pearls erupting on his brow. "Easy," he said, and pushed himself up with his left elbow and pried her open with his leg.

The room sailed off with them. He was into her. But when he looked at her face—"What in the world's the matter?" the male asked indignantly.

"What's the matter with *you?*" she asked.

He rowed her a little ways and stopped. "Well?"

"Go on," she said in a damp, bored voice.

"You ought to relax."

He listened to the sounds beyond the window. Myron was banging the milkers, getting them ready in the barn. It was Myron because he heard Curtiss leaving the house. Myron liked to be first.

He rowed faster and swore because suddenly he lost control and had to bail out. "What are you trying to do?" he asked after he had dropped away.

She didn't speak.

"Hell," he said, panting, the room returning to normal.

"Well," she said.

"You didn't feel nothin', did you?"

"Me?" she answered. She did not know what he wanted her to say. Then she spoke again. "Would you mind getting out now? I got to fix breakfast."

She'd behaved like a whore; he felt like one. "How'm I going to show you?" he murmured.

"Show me what?" she asked.

He laughed not very nicely, spoiling the mood, and after he went, she got up and looked to see if he'd left any money on the dresser.

The next morning he took it as slow as possible, and to her dismay, her body received a dim thrill she had never had before.

Dietche was fit to be tied: thirteen mornings of this, his nerves were shot. But it was the kind of patience he had. It was the kind of patience that had got him through the henhouse. He still believed in the succotash prize somehow and in her behavior and what Myron told him the day Myron knifed him. He knew there was something beyond money in this. He knew he was after something rare. "Oh," she said, and he almost hadn't heard it, he was so busy thinking. It struck him like a blow. With a jubilant feeling, he left her, cursing her for holding out on him so long, yet knowing with half his desperate brain that it wasn't hers but Myron's fault he was being put to so much trouble.

Oh, she thought, alone, lying hot and light-boned in the bed, wondering for a second why the walls of the green bedroom seemed freshly painted.

The hay was cut and stored now. Myron had brought over a silage cutter from a farm in the next valley and all that day they fed the long bundles of corn stalks to it. A blower drove the green bits up a tube and they fell lightly inside on the sweetening, decaying level reached the previous spring.

It was Curtiss's job to pile the silage evenly around the circular walls. The smell was sickening in the big cylinder and he disliked the work. When he came out he had to take off his shirt to pick the wet bits off his skin, and his lungs and nostrils were thick with the cloying, hot smell.

Sometimes Dietche would press a stick onto the drive belt outside, gagging the blower so a thick wad of silage would pile up in the barrel; then he would take the stick off and a heavy stinging rain of the junk would pour in on the young man who had been wondering a moment before why the spray had stopped. They heard him slam the shovel against the rounding boards in fury.

"Don't do it no more, John," Myron said. "He'll break the scoop." Both Myron and Dietche were feeling his impatience to be off and this made them pick on him.

When Cora told Myron she was feeling poorly and would rather not go to the fair, Myron said he wouldn't go either. He suspected nothing, and Dietche knew that he'd go if he wanted to, regardless of how she felt. Kean had him worried.

She had thirty-four dollars in the cuckoo clock. Each time the hired man made a deposit, of cash, she felt the satisfaction of earning something of her own, of acquiring, of possessing, and in spite of the momentary, beautiful fraction of a second that morning, that sound she'd not even heard yet, the sense of gain was uppermost in her mind once she got out of bed. But he'd felt the fraction as well that morning. And he'd learned how to talk to her.

She told herself she was aiming at fifty dollars—a hundred if he had it. A hundred would be a good sum to start raising pullets with. She'd let him in until a hundred dollars, even though she had to give him more and more each time to get it.

She'd ask Jim Lace to put the hens in when Myron wasn't looking.

CHAPTER THIRTEEN

The sun reached into Greenhalgh's freshly planted flower beds where there was no water and too much sand, and, putting its merciless tongue in the sweet young things, destroyed them.

Myron and the earth and the sun all worked the same, paradoxical racket in competition with each other, except that whatever they turned to was shortened in its growth, or killed, by one or the other. While Myron spoke, just before leaving for the fair, sunlight entered the house at him through the window, the back door and down the stairwell. "Don't worry," he was saying, his mouth moving in a streak of light, the upper face in shadow, "I'll just tell Kean we'll *pay*. That'll hold him a while. And when he asks for his money again, I'll say the same thing. It's all we can do."

There was this day; there would be the next day following upon that. That was what the word future meant to him. He lived inside the great clock of life. He never saw the moves marked on its face, being part of the works.

But his wife was wondering what would happen on the day after the day after tomorrow. "What if he don't allow you not to pay him?" she asked, seeing both her husband's head and above it the cuckoo clock stuffed with (what she thought was Dietche's) money.

Myron picked up his coat. "I told you."

"How much does he want?" she asked.

"A couple thousand dollars," he replied. "No need to worry. We can't pay it."

"You sure you want to go see Kean," she said at the table, head aslant, her ear on her palm.

Dietche was in the barn with Curtiss, repairing harness.

"You'll feel better tomorrow," Myron said. "The curse don't last forever. After Kean, I'll see the livestock and be back by sundown. If I'm late, Dietche will do the milking." He went feeling lord of all the fowl in the air and creatures on the earth; outside, as he crossed the lawn towards the garage, his proud eye brought him his faded barns, his silo, the long carpet of clover where he'd find pumpkins in the fall, and Dietche's cabin against the base of the pine woods. He went into the garage, got in the car, laid his town coat carefully over the back of the seat, rolled up his white sleeves, exposing his hard, brown forearms, and pushed the starter.

A few minutes later, Curtiss left the barn—the Buick had come with J.J.

"I had lunch," he said to his uncle as they walked to the house. "Have another."

"Can't afford it," Curtiss said. "I'll sit with you."

J.J. slapped his shoulder. "Don't you worry about affording anything; this is the day of the county fair, boy; we're going to have a ball. No holds barred. No whores barreled. No bars holed."

"It's only a lousy district fair, J.J.," he said severely. As usual his uncle tried too much to live up to his aunt's first husband, whom Curtiss had not known.

"I got plenty of dough."

"Don't kid me."

"Don't I? Remember I told you about this man McLeod manufactures those little plastic buttons …." Curtiss was holding the door open. Cora called to them to come in or go out because of the flies. J.J. continued, dropping his voice. "… that say you can play with my doggy but leave my pussy alone? It's not much on the Raleigh Drug job, but still," J.J. said, backing out. The door closed. Curtiss watched him through the screen. "I'm supposed to spread the buttons all over the state. Got a big campaign all mapped out. Sent me the initial outlay this morning. O.K. G'wan and change."

From the entrance of the barn, Dietche watched J.J. go to the car, and then Curtiss emerged from the house, and J.J. said to him, the wind carrying their voices up the hill, "We'll pick up your bag tonight. We're late—Grace's been waiting for us in town—she'll be—what's the word she uses—livid?"

"You aren't scared of her, are you?" Curtiss asked, getting in.

"No—we got to be careful, kid, that's all."

Then they were gone and at last the farm was his.

He hung up the harness, put the punch in the tool box, and went across the side of the hill to the trough and washed his hands and face and neck with a piece of soap Myron kept by the faucet. He closed the faucet slowly and deliberately and dried himself with his shirt and, slinging the shirt over his shoulder, made his way down to the house, scraping his ribs like his side was a banjo. He rubbed the red blotch where his shirt was open all day and his unweeded nipples which itched badly; his eye went up to the bedroom window. He saw her watching him.

She was standing by the table dressed as he came inside.

"You want them hens?" he asked.

"Yes," she said. White ones. Two hundred white, white hens.

"Then you want to get upstairs into bed, don't you," he said.

He left his hat on the top of the water cooler and pressed himself a glass of water. He heard the bed creak above his head. The giant bubbles exploded through the jug. He wiped his mouth and went upstairs, hanging his shirt on the stair post at the top.

"You got any money today?" she asked.

"We'll see," he said, leaving a bill on the dresser as he undressed.

"Everybody gone?" she asked.

"Don't be scared."

"No," she said, facing the wall under the covers. "I wish you'd give me the money without all this other stuff."

He talked to her a short while about chickens. After a moment, he touched her foot. 'If I don't get her this time, pore devil,' he thought, 'I never will. Can't keep it up forever.'

"Come on," he said. She turned. Once again the laws went away, leaving nothing but the purest human infinity in the room. The time: two thirty. The temperature: eighty-four degrees. The sun hot and bright. It was like in the henhouse.

"Easy," he said, rowing gently.

Her red hair streaked the covers. Her eyes were closed. Her mouth was dry and flaky. "I don't know what's to become of me," she said.

"Stop talking. Try and feel what's goin' on. Shh. Shh, honey," he said softly.

That started it. Faint—as far away as New York—she felt a slight glow which could have been a light, or a sound, and which was not unpleasant. Again. So far away. 'There's a funny light way off—no it's a noise,' she thought. Nor a comet, although she had seen one or two. Nothing pictorial; nothing 'like.' It was merely the multi-sensual approach of sexual ecstacy which, being the daddy of them all, had no similes. "Oh," she said, "you better get. Goin' to be sick."

"No," he said, dropping current. They went a little faster.

"Oh," she said—the light-sound was coming in.

It was like landing a trout with thread. "How you?" he asked.

She did not answer.

They lay covered on the rough sheet, perspiring.

"Courage," he said, when he felt she was going under. It came to the point again where she had to make up her mind whether to go on or swerve aside and take him.

"Easy," he said, knowing she wanted it but would try to harm it. No bird cares to leave the cage after fifteen years, without needing the encouragement and faith of its master. "Cora—I love you," he said. "You know that."

"What's happening to me?" she cried.

"Relax," he said softly. "Don't think of anything—except that I love you, I need you. Give yourself to me."

"I'm goin' to be *sick*," she said.

He rested on his oar. She put her legs out. "Jesus," he whispered, losing his temper.

"Don't say that. Gimme my money," she said angrily.

"Jesus, it's marvelous," he said.

"Oh. Oh. Is it?" she asked.

The pleasure grew ungainly. She feared she would be hurt. "Oh Lord," she said, suddenly jolted again by light and sound which was neither heard nor seen in the room although quite honestly she snapped her eyes open a second to look. "Oh Lord," she cried again, holding a bit of the sheet between her teeth.

"Shhh," he cautioned. And then he himself was rocked, relieved again and again of the load from the zone in his hips emptying himself of translucence.

He listened.

Shudders ran through her. He imagined she could be dying.

"Oh," she said again, smacked again and again by some huge unwinding iron steps. "Oh," she said. "I never, never."

"What's the matter?" he asked. Her face was sheeted in water. The torment passed and then she began really to cry. It was a terrible sound. She was breaking all up into water.

He was quite shaken. He sat, drooped on the edge of the bed and heard her talking through her tears, asking if she were dead. "What?" he complained. "You ain't dead. What's the matter with you?"

"Oh!" she cried again. "I'm still bleeding," she protested.

He came from the bathroom with a towel. "Why don't you stop crying?"

"Am I bleeding to death, do you think?"

"Ain't no blood," he said.

"No? What is it then, Johnny?"

"Well," he said, "you know—"

He left the room and went downstairs and sat on the grass in his bare feet. "Oh Lord," he said and lay down on his back. "I got her!"

"Mr. Dietche." The voice came through the bedroom window.

He sat up out of a doze.

She called him again.

He went in the house, cut grass hanging on his feet. "Hello?" he said at the stairs.

"Would you mind comin' up again?"

"What's the matter?"

"Oh well," she said.

He went to the foot of the stairs to say he'd have a drink of water and then he'd see how he felt.

"Come up. Please."

She went back into the room and drew the blind. The room became the color yellow, the cuckold's color, the color of flypaper. She shut the door.

"Leave it open," he said, "or we'll cook."

"You're welcome."

"No, I mean it," she said and burst into tears again.

"I can do this any old time you say," he said.

"Yes?" she said, and took his hand and held it to her cheek.

He appreciated the gesture, and fell asleep beside her, reluctantly, with his back to the wall, her chin on his shoulder, his long white legs and his ivory feet lying one before the other like a bas-relief Pharoah gone hunting, soiled from centuries' burial in the dirt. He breathed in a rasp, and dreamed and moved.

The dream was about his father, whom he imagined had come down the mountainside crying "John! John!" and no one was there to answer him, so the old man wrote a note in German telling how the chickens were et and he was sick of the taste of them and that he needed John's help now in getting him something more palatable. Putting the note under a stone, the old man went to the big barn and fell asleep in the hay.

Dietche woke. "Cora," he said, getting out from beside her. She was spread all over the bed. Her red hair was tangled over her eyes and stuck to her forehead. The sheet covered her nakedness. "Cora—how do you feel?"

"All right," she murmured; before she dropped off again, she said, "I'll tell Myron."

He nodded, thinking that it wouldn't hurt her to want to aim to, since he was now going to the fair to tell him himself. "Yes, you tell him," he whispered and patted her sheeted rump. He had to get away from there. He put his clothes on.

Downstairs, he saw the three people from New York sitting inside the Buick. He took his hat from the water cooler and went outside, closing the screen door quietly.

"Goin'?" he asked, approaching the car.

"We're on our way to the fair, John," Curtiss said; he had made them come back after lunch to fetch his suitcase.

"You got room for another?"

Grace opened the back door where she was sitting alone. Before he got in, Dietche spoke to Curtiss. "Go up quietly— Mrs. Greenhalgh is asleep."

"What's the matter with her?" Curtiss asked.

"Well, she's tired," Dietche said. "You know."

"Jesus Christ," Curtiss said at Dietche's tone of voice.

"Just call me John," the hired man said irritably and bent to get in the car.

Curtiss walked off like a judge who has discovered he's hung the wrong man.

"Hi," J.J. said to Dietche.

"Good-bye," Curtiss said quietly at the door, his suitcase in one hand, the unread, heavy red book in the other. He waited a moment and then tiptoed down the stairs and out to the car. "O.K.," he said. "Let's go."

"Put your bag in back," J.J. said.

The car behaved well, Dietche thought absently. It made him gloomy to see the sides of the passing hills going red and yellow, feeling the sun get softer. 'In case the kid's there,' he thought. 'I'll make Myron take her home with us. Then I'll have the cabin fixed up and I'll have my teeth cared for.' His teeth ached.

"This is sure nice country, John," J.J. said.

"Yeah," John said. "It's all right for the fellow that passes through, Mr. Tavener, but livin' here is something else."

"By God, I guess so," J.J. said.

Oh she was fat and greedy and it was money that got her. But still he couldn't step on her so easily, in his thoughts at least, any more. Not now.

"This is nice country, though," J.J. was saying again.

"Oh yeah," he mumbled. The cards were on the table. The bet was won. The game was over. But he was still John Dietche; for some reason that didn't mean what it did a day ago. He looked across the valley. Dust. He would try and find hope. "What are you all doin' tonight?" he asked. When he told Myron, that should pull his spirits up. Then he'd be busy again. It was like the way he'd felt with Louise. It would pass.

"Curtiss wants to see the daredevils," Grace was saying, "and we've got to get back to New York tomorrow; so we're going to see just a little of the show and leave."

"I'd be obliged if you let me out before the covered bridge— I'll show you," he said.

"Oh we can take you right on in if you like—we have a pass from a friend of Curtiss's uncle. Would you like to go with us?"

"No ma'am," he said, adjusting his hat. He saw that his boots weren't even tied. 'Lord,' he thought, grinning, 'looks like I just got out of bed.'

"Curtiss tells me you're a pretty good mechanic," J.J. said.

"I'm no wizard."

"How's the car sound?"

"What kind of gas do you use?" Dietche had his eye on a speck in the air ahead.

"Premium Extra."

"Well it should be all right, big engine like that," Dietche replied. "What's that over there, Mrs. Tavener?"

She followed the line of his finger. "Don't know," she said. She was blind as a bat.

"It's a hawk. It's a little early for owls—unless—see how low it's flyin'? No, it's an owl."

She saw it then. The brown bird dipped lower and lower and then pulled out over a bare stubble field below them, its beak hidden in its apple-shaped face. The beak was the point, however, and they all felt it in the car.

"Watch," Dietche said with delight, his head turning with the car so that his good eye could see.

J.J. slowed down.

"It's chasin' some pore feller."

The owl dropped below the car, turned down the trailing edges of its wings, the head swiveling to see round its legs. The crescent feet came out and picked up a crazed running rat off the ground. The owl beat its wings harder because of the new weight and bore the rat away from the tracks which had come frantically to an end.

"D'you all see?" Dietche asked. Grace felt a little ill. Curtiss and J.J. were thrilled—the great outdoors. "Y'see," the hired man insisted, and reached ahead and pushed Curtiss's shoulder.

"Yeah, yeah," Curtiss said.

Dietche sat back, depressed, and waited for them to bring him to Cannonville.

He held the hat over his face, pretending he was asleep, as they drove into town. The lights in the high school were on— there was a dance that night. The drugstores were open.

They crossed the river again—a small stream now running in a sand channel. "It's nothing," Curtiss said. "It's nothing— when I was here last—" They swung around the square and, following Dietche's directions, passed an ancient hotel with an endless porch on which old men, sitting behind gray posts, watched the car pass, their heavy turnips beating like hearts in their pockets.

It grew darker.

They passed a bar. The car went down a short incline, swooped up and they were at the square mouth of a covered bridge. "Stop," Dietche said, and got out. "Good-bye. Thanks."

Curtiss got out. They walked across the road. "So long, John." Dietche looked at him a moment. "Goodbye Curtiss," he said, and then walked down the bank and disappeared among the trees arching over the river bed.

He went downstream until he came to a tall broken chimney. There were a lot of these ruined mills along the river. He knew of six on the river between Cannonville and Peru. He'd done the river on logs as a boy. The trailers were all lit up and drawn in a ring as he climbed over the top of the bank. Far off, like a live crater, the grandstand. He sat down on the bank with his back to the trailers and drew out a cigarette. 'Poor thing,' he thought. Then he threw the cigarette away, got up and walked in towards the trailers, a tall, thin shape walking slowly and patiently in the darkness with the gait of a tramp. He would explain to Myron how she was his now and how things had to be different now she'd given herself to Dietche. He had to phrase it just right so

Myron wouldn't panic; so Myron would know he wasn't completely free to do as he pleased any more.

The man was standing ahead of him, his suit coat slung through one arm, peeing. Dietche stopped. "Who's that?"

"Jack Dempsey."

Dietche recognized the voice. "Hello, Cowboy. Ain't you killed yet?"

"No," Cowboy said. "How're you, John?"

"Fine. You got a new name."

"Jes' tryin' it out. How about a drink?"

They stopped at one of the trailers.

Cowboy was living in style now. He had a steady girl, too. She handed him the bottle through the door and went back to bed. They'd had a party all of them to Peru the night before, Cowboy explained, which had finished at noon.

They came to the parking lot, facing the stands. Tall floodlights made the speedway a rich, fertile brown, and spread a curtain of pale shantung on the people in the distant tiers of seats. An event had just been run off.

Dietche held the whisky out and sat on the running board of Myron's car. He took a drink but didn't give the bottle back. "You don't want to drink no more, Cowboy." Cowboy sat down beside Dietche and in a quiet, patient voice explained why he had to. "We don't get no insurance for our work here. You know that—"

Dietche nodded.

"And you know I drive the big ride."

"Yes."

"I'm the star now, you see. They all come to see the bus ride. I get a hunnert bucks a week now."

"You been raised."

"I asked for it."

Dietche's attention drifted to the stands.

It was the same old show. Only the names of the events had changed. The paint might have been brighter on the cars and there were one or two new doodads on the program … lady drivers … a clown …

A gust of laughter came from the slanted rows: the clown had fallen into a pail of whitewash. They wanted to laugh.

Dietche laughed, too, and turned his ear once more to Cowboy who was saying, "Then I get in the car and focus on the ramp and gun the engine and put my foot down and aim for the moon. Whiz. I'm over. It's all done with a hoot and a smile and I ain't hardly knowed it. But you can't do it over and over again sober. My stomach never was no good." He paused. "So your friend drinks for occupational reasons. Now let's have the bottle, how about it."

The hired man struck a match to light Cowboy's cigarette. "You ever missed yet, friend?"

"Never. Well—once."

"You sure did. Look at your nose!"

The bearded man inhaled and shrugged. "It's hard to blow is all."

"It's hard to blow. It's hard to blow," the hired man said. "Here," he said, handing him the bottle.

That afternoon they'd had trotting races and the smell of the horses stayed on the ground. Dietche thought of Myron. 'It's hard to blow,' he thought, and wouldn't trade his lot with all the Cowboys, J.J.'s, Curtisses and *Myrons* in the world.

The bright yellow bank of humanity lifted up and away into the dark, a thousand or more people, collars open, cheap cologne or perfume cooling the backs of the women's ears and the men's shaven jaws. The men were dressed in green and brown for the most part, and their women in all the light, cheap, simple colors. Pony tails swept back and forth and low whistles came from anonymous packs of boys as a tall doctor and his pretty fragile wife in a sky-blue dress walked below the stands. She looked good enough to drink. The doctor was proud of her looks and shy of the mass above him. He chose a seat at the edge of the stands. It was a good place to be in case a call came, he thought. A man-sized dog lay down at their feet in the cool dirt.

Halfway up the bank, J.J. was reading the doctor. He added up the dog and the little wife and the clothing with a certain amount of envy. J.J. belonged to that part of the pot which is most melted—the verticals, men of the twenties, men of Harvard, men of Hoboken, who had never made it—melted down from all classes and eras, men who were unable to "do" anything "really successful" except possibly perform small miracles of charity; the kind of people who give more than they take, and not necessarily by choice; men who might have lost hope of being "anything" but who had not quite lost their sense of humor. Bad opera singers, magicians, men who hired out the boats they lived on. Socially beneath the great, pasty mass who had managed to finish first, and, in their own minds, socially above the workmen whose associations they suspected. Shipwrecks of all classes, with clean faces and unmatched luggage.

Grace, sitting bored beside her husband, had come down late to the club. She brought terrific flexibility, but it was J.J.'s look of tenacity, of lower-middle-class morality, that was the lock that was supposed to hold the marriage together, whenever it was together. She married him because of this lockishness. He did look strong and decisive. That's why it hadn't ever been hard for him to get a job, and he'd had a lot of jobs.

J.J. and Myron did not feel comfortable in each other's company. Myron was a glowering little man in a white shirt, his coat over his arm. A white arch framed each ear where the barber's clippers had moved and a white swath swung round his neck. Myron looked like anybody there. He wanted to go home and get a good sleep because he'd decided to dig the potatoes on Saturday. But he had to wait until after the show to see Kean. He resented that. J.J. was saying something to him about beer. He made a shy smile and shook his head. "No thank you," the king said and pulled his legs sideways as J.J. rose.

Dietche was king too. He watched a man pass the stands on the hood of a car. The head struck a board fence and then went into a pile of flaming hay. The car stopped. The man rolled onto the track, putting the flames out, stood up, took off his helmet and rode slowly past the stands. Dietche asked Cowboy if that was hard to do. "No," Cowboy said. The stands applauded.

The daredevils had put too many items on the program. By the time the, Fall-De-Roll was lined up, the crowd was starting to clap for Cowboy. Fall-De-Roll was a moving sequence of cars passing the stands, swerving violently and rolling over and over one after the other in rapid succession. Then it happened, and in a few moments the track was strewn with cars on their backs and sides. "Is that hard?" Dietche asked.

"That's pretty hard, yes," Cowboy replied.

Myron glanced at Curtiss. The young man was involved in the cars. He'd paid him back. Myron would not miss him. Myron refused a cigarette from Grace and waited patiently for the whole damn thing to be over.

Dietche saw J.J. climb up the center gangway with three white containers of beer. He followed the silver head until it stopped at Myron. There he was, Dietche thought, and pulled the hat farther down on his nose and counted the alternatives before him. He could run off to Buffalo. He could go back to Myron's with her as hostage. Or he could go back to prison. He smiled. He would kill himself before that happened. He would blow his brains out. Was he thinking of Rolly? he wondered.

Myron's car moved as Cowboy got off the running board. "You goin'?" Dietche asked.

"Yep."

"So long," Dietche said.

"Bye, boy."

Cowboy walked to the back stretch of the track where his small yellow two-door sat with huge red wings like those of a mythical Chinese dragon painted on the doors and spreading over the fenders and ending at the tail lights. It was almost alive. A mechanic lay half-eaten under the hood.

"What're you doin', Oil?"

The man looked out at Cowboy and said, without respect, "I'm tightenin' the steerin' for you. Last night you said the steerin' was loose. Well, I'm fixin' it. But it *ain't* loose, Will. It's you."

Cowboy very slowly frowned. "You got to be such an arrogant, precious snot all the time, Oil?"

"No I don't," the voice said and bent fiercely back under the raised jaw.

Cowboy got inside. There was nothing left to speak of, of the interior except the seat, the safety belt, the steering wheel, the shift, and the pedals. There wasn't any glass in the windows or the windshield. The track showed through the floor under his heels. Cowboy pulled the starter. The cylinders rang.

"O.K.," Oil said, closing the car's mouth. "Kill yourself."

"Much obliged," Cowboy said dreamily and rolled away.

The huge silver carcass lay in front of the crowd now. At either end were eight wrecks. A long triangular ramp was wheeled out and its vertical face pushed up to the first of the wrecks. Dance music coming from the two amplifiers at the back of the stands cut out and it began to grow quiet.

This was the final event. The people hadn't let them show this on the Fourth of July because of Daville and Howard Lace and Dietche, all of which items now, save Dietche perhaps, were no longer so close to their hearts.

The oval beam of milk rested at the end of the track, as far as its eye could turn, waiting for the little yellow car to round the corner where it could pick it up.

The ramp, carefully aligned and pointing at the moon, was dropped off its transfer wheels.

The speedway cleared.

Cowboy fastened his seat belt.

The jump was supposed to be over one hundred feet, the loudspeakers claimed, from where the car left the lip of the ascension ramp to the spot the car usually landed, which would be, if all went well, on the roof of the last wreck at the other end of the bus. As the lights went out, and the stands and track and environs were dropped to darkness, the bus shone a sudden, looming silver by itself.

Softly, a drum began to roll through the amplifiers.

Far away in the dark distance sat Cowboy. They couldn't see him yet, but they heard him out there somewhere.

Dietche got inside Myron's car. When this was over, Myron would come.

Through the haze in his head, Cowboy could just make out the ramp. "There ain't nothin' to it," he told himself. He had just the right amount of alcohol in his stomach. His leg was not shuddering on the accelerator. He smoothed his beard and then getting the signal from the pits that the people were more than ready for him, he started.

The car swam into the waiting spill of light. It began to race it. The exhaust pipe had been treated for loud noises: he came at the ramp roaring, stifling a sudden yawn.

With fifty feet to go—the car racing towards the ramp—a man ran below the silent crowd waving a linen hat at someone in the stands. "Myron!" the man cried.

Cowboy cut the motor.

"Myron!"

The car ran quietly up the sharp incline, soared high over the eight junks and then began crossing the long silver table. It thrilled Dietche. This was the true meaning of freedom—that one moment between taking off and landing, the moment of peace and joy and abandonment. It was what he tried to divide his whole life out into. He watched the car come slowly down like a yellow-and-red butterfly. For a moment he wanted to congratulate Cowboy and apologize for despising him. Later he remembered noticing the man on the track as Cowboy landed.

"Your barn's on fire!" the man cried.

Myron stood up in the still silent crowd. "What?"

"Your barn's on fire!"

"Which one?" Myron called coldly, feeling the eyes of thousands on him.

"She didn't say," the postmaster cried back.

A fire engine could be heard racing through the dark town across the river.

"Which one did he say?" Myron asked Curtiss. Curtiss shook his head. People began standing up by the hundreds. The lights went on.

'Couldn't be Dietche,' he thought.

Grace put on her hat.

Myron went leaping down a channel people made for him. "We're coming with you, Myron," they said.

"How'd it happen, Ernie?" Myron asked when he arrived at the bottom. "How'd it happen?" The two men walked quickly through the crowds, ducked under the white rail and ran across the tanbark towards the parking lot.

"She didn't say anything, Myron," the postmaster said. He was very excited. "She said, 'Will you tell my husband the barn is on fire, please?' "

"She did, eh?"

"You want to use the phone here?"

"No, I want to get started," Myron said.

Cowboy was leaning on the fender when Myron got to his car. All around them men driving out, pulling up dust. People were shouting, there was a dog barking somewhere and above it all, the dance music was going again.

"Wish I could help," Cowboy said.

"Who are you?" Myron asked, climbing in behind the wheel.

"Friend," the daredevil said.

"Get out of here," Myron said. Cowboy stood off. He watched Myron go and then smiled stupidly and went to his trailer to get ready to move on.

Myron drove carefully through the covered bridge. But he couldn't wait to know. He stopped at the Concord House.

"Excuse me," he said, tapping the linen shoulder at the telephone stand. The doctor with the pretty wife was about to call the police.

"What do you want?" the doctor said, holding the receiver.

"My barn is on fire. Gimme the phone."

"Well, Myron, my dog has run away because of all the commotion." Perrin was tired and irritated. He wanted Myron to let him call for help and he knew Myron's was a more important call, but in a way, Myron was to blame for his losing his dog. Please just let me get my *dog* back. "Oh here," he said weakly, handing Myron the phone.

"Thank you, Doctor."

"Don't mention it. Hope it isn't serious."

Myron told the operator to get him Valley 2-3. He put in twenty cents. "Cora?" he asked.

"This is the operator. Hang on, Myron."

"Get my *wife*."

"Go ahead."

"Cora?"

"Hello."

"What's goin' on? Is the fire department there?"

"No," she said quietly.

"*Tell* me something!" Myron swore.

"The barn is on fire—the little one—just the little one."

"Oh thank the Lord. How bad is it? What's the matter with you?"

"I'm scart."

Myron blurted out, "The tractor! Is the tractor outside?"

"If you or John took it out it is. I'm not goin' up there."

"Tell them to get it out!"

"There isn't anybody here."

"Oh Lord. Tell me," he whispered, "did John do it?"

He thought he heard something that sounded like an explosion. "What was that?" he demanded, frantic. The people in the hotel lobby, pretending not to be listening, looked up.

"Just a minute," she said. There was silence for a moment. "The roof's blown up, Myron. It's terrible. It's just terrible!"

He hung up, and asked the operator for the State Police. "That's a free call, y'know," he said.

"Go ahead, Myron."

"Hello, police. This is Myron Greenhalgh."

"Your barn is on fire, Myron."

"You don't say—listen—I want you to get this straight. So listen. There's an escaped prisoner or something come ...." The story rose from its file exactly as he had prepared it, months ago, for just such an emergency. "He came to my farm and slept in an old cabin I keep beyond the barns. His name is John Dietche."

"Any more?" the man in the gray uniform and headphones said quietly.

"He said we would have to do what he said or he would murder us."

"Who's us?"

"My wife and me. We had a boy helpin' us from the city but he's gone back."

"Where are you?"

"I'm at the hotel in Cannonville."

"You say Dietche's at your farm now?"

"My wife—my wife just told me she saw him."

"Did he set the fire?"

"I think so."

"You best go home now, Myron. We'll see you later."

"I just want you to know about this man—"

"Go home, Myron."

CHAPTER FOURTEEN

The pickup rushed down the road between the trees. He sat pressed against the cab so as not to be seen from inside, his long legs stretched underneath the window.

He had made his way out of the parking lot, in hopes of beating Myron to her (a dog knocked him down on the way), ran, and jumped on the back of a moving truck marked KEAN. He took a look in the cab when the street lights were gone. Three men were talking inside. One of them was Jim Lace. Dietche was amazed to see how he had changed in ten years. His hair was pure white.

The truck rocked on the curves, the moon shifting around through the trees. It was a little like being pleasantly drunk.

'What would make her do a thing like that?' he wondered. If she had done it. It might have been an accident.

'Come on, Jimmy Daddy,' he thought, his head tapping the cab. Lace swerved out, passing a line of automobiles. "That's the boy," he said and lay down in the truck before the headlights could strike him. Two two two two two. Then they were back on the right side again.

A pair of lights overtook them. The Buick. And was gone. "Jesus," Dietche said with a grin, "J.J.'s goin', ain't he?" The truck sped on, turning in the cool wind. And then he saw Myron, who never drove fast, pass them. If only she wouldn't tell him. She'd say that was an accident, too.

Myron left Sage at the garage and went in his house.

Cora was upstairs. The bedroom was orange. Her shiny face was red.

"How did it start?" he demanded.

"I'd like you to know," she said carefully, "that I did it."

He jumped. "You set fire to my barn? What made you do a thing like that?" He felt he should hit her. But he was held back this time for want of a reason. "Why did you do it? Was it an accident?"

"I know we're married," she began, her voice low and infirm, trembling. "I know all that," she groaned, "but Mr. Dietche and I slept here this afternoon while you were to the fair. We *slep—*"

"Your Mr. Dietche's going to jail tonight if we catch him!" he yelled. 'What's she mean?' he wondered.

"Well," she said and paused. "He ain't my Mr. Dietche—and jail's his lookout. He showed me, Myron, somethin'; and I showed you."

Myron noticed a two-dollar bill by his shoe. "How did that get there?" he asked; he knelt and peered under the bed. All his money lay heaped around the black box. "What the hell's going on?"

"He gave me money to get in bed with me. I'm givin' it to you, Myron."

"But it's my money!" Myron said. Violently, he opened the drawer in the dresser where the key had lain hidden for years, bent down, and opened the empty black strongbox. He showed her it was empty. "He never had nothin'!"

"Well," she said and almost laughed. "I didn't know. But it don't matter. I don't want them hens now."

Myron got off his knees. The only motive for the fire was himself, it appeared, from the tone of her voice. But he couldn't be a reason.

"I don't love him," she was saying.

He hit her then.

She held the place on her cheek where it hurt and lifted her eyes to the fire again.

"Why in heck would you do such a thing?" he asked.

"Well," she said, straightening her skirts and setting the chair close to the window, "I told you, didn't I?"

"No you didn't!"

"I did."

"What do you think you're going to do now?"

"I'm stayin' with you, Myron," she said and looked him in the eye, and then turned her large copper-haired head away to the fire again.

He ran downstairs. The fire was all he understood at that moment.

He saw orange light on his shoes and turned and looked beyond the cab. "Lord God," he murmured, and then crawled to the back of the truck. He felt the heat, and he could hear the flames now. A short ways down the road the traffic was being halted until a ramp could be laid over the hoses crossing the road from the river. The truck slowed down. He jumped off.

Running low into the hayfield by the road, he made his way to a haystack he and Myron had made the day before. 'They best get the animals out,' he thought, kneeling and lacing his boots tighter. The horses were screaming in their stalls, like women practicing singing.

Passing the house, he saw the women in Greenhalgh's kitchen. He couldn't possibly get to her now with all those people there. Retreating, he took a long, circular course, ending up at the henhouse, and waited, watching, his face an orange mask hanging in the night, the rest of him darkness. The small barn burned thirty yards away. He could smell the tractor tires. From the roof of the barn sparks dripped upwards into the night. Had he done that?

The frame contained the furnace until the roof beams fell and, with a surge of red, brought the fire down. As the life went out of the small barn, the light rose on the big dark shape farther across the hill. That was also on fire.

The driveway, jammed with people, finally overflowed into the clover field below the big barn. Up by the trough now a team of three firemen held a nozzle, yellow gold in the glare. No water was coming out of it. They waited like a group statue. Dietche asked a man why they didn't turn the water on, and was told the river was dry. Before he disagreed, he turned his head slightly and saw he was talking to a policeman. The hired man walked away as carefully as possible.

"One at a time!" Myron yelled through the stalls. "They'll kill each other if you don't let 'em go slow." A cow went past him, its missing ear out of Myron's sight.

"I am," a voice cried to him through the smoke. "She broke out herself, Myron."

Myron went in between two demented cows. "O.K.," he said to the man who was there. "Easy now. It'll take both of us," he said and cooed to the cow whose ears were bleeding and whose eyes had reverted into its head. He took the stanchion in both hands, pushed the frame together on the cow's twisting neck. Brunet undid the clasp at the top. The unlocked bars flew apart. The cow ran out into the yard and stood, coughing, her mouth dripping blue in the firelight.

One by one they freed the rest of them that way, slowly, so as to give each plenty of time and space to get out. The wind changed; the bull began charging his smoky pen.

Outside, the water was at last coming through the hoses. "Put it on the roof," ordered the chief, "and take one more—we got the others?"

"Comin', Fred," a man called from the crowd. A space appeared—four men charged into the yard with a second hose and were brought up short because it got caught in the gate. "Come ON!" Fred yelled impatiently, running down to them. "Get inside the stalls—you got length?"

"Yeah O.K., hang on, Fred—let's get it unhooked here," said one of the volunteers sweating at the gate.

Fred turned to another team coming through. "You get that up around at the top if you can and hit the lofts. The east side's caught. It's *silly* having to go so far for water. We'll save the stalls if we can. We ain't got much time."

Dietche had sat on the lower pasture, puzzled, bewildered, watching the fire eat through the east wall. The freed horses stood nearby, cropping grass. Suddenly, 'way down, he saw Myron run out of the barn and speak to the fire chief, and point up in Dietche's direction. Men immediately sprang out of the crowd and began running up the hill with pails from the milkroom. Dietche filtered away.

The bull smashed his way out, and stopped outside seeing the crowds. A disk of hot ash fell out of the wind on his back. He started, his legs splaying out, and then ran blindly at the people. They divided and he patted down to Myron's back door where he stopped again, listening to the women inside the house. They found him later in the river.

Meanwhile, a single line had formed up the side of the hill. The pails began swinging down, originating from the spring.

"How'd it start?"

"Don't know."

"I spoke to Roy and he said they was lookin' for John Dietche."

"Huh. Orilla Ano's jaw."

"No, he said Myron'd reported seein' him round here."

"I'll be—"

"Yes you will."

"Who started the fire though?"

"Well, John Dietche. Gettin' revenge on Myron for drivin' him out so long ago."

"John never cared."

"Who said so?"

"Don't slop the water!" a little man cried.

"No one said."

"Well then."

"How'd the big'un catch?"

"Myron was up there with wet blankets on the roof but a piece come from the littl'un and went inside a window."

"Look at that!" a man said up at the spring near Curtiss who'd come to open the sluice pipe to feed the back yard hose. They looked down through the trees.

The entire roof was blazing. The silo was on fire.

"Biggest fire I ever saw," the man said.

In one of the cars in the clover, J.J. and Grace were fighting. "They don't need you," she said and paused while a raging sigh came through the hatches on the roof. "They have all the help they need. You stay here with me, J.J." She was holding him by the sleeve.

"I got to help."

"That's the beer talking."

"Grace, it is not. Dammit."

"No, stay here with me, J.J. You'll just get into trouble. Your place is here." She laughed. "Please."

He got out and went off. She began examining the dirt beside the car, her eyes bleary.

With five cows still to free, Myron was overcome. "Take me out, John-Paul!" he cried. But John-Paul was himself out on the lawn, receiving medical treatment from a young man in a white coat with red crosses on the lapels.

Myron felt his way past the milkroom.

It was a complex building and there was a lot of surface for the flames to cover. Nevertheless the fire was gradually capturing the whole barn. It appeared to the crowd, however, that there was hope still. But Myron had been inside. Nobody out there could feel what was going on inside. Jack Kean said there was hope, from where he sat on the road behind the wheel of a big new car, some distance from the farm. "It's a shame he don't have a clean insurance," he kept muttering. "It's a damn shame." Jim Lace, standing outside with his elbow on Kean's window, nodded in agreement. "A fire is a sad thing from a distance," he said. "Up close you don't feel much."

The firemen led Myron to the medic who washed his eyes with boric acid, whereupon the farmer broke away and ran back inside, hope or not. He found flames in the smoke now. The fire had dropped down the chute. "Water!" he cried.

"We're saving what we can, Myron," the fireman who had followed him in, to take care of him, said. "You're not supposed to be here."

"Save the rest of my cattle."

"Let's see what Fred says."

"You see what Fred says," Myron said and ran back outside and down across the face of the barn to try to get through the back doors.

"Where you goin'?" a voice called from the large bowl of faces in the clover field below him.

"I'm goin' to save them cows," Myron said.

"We help?"

"No."

"Whatever you say," they said.

When he got there the future was apparent: the back of the barn was gone and he could see into the lofts. Through the flaming slats, the new hay was a huge sea of red torment.

"Myron!"

The farmer turned.

Dietche was standing on the stone wall above him.

"Hey there!" Myron said.

"I didn't do it. O.K.? So don't do nothin' foolish."

Myron ran away below the barn.

"Where you going?" Dietche called. But Myron was gone. She'd told him, by God.

(Myron's face, a woman in the crowd remembered later, reminded her of the devil.)

Hat down, Dietche slid through the bucket brigade which was getting an air of futility about it. He did not answer when they called him names for not relieving them. They knew the barn was lost and that their labor was only a gesture—they saw how the fire was going—and they weren't charitable people when charity had no point. They quit passing the buckets. Highly strung by the events of the night, Curtiss came down from the spring and called them all jackasses. They told him to shut up.

Dietche stood by the kitchen window. She was sitting in a circle of women in her bathrobe. On the stove a large tub of coffee was heating. She looked as if she had waked from a long sleep.

She looked alarmed; it *was* Dietche she'd seen for a moment looking in the window. She went outside.

They went behind the house where it was quiet and cool, and only the violent sound of flames was evidence of a fire going nearby.

"Did you do it?" he asked.

"You got to go, John."

"What for?"

"He's told the police. They blocked all the roads."

"Did you set fire to the barns?"

"You don't want to be caught," she said. She felt the minutes passing. She felt him passing. Her face was full of sympathy for him.

"Mrs. Greenhalgh!"

"Shhh."

"Did you set fire to the barns?" he said.

"Yes I did."

"What in hell did you do that for?" he cried.

"They ain't your barns are they?"

"Somebody could catch me—they could take me away," he said. "Why didn't you ask me?"

"It didn't have anything to do with you. You best go, John."

"Mrs. Greenhalgh, for the love of God, why did you set fire to that barn? You knew I was wanted. I told you."

"It came over me."

"But it was you and me all the time!" he said. "I love you, don't I?"

Then, suddenly, the third one was there, his mouth a ring of black, his shirt a scorched rag. "It's about gone," he told them. He appeared to relax. "What have you all been talking about?"

"Myron," Dietche began, "you know I didn't do this. You can't say I done it."

Myron did not speak for a moment. "Don't see why I shouldn't," he said at last. 'Where were the police?' he wondered.

"*She* done it," Dietche said.

"Oh I know all about it. I bet she's pregnant too."

Cora blushed, surprised, and then alarmed by the idea.

"What got into you, Dietche? Look what's happened. The barn's gone. Everybody's here for miles around. Five of my cows are choked to death."

"She done it," Dietche protested. "I was at the fair."

"I don't get it," Myron said bitterly. "She put them cows in too." He walked back towards the fire. These people, these problems were nothing compared to that. Or weren't they? Maybe there was a chance, he hoped. On his way, he looked for a cop.

The people below the barn were spreading back now from the heat. There was no chance. The firemen had rolled up all the hoses except one. The fire roared stronger and stronger. The fences had been cut and the cows walked safely in the clover and on the road and among the cars.

Upon the side of the lower pasture the bucket brigade sat silent, their faces reflecting the passion of the fire.

Lieutenant Klein had arrived. Klein disliked fires and went down to the river to speak to the fire chief who was guiding the pump truck farther back into the water.

It was still the big barn, in shape, a shape made entirely of fire. The trough was burning as if it had been filled with gasoline. People as far away as the lawn felt the dirt warm under their soles. On his way to find a cop Myron yelled above the roaring to Sage that Cora had set the fire by accident. She had been smoking a cigarette and a spark flew off from the match into an open kerosene can and so forth. He had to tell an approximate truth because the way she'd told him, she'd tell anybody. She wasn't even ashamed. Myron had thought it all out. It didn't change anything, however, in *his* mind.

"If you don't mind my saying so, she's a damn fool, Myron. You can take that as a criticism or not."

Myron answered, suffering, watching a beam fall fifty feet into the inferno. "No, I don't mind." He went on.

The flames fell at last and the heat began to diminish. But, somehow, as on the smaller barn, the roof still held up. The barns were built strong. A sweet smell blew through the crowd. The silage. Baking.

Dietche decided to cross the highway, skate south, circle round, and come back. To see what the cops were up to. There were no dogs at Myron's, but he remembered seeing a dog somewhere that night, so he ran part of the way in the river. He knew dogs would get him if he wasn't quick.

There were no dogs, and when they arrived the police were much more interested in the fire; they half forgot Dietche. He'd only jumped parole anyhow. It would merely cost him the rest of the sentence. Myron went up to one of them. "I just saw your man."

"Who's that?" the trooper asked.

"John Dietche. He's got some of my money on him," he lied.

"Does he," the trooper said.

"Why don't you go after him?"

"Waitin' for Lieutenant Klein."

"Where's *him?*"

The cop did not answer.

"Jesus you fellers!" Myron swore and went off.

The cop, whose name was Handyside, shifted in his leather leggings, folded his arms, and spat and watched the roof creak, preparing to fall. He wondered how a woman could be so stupid as to start a fire like this—and then let her husband tell everybody about it. The crowd backed away. Smoke canopied the farm, blotting out the stars. The milking equipment was all piled on the lawn.

The news had come to the women inside the kitchen. They found it difficult to speak to her. She sat in a corner by herself while the coffee was served to the firemen. They came through, single file, received their cups and went out the newly unlocked front door of the living room.

The farm grew smaller behind Dietche. As he walked out of the river there was a flash of light. He looked over his shoulder. The roof of the big barn was falling. And then the crash came.

Cars began moving away from the farm, guided by the police. A token stream was kept on the fire to the last, to damp the embers. It was all over.

When Myron found him, Lieutenant Klein, only slightly taller, was finishing a cigar by the river. He wore a clean, gray coat, and a thick belt to hold it straight. A black silk ribbon ran down the seam of his trousers to his shoes, one of which was propped up on a log. Myron asked him if he was thinking of going fishing. In a mild, evening voice, the lieutenant asked what Myron meant.

"You don't take your duties very seriously, Lieutenant. There's an escaped prisoner on my land and you don't seem to want to go after him. Why not?"

"Mr. Greenhalgh, we don't have hardly enough men to direct the traffic. I didn't realize how many friends you got. In the second place, every car going out of the district is being stopped. In the third place, have you ever looked for a man in the dark?"

"I pay taxes for you to do your job. The fire department don't ask if it's dark or not—they come and do the job."

"The police aren't volunteers, Mr. Greenhalgh," Klein said.

"I know. I know. They lack the spirit."

The cigar reddened and dimmed and then the soft voice came again in the local tenor accent. "We are servants of the State of New York, Mr. Greenhalgh. I've caught men before. Don't worry." He cut the ash of the cigar on the leaf of a bush. "I'm sorry about your barns. I hope you'll be all right."

Myron was very upset. "Look, mister! You got nothin' to lose—you got no farm—but for Lord's sake help me a little, won't you?"

The lieutenant looked at him. "Help you?" he asked puzzled. His face was as dark as Myron's, but soft, and intelligent. Not a mysterious face, not a face in motion; a simple picture of the man. "Myron, there's nothing to do until the crowd goes. You say you saw him. How long ago was that?"

"Two minutes ago."

"You sure?"

"I'm sure."

"Where is he now, do you think?"

"I don't know."

"Myron, if one of my men sees Dietche, he'll take him. But a big mob like this is a godsend to the boy and he'll use it to his advantage. He's been in prison seven years, don't forget—he's learned a lot. When that crowd goes we'll look for him. But now we're hogtied because if the crowd gets wind of Dietche someone's bound to get hurt."

"People are leaving. The fire's goin' out, Lieutenant. Let's go get him now."

"No," the officer said, his head jerking to one side to clear a bug from his eye. Neatly and slowly was his motto. He was a smart officer, condescending to his masters, the people of the State of New York, as good servants are. Nothing amused him. "Wait," he said. And he didn't have enough men.

Below them the red pump truck shook gently, pushing water into the remaining hose. A lot of mud was going on the embers.

"He could be in the next county by now," Myron said.

The cigar hissed, spun, floated downstream, and was drawn into the hose and blown onto the fire. Klein walked away, saying he was going to have a look at the barn.

The crowd had not diminished as much as Klein had hoped. The barn was all down. It was a terrible sight to them. He thought they stayed for the love of it. "Myron," he said over his shoulder, coming to the road, "if you tell me why Dietche come all the way out here from New Jersey, it'd help us."

"Nobody's ever been caught standin' still."

"It's a matter of brainwork too, y'know."

"And the feet."

"How would you like to go lookin' for him for me?" Klein asked.

"Wouldn't mind," Myron replied after a moment. "Alone?"

"No, not alone. Now look—"

"He came up here to get even with me—he thinks I helped chase his Pa out of Spring Valley after the first war 'cause they was Germans."

"Did you?"

"Dammit Lieutenant, what does that matter? I was eight," Myron said, turning on him.

"O.K. O.K." Klein wore the uniform from fear of a man like Myron.

They walked up Myron's driveway. Hoses littered the lawn and people were drifting away to their cars. A white smoke like steam rose from the hillside ruin.

Handyside, the large scar-faced brute Myron had spoken to earlier, greeted Klein with a moronic grin and reported he had not seen anyone answering to Dietche's description. " 'Cept for that eye, you could lock them all up. Farmers all come from the same mother." He itched himself, watching Myron. " 'Sides the trash wouldn't tell us if they saw him anyhow. Such a little reward."

Myron paid no attention. He was going to build again. If there was any reward, and Myron found him, he'd put the money into a new barn. He would build again. Dietche was finished. He cast his eye over the faces of the people who were leaving, wondering if there was somebody around he could hire to help him get started.

Klein decided they should start moving. Myron'd be given four men.

"What?" Myron asked, surprised and pleased. "You're puttin' me in charge?"

"You said you'd help," Klein said. "You know the land."

"Yes, I do—"

"O.K. then Myron. You lead."

"O.K. Sure will."

"I'll stay here," Klein continued. "How much money did he take?"

"I don't know," Myron said nervously. "Haven't counted."

Handyside was about to object to Myron as leader of the expedition when a woman arrived, moving contrary to the departing crowds, and spoke to Myron.

"What did she say?" Klein asked Handyside quietly, seeing Myron lift his head stiffly, suddenly.

He was alone and free—except for this business of Mrs. Greenhalgh and the police. Going alone through the darkness, he felt good. But he was being chased and that diminished the pleasure.

He came quietly in alongside the cabin, his hat on low to cut the moonlight out of his face. The barns were nothing and the fire almost out in the two stone pits where the barns had been; quite a few people were still there. He couldn't see the trooper car or Myron. He crept down among the cars in the clover, trying to find one to hide in. He reached Curtiss's. Salvation. The hired man got in back.

"We're just going," Curtiss said.

"Let me sit a second, Curtiss," Dietche said. "You got a cigarette?"

Grace sensed something wrong. The hired man smelled of weeds and mud. J.J. didn't see anything because he didn't want to. He held his eye fastened to the ruins. "How are you?" he said.

Curtiss gave him a cigarette. "I guess we're going off now, John."

"Curtiss," he said, exhaling; he leaned forward to Curtiss's ear; his voice dropped to a whisper. "Take me with you." He waited. He lifted his blank, unaccusing, unfriendly eye to Curtiss's face. It was the same old face. "O.K.," he said, and got out of the car, and slammed the door shut.

The last Curtiss saw of him was when a young woman took hold of him and looked at his eye. Dietche stared at her in fury; he said something the boy couldn't understand, tore her arm off him, and ran up past the stone ruins. The woman thought a moment, and then made her way through the crowd to Myron.

"Drive off, Curtiss called from the back seat.

"Don't you want to say goodbye?" J.J. asked.

"I've said it."

"I think he's right," Grace said. J.J. backed the car onto the road, smiled at a traffic cop and asked the way to New York. Curtiss sat quietly and did not feel like speaking until they were several miles beyond the motorcycle checkpoint on the road away. He knew there had been a chance for Dietche in the car. There was nothing risked. And Dietche could have gotten out before the rather unimpressive roadblocks and gone into the country. But the three of them drove on through the night to New York, and Dietche remained behind. Curtiss felt he'd adjusted the balance; that's what he kept telling himself. In any event, the young man was unable to forget what he had done. To his perpetual irritation he would find he could never forget Dietche. He had not learned that in a crisis an act of charity rids you of people more easily than an act of desertion, genuine or not. One denial and you're brothers for life.

"She said she seen him," Myron said, turning from Orilla Ano's scared face.

"Handyside," Klein said, "bring up Tait and Morelli and Ferguson. You'll be walking a little this morning. Myron, ask her which way he was headed."

Myron turned to the woman, wondering why Klein didn't ask her himself.

"She says she thinks she saw him go up the pasture."

"Bill," the Lieutenant called.

"Sir?"

Klein put a cigar in his mouth and the two men walked away, helping each other unfold a survey map. "Tell the motorcycle officers to go to either end of this back road and wait. Take the map," Klein said.

"Yes, sir. Can we shoot him?" Handyside asked.

"No, you can't."

"What's it all about?" several people asked. Myron explained about Dietche. Their faces lit up. The rumor had been true. "What rumor?" Myron asked. But they'd lost hold of it. "Something about you—" They didn't remember very clearly. Some asked if Dietche had set the fire, and Myron wished he could have said yes. "Want to help git him?" he said instead.

They looked at each other.

"He set fire to the barns?" they asked again.

Again Myron did not answer, so they went thinking Dietche had done it, wanting to see him again.

Klein found Myron at the head of a gang of twenty when he returned. He became angry. "Myron, I don't want a posse. I said you could take four of my men and that's all. The rest of you guys scram."

"Scram yourself, Chief," one tall, moody farmer said.

"I'll lock you up," Klein replied, his eyes on the ground, "if you talk to me like that again."

The men whispered to Myron's neck that they'd meet him in the woods, and walked off.

"O.K.?" Myron said to the four policemen. "Let's go. We'll head for his Pa's house."

Klein told him to be pacific. Myron didn't know what that meant, but nodded, and went away.

Dietche knelt and drank at the muddied spring.

'I hope they don't remember Pa's for just a while,' he thought, dipping his face in the pool. 'Myron'll be with them though—maybe he'll think I've figured he'd go there and so I'd go somewheres else.' His best chance of escape, and the most immediate, was through the mountains behind his father's house. But Walter would have to lead him. He'd forgotten the way through.

Myron entered the woods on the cow path. Handyside disagreed with the direction. "If you knew prisoners as well as you know your land, Myron, you'd know they don't think like you think they think."

"How do they think, Mr. Handyside?" Myron asked politely.

"When he don't hear dogs, he'll double back, stickin' close to the main road where a car might pick him up."

"That's just what I figured he'd think we thought," Myron said.

Handyside lost track of the thought. "I bet you my last dollar if we all sat down by that nice warm outdoor fire down there, he'd pass us in an hour."

Myron pretended to laugh. "That's what you'd like, is it? Set down and wait?" The other farmers laughed too.

They continued on, quietly, slowly, like Myron, towards Walter's.

The hired man bent under the fence at the back road and laid out two long steps in the soft yellow dust and took a branch on the other side and rubbed them out again.

They were all in the pasture now. The moon made a blue-white zone of the grass. Myron, who was picking up tricks of hunting as if he'd done it all his life, kept the men close together to travel faster.

Dietche hurried across the desert and approached his father's house from behind. The car was in its place, cold and empty on its blocks. The old man lay on the brass bed.

"Pa," he whispered. From far off he heard the rattle of a motorcycle, and then silence. He knelt, afraid, at his father's side.

"Pa!" he hissed.

Behind him the woods stretched eighty miles into Canada. There was (a way many of the lovers used to come to the upper pasture) a trail. But he could get lost unless he knew the way in. His father's eyes opened slowly. "Pa," Dietche said, encouraged. "They're after me now. They'll get my tracks out here soon. Take me through the woods."

"They'll come here," the old man said, drunkenly. "This is my house."

Dietche swore at him.

"—is my house and it's all I got," the old peasant mumbled on. He said he would give Dietche up if he was there when they came because if they found him they'd tear the house down and hang him in the ruins. "It's my house," he explained. "Now go on. You'll make it. You'll make it."

"Take me," Dietche said.

"They'll catch you if you don't get through?"

"They might."

"Well, you try, son. You try."

"Ain't you goin' to help me?"

"No."

"Why not?"

"They're after you ain't they?"

Dietche left him in disgust and fear and went out into the desert to see if anybody had come down yet. He was still moving, still free and alone. 'It'll turn out all right,' he thought. 'It'll be all right. I best go back to Myron's and get on the road an' get a car,' he thought. Myron's was all he knew.

And so, walking very slowly, he turned another long circle, heading under the mountains, figuring that the larger the circle he turned and the more time he used in turning it, the wider the net would become, and therefore the bigger the spaces in it. Eventually they'd have to call off the hunt.

By the time Myron got to Walter's the night sky had broken up.

The men gathered round shining their lights on him in the diminishing blackness and wondering at the field of scattered, bleached chicken bones around the bed. They did not make any noise, standing in the sand. Myron spoke loudly. "Search the house."

"No! Don't have to!" Walter yelled. "You leave off my house." He stood up stark naked as the blanket fell off him. "He ain't here. I promise you. He's out there! You wreck my house, I'll kill you."

"Take up the floor," Handyside said, looking up at the crazy old angel whose gray eyes flashed from face to face, his pink tongue stuck between his lips, his arm extended pointing into the waste.

Myron and Handyside went inside, not believing that the father would give up his son.

At Myron's suggestion, a policeman brought an enormous pair of trousers to the old man. Walter dragged them on, and then led the young man out into the sand by the car and showed him footprints. "Them's us," the young policeman said.

"Waal look here then!" the old man said, dancing ahead. "And here and here! Look—he's all over the place." The young policeman couldn't believe him.

The eyelids of the two remaining, uneaten chickens had dropped open, revealing cold green circles of glass. They'd have believed him.

"What are you doing, Younger?" Handyside called from the doorway.

"He says he's got Dietche's tracks out here."

"Leave him be—you come on back and help us in here. Hurry up. We're losin' on him."

The young policeman joined Myron and the men inside. Two patrolmen stood with their guns out while the others peered under the broken floor boards.

All at once they heard the old man howl. "Hey!" the old cracked voice came again, followed by its owner, beard flying. "Look!" he shouted, bending through the doorway, holding something aloft at the end of a very long arm.

"What's that?" Handyside asked.

"It's a hat," Myron said.

"Whose is it?"

The father came to Myron, a swath of red anger across his face, shaking the hat in Myron's face. "WAAL?"

Handyside looked at Myron. They all looked at Myron. "It's John's," he said. He went to the back door filled now with gray light. "He's out there," he said, gazing into the waste.

Dietche was not to be seen on it anywhere.

Myron asked the father if John had gone into the woods. The old man said no; he led them out beyond the car and showed them Dietche's tracks.

His feet were so badly blistered from having run in the river he had to remove his boots. He sat in a brake of bushes on the rim of the dump, cursing his feet and his blindness. They slowed him terribly.

He had just seen them. He threw the damp, torn socks away and put his boots on again. Wiping his forehead, he found he had lost his hat—it had been too dark to know if he had a hat on or not. He looked about for it and made his way back onto the naked waste. Far away, before the house, he saw them all coming on, like pine cones. He could still not walk in the boots. He removed them again, tied the laces together and hung them round his neck and held them still with both hands as he ran.

She sat in the gray kitchen, watching the sun rise, in the space created by her destruction, from the mountains. It was the first time she'd seen it that way in her life.

With the coming of the sun, the hills entered the third dimension, and then the henhouse and Dietche's cabin.

The sun's heat made her feel her tiredness. She left the window and put away the cups the long departed women had washed for her and walked slowly, wearily up to her bed.

Klein sat in the patrol car, smoking a cigar, listening to the morning come in with the first sharp, cold caw of the crows; then the cows, still loose, began protesting their unwanted freedom.

The clover field was trampled like an old dish rag. The bark of the elm trees was cut and slashed. The trough was a charred dugout. It was as if a war had gone on, just there.

The heat of the morning extended to John Dietche, whose skinny chest ached from running and whose watchful brain was telling him how he'd gotten there that day. It didn't help to know. He was standing in the quarry, full of fear, watching Myron Greenhalgh on the road below.

"John!" the voice called a second time. The high syllable fell off the rock face of the quarry.

Dietche waited to move until Myron bent down to get under the barbed-wire fence. Behind him was a cave in the rock, used at one time to store dynamite. Myron moved. The hired man slunk into it through a door of elder and blackberry wire and crouched down.

Myron came up the side of the low hill leading to the quarry floor. "John!" he called.

Dietche felt his only chance now was to make the highway and somehow get to Cowboy.

He could handle Myron if he came any closer. He had his hand around a slice of rock. But looking out of the cave again, he saw eight men enter the road, spaced twenty yards apart, like a giant comb coming across the land. Myron's net. Two of them were cops, with pistol holsters. He swore and tried to keep his chest from heaving too noisily while he thought of what to do immediately.

"John!"

Soon they would search the quarry, and they would find him. He had better move before they got too far up the hill. He wanted most of all to go to the toilet. He rose out of the cave and ran up the rocky side of the quarry in his bare feet, leaving his boots behind.

Myron forgot to call out when he saw Dietche. He chased after him in silence, in a cold wrath. Dietche stopped up on the sod heights of the quarry face and tried to push a big boulder over the edge. Myron took cover behind the broken conveyor, and when he looked out to see why the boulder hadn't fallen, Dietche had disappeared, deciding that the boulder would attract too much attention.

It was cool to run in the pine woods and easy on his bleeding feet. He ran and ran, until he fell, exhausted, in a dry gully. All was silence and peace, and he thought he'd made it when he saw two men on the road below, running *back* towards the posse. 'How many are there *want* me?' he wondered. He staggered up the side of the gully, leaving long, telltale gray streaks up the virgin sand.

For a time he ran downhill through spruce trees, and then on open, confident, grassy earth. He traversed a large clearing of wild hay and entered a dark and sweet-smelling pine wood through a gray gate. He thought he'd lost them. He would like to have lain down, but he didn't think the highway was far now. Pine branches swopped his face. The smaller, brittle ones broke off. Several times the larger, jagged ones opened small cuts when he did not see them because of his eye.

He ran on, soaking urine and sweat. The slim, polished needles cooled his seared feet.

"John!" came a cry. It was almost amusing. '*Lord,*' he thought, 'I'm not running fast enough.' He fell down terrified as his foot went soft in a bank of loose dirt. He rolled over, knelt, and listened.

Silence.

He flung himself down the side of a pasture, through a herd.

When Myron arrived there two minutes later, they found the strange cows standing up, watching, not eating, dumbly facing the direction Dietche had taken. Everything betrayed him that morning.

Hoping he'd made it, Dietche kneeled under a pine tree to rest. His head felt quite small and tight. His legs and his stomach were shaking with exhaustion. He pulled his head up.

It was Handyside. The near-sighted policeman was only a hundred feet away.

"Hey you!" Handyside said.

'Jesus,' Dietche thought, 'he's close.'

Handyside called for Myron.

Screaming softly, Dietche stood and made his bare feet run straight through a blackberry bush. Screaming still more softly from fear of being caught, he went under an ancient board fence and knelt again to rest in a dirt road.

He looked up.

The men were all on the road watching him.

He was sitting on his hips, his legs lying out together as if paralyzed, but he got up again; he lifted himself on pure fear and ran away in a crazy, slow, light-headed course through the dirt, leaving tracks like a snake with his toes, his head swinging back and forth on his neck to show him where he was going, his mouth open. They were on all sides of him, and told him so. He heard their voices crossing to each other over his head.

"John. Come back here."

"Let him come on, Myron."

Dietche realized he was heading right into them. He dove off the road, praying under the barbed-wire fence, and struggled through the wild hay towards a distant pine forest where it looked green and cool.

"We can't chase him no more," Myron said. "Shoot him."

Handyside called on Dietche to stop.

Myron's shrill voice rose, picking out another policeman. "Shoot him, Younger. He'll get away from us. Shoot him!"

"No," Handyside said, though the temptation and the target were great.

"I'll just shoot over his head," Younger said.

"Shoot him!" Myron cried. "He's gettin' to them woods!"

"He ain't done nothin' that *important,* Myron," Handyside said impatiently, firing a shot into the air.

Hearing the gunfire, Dietche lurched about, his arms swinging out from his sides, and cried in a sharp voice, "Don't! Don't shoot me! I'm innocent." He swayed a moment on his aching legs, and then he collapsed, and they went through the grass and took him.